THE
REALM

the
Awakening Begins

A novel by
K.L. GLANVILLE

LUMINATIONS
MEDIA GROUP INC.
Monterey Park, California

THE REALM: THE AWAKENING BEGINS
by K.L. Glanville

Published by Luminations Media Group Inc, Monterey Park, CA
www.LuminationsMediaGroup.com
Printed in the United States of America

Cover design by Jeff Milam www.MilamDesigns.com
Page layout by Jeff Simons j_simons7@yahoo.com & K.L. Glanville
Interior illustrations by K.L. Glanville
Seal by K.L. Glanville & V. Lindstrom v_lindstrom@yahoo.com

Publisher's Cataloging-in-Publication
(Provided by Quality Books, Inc.)
Glanville, K. L.
    The realm : the awakening begins : a novel / by K.L. Glanville.
    p. cm.
    SUMMARY: In the slum town of Sawtong, a place where spirit priests have ruled through fear for generations, fifteen-year-old Adan tries to hold onto his family's power. He and Graisia, a twelve-year-old orphan, struggle on opposite sides of supernatural forces that vie for control of their community. Somehow, Graisia has discovered a power greater than Adan has ever seen.
    Audience: Ages 10-15.
    LCCN 2008907819
    ISBN-13: 978-0-9821199-1-4
    ISBN-10: 0-9821199-1-7

    1. Good and evil--Juvenile fiction. 2. Supernatural --Juvenile fiction. 3. Fantasy fiction. [1. Good and evil--Fiction. 2. Supernatural--Fiction. 3. Spirits-- Fiction. 4. Fantasy.]   I. Title.

PZ7.G48035Rea 2008   [Fic]
                      QBI08-600254

WHAT OTHERS ARE SAYING ABOUT:
The Realm: the Awakening Begins

"Startlingly vivid, full of terror and consolation, The Realm: the Awakening Begins offers a glimpse behind spiritual doors into horrific darkness and resplendent light." – **Kathy Tyers, author of Shivering World and the Firebird trilogy**

"The Realm: the Awakening Begins by K.L. Glanville is a groundbreaking fantasy book which doesn't shy away from the dark spiritualism and real world pressures of life. This book takes readers by the hand and walks them into shadowy places where they don't want to go, only to show them the glorious beauty, awaiting on the other side. If you like roller coasters, scary movies, and an overcoming faith then you'll love The Realm: the Awakening Begins. I highly recommend this book." – **Robert Martinez, screenwriter, Victim and Gulag**

"Life on a garbage dump is about more than poverty. There are spiritual forces at work keeping people poor. K.L. Glanville, drawing from her real life experiences has woven a fascinating tapestry of human and spiritual factors that just might be what really goes on beneath the visible. Like Frank Peretti (This Present Darkness) K.L. Glanville sees beyond the human and material to a reality that few Westerners know how to deal with. There is drama here, and suspense and just plain good writing with a surprising climax. The book was hard to put down from the start but impossible to put down toward the end." – **Charles H. Kraft, anthropologist and author of Defeating Dark Angels**

"I was amazed at this book! Though it is an imaginary place – vividly described and incredibly supernatural – it is unbelievably, very much like our own. Shape-shifting, transportations, dreams, and another dimension... it's all there, superbly crafted into a supernatural thriller bound to keep you on the edge of your seat until the last page is turned... and make you question the reality you thought you knew." – **Doug Addison, inspirational speaker and comedian**

"Take a step inside The Realm and you will find a story that is cinematic in its scope. As a film maker I appreciate the imagery in K.L. Glanville's book. Her characters seem to jump off the page. The story is one that will have you on the edge of your seat!" – **Diane Wigstone, movie producer, President DNA Studios**

Dedication

 To the first travelers through the fifth room, you were a major inspiration for the writing of this story and are still in my heart.

To the countless others whose stories and paths have been interwoven with my own, your lasting imprints have been felt and not forgotten. Especially, Dad, Mom, Jenny, Nels, Peter, John W., Viv, Satya, Jim, J.P., Doug & Rick.

 To those who have ever dreamed of being someone special, a superhero, queen or king, I'd pay attention to those dreams if I were you.

May your hearts and dreams be awakened...

the Awakening Begins

I contract my life and my blood to Mahalan.
Ivah is forsaken. From this day on Mahalan
is given the power over the town of Sawtong.
I pledge my family to serve him for all generations.
We dedicate our family to being the priests
and guardians of Mahalan's power over this town.
Each successive Spirit Priest shall affirm the
resealing of this contract with their own blood.
Mahalan may have the blood of any of my
descendants. If it is not given willingly,
he may take it by force.
Let any who forsake Mahalan be cursed.
With my life I sign this,

Ramél

 Graisia stared in horror at Adan's eyes. They flickered like flames, reflecting the blood-red, eerie light of the darkened sky. His face hovered so close she could feel his stale, warm breath that seemed full of slithering worms. She wanted to turn and run, but there was no place to go. She stood backed up against the wall of someone's shack of a home, trapped at the dead end of one of the winding dirt paths that snaked through their makeshift town near the dump. Terror raced up and down her spine like needle pricks, and splinters pressed into her back from the rough wood. Her thin, worn dress gave her about as much protection as a flimsy layer of onion skin.

She had no way to defend herself against Adan, the second deadliest person in this pathetic town. He could stop her breath with the power of the spirits, or sell her off to someone in the city.... *Maybe he'll put a spell on me, or... I'll disappear and no one will see me again.... Maybe he'll take me back to his father and let* him *torture me....* She was sure Adan's father, Danjall, the local Spirit Priest, would never show her mercy.

And no one would even miss you... the thought floated through her mind unbidden. Her heart sank, knowing it was true.

The scarlet flames in his eyes grew brighter and larger, feeding off her fear and dejection. Paralysis began to take over her body, starting at her nose and working its way down like a tingly electric current, shutting down all her muscles as it went. Her mind raced futilely to think of someone who hated her enough to hire Danjall or Adan to put a spell on her. *I've never hurt anyone!* She tried to tear her eyes away from Adan's, but he held them, locked in a prison of panic.

Adan twisted his lips into a pitiless and cruel smile of victory. Graisia watched with alarm as his arms rose slowly to grab her.

Crash. A metal bucket hit the opposite side of the thin wall next to Graisia's head.

She sat up petrified, sweat dripping down her face. She looked around at her surroundings and saw she was sitting in her tiny cubbyhole, on the same worn piece of cardboard she always slept on. The morning sun forced its way through the cracks on two of the low walls around her. She had been dreaming. But her heart still pounded in her ribcage. She knew the truth... dreams like that were more real than not.

She tried to calm her breathing. Adan may have been a dream, but the bucket hitting the wall wasn't.

"You still in there, lazy trash girl?" Opana's

abrasive voice came from the other side of the wall.

Graisia looked down at her trembling hands. Opana was the "mean giant" who fed her. At least that's how Graisia thought of her, though she would never dare to tell her to her face. Opana claimed she had found Graisia as a toddler, crying by the roadside on her way home from taking laundry to the city. She said Graisia had probably been dumped off on the main road by someone who couldn't be bothered to walk all the way in to the dump to finish their business.

Why Opana took her into an already crowded shack, Graisia didn't fully know. Opana seemed to have enough on her hands, between her own kids, the laundry she did for city people, and, in her spare moments, reading people's omens in tea leaves and *takra* sticks. She remembered Opana saying something about the tea leaves foretelling her coming, and Graisia having "the gift" that "shouldn't be wasted." Opana told her one day her gift would become obvious, and hopefully useful. As far as Graisia could tell, her greatest gift was bringing in some extra coins by sorting through garbage at the dump for goods that could be recycled. Graisia was beginning to think that maybe Opana was using the whole "gift" excuse just to get her to stay and keep bringing coins home.

Graisia took a deep shaky breath. There was nothing she wanted more than a real mother. Even if she did have a gift, what good was it if no one was there to love her? She would do anything to have someone care for her, even if it meant giving up a potential gift, whatever it might be.

With Opana yelling at her own kids inside the shack, Graisia stuffed her thoughts down deep where she wouldn't feel their nagging pinpricks. She didn't have time for daydreaming and wishful thinking. She had to focus on surviving.

Her heart still hadn't slowed down from the nightmare. She shuddered. *Why do I keep dreaming about him? What did I do? Why is he after me?* A beetle skittered across the toes of her left foot. She jerked her knee up toward her body, shaking it off. She knew that dreams about the Spirit Priest or his son being after you were not good. Too often when people had dreams like that, it meant they really did want to do something bad to you. The dreams were stacking up, mounting like a tsunami that would crash over her at any moment and wipe out life as she knew it.

The bucket hit the wall again, making Graisia jump. She deftly moved the little piece of wood that covered her door leading out of her cubbyhole.

"Just about to leave, Opana!" Graisia scrambled out of the little shelter that she'd built onto the side of Opana's shack. She wondered how much longer her walls would withstand the bucket's abuse. She was actually glad Opana had decided there wasn't enough room for her inside the larger, one-room shack filled with Opana's five children. It had been crowded and noisy. In the shack, the bucket had been more likely to hit her head instead of the wall next to it. She remembered the day Opana told her to start bringing home some wood from the dump so she could build her own space. She had to get her friends to help carry it. But she was lucky enough to have a roof to sleep under, even if she did almost hit her head on it when she sat up.

Graisia squinted and glanced around the slum town with a frown. The town didn't officially have a name. Most people simply called it, "Sawtong," meaning "so what." It was the only place in which Graisia could remember living. The sun was barely coming up, and the rest of Sawtong was beginning to rouse.

Old lady Flora was shouting next door and kicking her husband. In a drunken stupor and with nothing to show for a day's work, he had passed out the night before on their doorstep. He grunted some incoherent response to his wife's assault. A dog yelped in the distance. People shuffled along the dirt path lined with shacks, heading off to try and make money. Some of their efforts would be legal, while many other dealings would be a bit shadier. Various neighbors were also setting up "shops" in front of their shacks to sell whatever they could find or cook. It might be a pair of used shoes, a glob of sticky rice wrapped in a leaf, or a dented radio stolen from somewhere in the city.

Graisia squatted down and reached back into her cubbyhole. She pulled out her too-big flip-flops and the well-worn, grubby rice sack she used for collecting recyclables at the dump. Graisia wasn't exactly sure how old she was, but at somewhere around 12, dump-digging was about the only reliable, half-way decent job a girl could have in the slum. It's what all her friends did.

She heard Opana rummaging around in the main part of the shack. Opana would be leaving soon to get in line for water at the nearest pump. She had to get the laundry done for those rich people in Kutah, the capital city, or there'd be no dinner tonight. It would be good if Graisia was gone by the time Opana came out the door. She spotted Cuni, Opana's youngest son, sitting in the doorway, gnawing a bit of pulp off a mango pit. It looked delicious. She leaned over to try and take it from him.

"Don't do anything stupid!" Opana yelled from somewhere inside the shack.

Graisia froze.

"The omen for you this morning was dark." Opana began each day seeking the omen for those in her household, and sometimes she shared what she discovered.

Graisia pulled her hand back. *And my life hasn't been awful the last few days? How bad can it get?* Her heart sank. Along the outside of the shack, Opana kept a little altar to her favored goddess, Harapkan, the goddess of fate. Graisia turned and bowed her head as she passed the altar. With her fingers she touched her own forehead and then her heart. Maybe honoring Harapkan would help her fate today.

Would Adan actually do something to her today? *Lakás... why does Kaly have to live so close to the Spirit Priest!* Every morning she had to stop by her friend Kaly's on the way to the dump. They worked together, along with a few others. Graisia thought momentarily about not going by Kaly's, but then Kaly would get mad at her and harass her all day long.

The warm humid air foretold another sweltering day in the sun. Graisia's torn and grubby dress, two sizes too small, clung to her already sweating body in the heat. Her feet kicked up dust as she headed off, flip-flops flapping awkwardly against her heels, like newly caught fish slapping in a bucket.

Even though she seemed to wake up just before Adan got her, she felt like he already had her in his steely grip. His raven hair, callous eyes, and towering frame hovered over her... and the *lakás*, the power he got from the spirits – he knew how to use it almost as well as his father. *What did I do to make him so mad? I'm always careful around him. Why would he notice me?* Whenever he was nearby, she made sure to look at the ground respectfully. Of course she did it mostly because she didn't want him to stare into her eyes and use *lakás* to paralyze her. But still, she'd respected him!

Graisia brushed a strand of her dark tangled hair from her face as she made her way around some broken glass and a large green iguana that had parked itself in the middle of the path. She would have to be particularly careful around animals today. It could be a *basyo*, or spiritualist, that worked with Danjall. One of them might have decided to take another form for a while – if she believed what Opana said, anyway.

"It's been there all night, girl," an old man commented from a doorway nearby, "like it's been waiting for someone."

Graisia glanced back only to see the iguana move in her direction. She didn't wait to see if it would continue on toward her. She took off running. A little farther down the path, a crow swooped over her. She instinctively ducked and looked over her shoulder to make sure it wasn't coming back. She hated crows. Every priestly family had a totem animal – the crow was Adan's. She wished they weren't so prevalent. She also wished she wasn't alone with her mind free to wander. The last time Opana had seen a dark omen for her she was sick for two weeks and almost died. Graisia furrowed her brow. She checked behind her to make sure the iguana still wasn't following her.

As she got closer to where Adan and Kaly lived, her heart started beating harder and louder, like a war drum. But fighting was the last thing she wanted to do. She'd rather run as far away as she could, but that wasn't an option. Surviving on her own in the big city would be nearly impossible. It would be foolish for her to think she might find another place to live or even another job to do. And if she wanted to find the mother who had deserted her in this forsaken slum town, she had no idea where to start.

Graisia walked slower as she approached Kaly's home. She hoped Opana had read her omen wrong.

Just as she reached Kaly's doorway, which looked like a mouth caught in a crooked yawn, Kaly bounded out and hopped over the open sewer that ran along in front of it. A few other kids spilled out of the doorway behind her and headed off in different directions. At 14, Kaly was quite a bit taller than Graisia. Her shoulder-length straggly brown hair didn't seem to know which way to hang, and the long t-shirt she wore covered her cut-offs as well as her still girlish figure.

"You look horrible this morning," Kaly said matter-of-factly.

"Hardly slept," Graisia mumbled to her friend.

"Another nightmare about *Adan*?" Kaly asked, sneering and rolling her eyes in exasperation.

"Shhh!" Graisia looked beyond Kaly to where the Spirit Priest's shack stood, across the path and about four doors down. It looked like everyone else's, except for the *dusanays* symbol of two broken triangles over the door – the symbol of the Spirit Priest in this area. Also, no one else's shack adjoined it. Many shacks were built right up against someone else's, but no one dared build their shack connecting to the Spirit Priest's.

Blood drained from Graisia's face as her worst fear materialized at the shack's door. Adan slipped out of the shadows and stood in the open doorway. He leaned against the doorframe and surveyed the people going up and down the path. He looked grumpy, and his hair was mussed as if he'd just woken up. He wore an old pair of jeans ripped on one knee and a dirty blue t-shirt. But he also wore something that set him apart, a gold chain around his neck. Hanging from the chain was a replica of the *dusanays* symbol. Rumor was that his dad had given it to him for his 15th birthday. It sparkled in the morning sun as Graisia tore her frightened eyes away.

Kaly turned and headed in his direction, the direction they walked every day to get to the garbage dump. From sunup to sundown, they worked like pack rats, scavenging for things that could be recycled for a few coins. Every morning, Graisia and Kaly walked together to collect the other members of their *bandhu,* or group of friends. It was safer to work in numbers.

Graisia followed tentatively behind Kaly, trying to stay out of Adan's view. "Why do you have to live here?" Graisia whispered fiercely, trying to hide behind Kaly's extra bit of height.

"Well... let's see," Kaly said dryly, "when I was looking for a home, the mansion next to *yours* wasn't available."

Kaly seemed annoyed she was being used to hide behind, but Graisia didn't care. She turned to look at the sewer that ran along the side of the path, feigning intense interest.

"You're as scared as a cockroach in the sun!" Kaly accused, too loudly for Graisia's liking.

"Would you be quiet? He'll hear you!" Graisia whispered back.

Kaly turned to her, exasperated. "Oh get over it! The worst he'll do is focus his eyes on you and use *lakás* to make you stop breathing for a few seconds." Kaly turned her back and stepped over a smelly dog pile. "He's never hurt anyone."

Graisia wasn't too sure about that, and she hated that Kaly never seemed to care about her fears. Graisia tended to believe any rumor that implicated his cruelty.

A door slammed. She looked up, horrified to see Adan looking directly at them. At her... she was sure of it. Graisia held her breath and stood frozen, not knowing what to do. He didn't need to use *lakás* to make her stop breathing; she did it on her own.

He was about to move his gaze somewhere else when he raised his eyebrows at her. His lips formed into a crooked smile.

He knows! Instantaneously, she knew Adan had seen her in the dreams, and she could tell he knew she had dreamed them too. She looked away as fast as she could. From the corner of her eye she watched him casually step off his doorstep. Graisia wanted to run down the path and hide in the first box she could find. But her body wouldn't cooperate. He came closer and began to circle around her. She felt her lungs beg for breath. He continued circling, like a hawk around a half-dead mouse.

Kaly stopped a short ways away and turned back for her. Next thing she knew Kaly was taking her hand and pulling her slowly away from Adan.

"She didn't do anything wrong. I'll try and keep her out of your way," Kaly stated simply, continuing to drag her away.

He looked at Kaly with eyes that could burn holes through a wall. Kaly immediately stopped and dropped Graisia's hand in momentary deference.

Adan seemed satisfied with Kaly's reaction. He turned back to Graisia and leaned in close. His warm breath grazed her cheek as he spoke just loud enough for her to hear, "It won't end the same next time...."

The dreams are real! I knew *it*! Graisia's thoughts screamed. Graisia's mouth felt like newspaper left to dry in the sun. She couldn't swallow, let alone speak to defend herself. She didn't dare to look up into Adan's face. Kaly grabbed her hand again and pulled. Graisia let herself be drawn away down the street, hoping Adan wouldn't stop them again. The flaps of her flip-flops now sounded like gunshots in her ears as they hurried on.

"You look so scared – he thinks you're guilty!" Kaly shook her head in disgust.

"Did you... hear him?" Graisia could barely get the words out in a petrified whisper. "He knows... the dreams!"

"He didn't say anything about dreams, stupid! He thought you were hiding something – you don't know how to keep out of trouble. Sometimes, Graisia, you are just so stupid. You know that? Just stupid!"

Graisia's heart dropped. Kaly never understood.

"If it wasn't for me, roach girl... I don't think you'd even survive in this town!"

2

Adan watched the girls hurry away. *What was the rest of that dream?* When he had seen that girl a moment ago, only one part of the dream had come back to him: having her backed against a shack in terror. *I'll have to ask the spirits about her. She's a worthless little rat. I can't imagine her being a threat, but it is nice having her fear me.* He smiled and looked toward Kutah, the capital city of Kahitsa'an – the pride and joy of their island nation.

The sun hovered near the horizon, streaming flame-colored light through a blanket of pollution and smog and bathing the distant skyscrapers in glory. Adan returned to his doorway and looked out over Sawtong. Brilliant reds reflected off the scrap-metal roofs of their makeshift town like an iron quilt. The colors were an odd contrast to the waft of garbage and sewage that constantly drifted through the air. The smell didn't bother him much though. He was used to it.

Sawtong was only one of the numerous slum towns ringing the enormous city of Kutah. People came to places like Sawtong when they lost a farm in the country to creditors or couldn't find a job that paid enough in the city. Everyone hoped to leave Sawtong someday, but families that had lived here for generations proved how difficult it was to escape the grip of poverty.

Adan wasn't enjoying the glowing roofs right now, or how beautiful the city looked in its morning radiance, or even thinking about getting out of the slum town. His thoughts were on his territory, or rather, his father's territory. "Sawtong" might mean "so what," but to him, the little town meant everything. It was where people feared him, where he could do whatever he wanted, and where he had purpose.

Adan looked up at the door frame over his head. The *dusanays* symbol was etched on the wooden beam. These not-so-subtle markings let the people of Sawtong know where the town's power resided. Adan reached up and ran his finger over the triangles. He often wondered about their original meaning, but when he had asked his father, he was simply told 'the spirits gave it to Ramél.' Ramél was Adan's grandfather, the Spirit Priest who had introduced the worship of Mahalan to this area. He had dedicated his entire family to Mahalan's service. There were other spirits and gods that they might honor, but the primary one Adan's family served was Mahalan.

Spirit Priest, Adan mulled the words over in his head. *One day the title of Spirit Priest will belong to me! And I'll get to rule this town.* Adan pictured himself walking the paths of Sawtong like a king, viewing a thousand families as his subjects. The town might not be Kutah, but ruling over people is satisfying anywhere. He'd be able to make people do whatever he wanted through spells, curses and threats. Everyone would fear him, like they did his father. All of his father's helpers, the spirit leaders, or *basyo* as they were called, would have to pay him and help enforce his leadership. *I'll show them.... They think I'm just a kid, but one day... I'll show them I'm more powerful than all of them.*

When Adan became Spirit Priest, he would get to lead the monthly ring gatherings of all the *basyo*. He would get to oversee them in the sacrifices to their ominous and powerful spirit god, Mahalan. Since he was a toddler, his father had taken him to the ring gatherings and taught him the traditional incantations, spells and spiritual protocol. He'd dreamt for years of being Mahalan's spokesperson and representative. He would get to feel the full power of Mahalan coursing through his body.

It was a terrifying yet thrilling thought. Mahalan was a fierce and demanding master, but he gave immense power in compensation. Adan would ascend to the highest levels of spiritual work with Mahalan. *No more messing with little spirits.* Lesser spirits already resided in him and helped him do much of the work he did with his father. A smile played at the corner of his lips as he thought of how much more he could do. The exploits of Mahalan were legendary. He couldn't wait.

On the other hand... it would mean his father would have to die, and he didn't want that to happen. His father was the only friend he really had. There was no one else he could trust, no one else who had his best interest in mind. When the time came, Adan would get his chance to rule with Mahalan. When he gained power some day, he meant to expand his control to other towns and have the satisfaction of hundreds of *basyo* following his leadership.

He stared down the dirt path lined on either side with shacks. People were shuffling to and from work wearing the telltale clothes of slum dwellers – mostly dirty, dull, ill-fitting and mismatched outfits that consisted of whatever people had found or stolen. Many people didn't have work and simply drifted about or sat on their door stoops ready to stare away another day. He despised them for not working.

However, he did admire the ones who took easy jobs of selling drugs or stealing. That was more Adan's route. He had the spirits to make his life easier and help him get what he wanted. *Being good might be good,* Adan argued when his conscience would trouble him, *but being bad is a whole lot easier.* He smiled at his own logic. *Anyway, someone has to be the Spirit Priest and look after the townspeople.*

The neighbor's television that had kept him awake last night was now quiet. His curse on their appliances must have worked. They hadn't turned the blasted TV off since they got it two days ago, and it had annoyed him. The people of Sawtong might not have much money, but somehow many found enough to buy an old TV, or steal it, and enough wire to tap into the city electric poles. They weren't totally left out of the 21st century in this slum, or in any of the other slum towns around Kutah for that matter.

The land the slums were built on was worthless, usually either near a dump, along a railroad track, or next to a river that flooded every few years. Sawtong was lucky enough to be bordered by all three. It surrounded one side of a dump, had the flooding river bordering it on the edge nearest Kutah, and was hemmed in on the other side by a train track. The fourth informal border of their town was a main road that led into the city.

Adan's thoughts were cut short as he spotted Soliel scurrying down the path in his direction. Soliel was the striking teenage daughter of Jandro. Though he'd never admit it to anyone, he thought she was the most beautiful girl in Sawtong. Her father, Jandro, was a *basyo* who supposedly followed his father, Danjall. But that was debatable. Everyone knew he wanted to be Spirit Priest himself.

All of the *basyo* used some of the same secrets to cast spells, but they were not nearly as powerful as the Spirit Priest. At least they weren't supposed to be. Adan knew Jandro was quietly gathering friends and alliances amongst other *basyo*. But he also knew that Jandro's power was nowhere near that of his father's. *He can't be more powerful,* Adan thought, *We're the ones with the alliance to Mahalan. No spirit is more powerful than Mahalan in this area.*

Soliel continued to walk quickly, in spurts. She kept her head down and hesitated occasionally, like a mangy stray dog that had been beaten one too many times. A familiar anger toward Jandro simmered in Adan's chest. He'd heard how harsh Jandro was with her. He wished his dad would just get rid of Jandro.

Her long black braid bounced lightly on the back of her lithe, petite frame. Adan usually felt nothing but scorn for people as timid as her. But when it came to Soliel, he felt unusually protective and drawn towards her instead. Maybe it was because she seemed to have no parents really caring for her, and he knew what it was like to miss a mother. Or maybe it was because she just seemed like a beautiful flower waiting to bloom, needing only the warmth of the sun to blossom, but instead she was frozen closed by those around her.

If only she wasn't Jandro's daughter. Then it wouldn't matter to his father if he liked her or not. Two years ago, Jandro had suggested arranging a marriage between the two of them, but Danjall would have nothing to do with it. Danjall had recognized Jandro's power play and chose to deeply offend Jandro rather than agree to the marriage. Jandro could have hoped for a grandson as Spirit Priest, but instead he was now Danjall's most loyal enemy.

Adan sighed. She was coming to their shack. *I wonder what trouble she brings from her father this time.*

Graisia and Kaly rounded a bend in the path and were now out of Adan's eyesight. Graisia began to breathe a bit more normally.

Kaly dropped Graisia's hand. "I don't know what you'd do without me, roach."

Graisia bit her lower lip and stayed close to Kaly. She wanted to take Kaly's hand again, but knew it was out of the question. Kaly wasn't exactly known for her compassion.

Just then they heard the pitter-patter of small sandaled feet running on the dirt path behind them. Graisia turned to see seven-year-old Mitina trying to catch up, soft dark hair flying everywhere around her face. Mitina's sack smacked awkwardly against her legs as she ran. She was almost small enough to fit into her bag. Her nickname, Teeny, really was appropriate.

Mitina's big brown eyes were wide open in anticipation, totally unaware of the drama she had just missed.

Despite her recent scare, Graisia gave a smile to Mitina and paused a moment for her to catch up. Kaly kept walking. Mitina was a new arrival from the countryside and, of her own accord, had attached herself to their little *bandhu*. Her family had lost their farm and been forced to move closer to the city of Kutah for jobs. Her father's income wasn't enough for the family, so Mitina was sent to work each day as well.

They rounded another bend in the path, and Graisia almost ran right into a towering old man. She looked up and gasped. Salim stood looking down at her vacantly with his wife Estar at his side. *The crazy, old witch-couple!* They stood right in front of her, blocking her way. She instinctively reached out for Kaly's hand. Everyone knew that the crazy, old witch-couple kidnapped kids, locked them up and used them for their magic. She'd heard too that if you ate their food, it could make you go insane.

Kaly tried to pull her hand away, but Graisia held on and ended up getting yanked out of the couple's way in the process. *Why does everything have to go wrong today?* Her heartbeat pounded in her ears. But the couple walked on, not giving Graisia another glance.

As if to read Graisia's thoughts, Kaly laughed at her side. "I don't think you're even going to make it to the dump without dying today!" She gave her arm a final tug away from Graisia and lifted both her hands to make wavy, ghost-like gestures, mocking Graisia's fear. "The spirits are going to get you and squeeze you till your eyeballs bulge out!" She laughed again and turned away, shaking her head.

Graisia cringed at Kaly's words, remembering Opana's warning at the same time. She wondered if she really would make it through the day.

The three continued down the path to collect Tayzor, the oldest member of their *bandhu.*

Adan turned and called into the shack, "Someone comes for you, Dad."

"Let Soliel in," Danjall replied from inside.

Of course Dad knows who's coming. He doesn't have to be told.

When Soliel reached the door, Adan, a head

taller than her, held the door partly closed for a moment, keeping her from entering. He wanted her to look up into his eyes and see he wasn't looking harshly at her. But it didn't work. She looked at the ground and chewed on her lip, probably thinking he was trying to intimidate her. When he'd waited as long as he dared, he opened the door all the way and then followed her into the darkened, single-roomed shack. *Maybe it's better she doesn't know,* he concluded, almost relieved she hadn't looked up.

Adan's father had lit some crude handmade candles, which now burned in a few places around the room. The waft of incense drifted from a far corner. Adan quickly shut the only window that was open, sealing the room from unwanted eyes and ears.

Danjall sat cross-legged in the middle of the floor, back straight, head held high. He looked at Soliel with piercing and lightless eyes. He dominated the room even from his lowly position. He motioned for her to take a seat across from him. Soliel lowered herself hesitantly, being careful not to look Danjall in the face or sit too close.

"What trouble has your father sent me now?" Danjall asked.

Soliel looked quickly from one place on the floor to another, avoiding Danjall's eyes. "Felirnu owes him money and won't pay."

"What does your old fool want of me? Is his power so weak now?" Danjall sneered. Almost laughing, he continued half to himself, "And he wants *my* position!"

Soliel fidgeted with her fingers. She opened her mouth and then spoke again, quietly, "Father wants Felirnu's son, Vic, to get sick."

Adan walked over to a cupboard in the room and started gathering ingredients his father would need for the spell.

"He troubles me for sickness? My son could do that!" Danjall paused and narrowed his eyes at Soliel.

Danjall had taught him all the rituals he knew regarding how to invite spirits into his body and summon them for their power, how to control animals, travel through the air outside his body, and even how to change his human form to that of another creature. Adan could battle people of lesser power and stop enemies in their tracks with his gaze. All these secrets had been passed down from generation to generation through Adan's ancestors. *Sickness is nothing!*

Adan wondered if the real reason Jandro had for sending his daughter was so Jandro would look weak to his father, and his father would let down his guard. *My father will see right through it. Jandro's a fool.* His father appeared to come to the same conclusion. Adan watched his face relax into a bored expression, as if he was listening to a child explain for the hundredth time how he could become a millionaire in a day.

"Does he want Vic to die?" Danjall asked calmly.

Soliel looked up quickly and shook her head. Then just as fast, she looked back down at the floor. "No... just scare Felirnu." Soliel paused and seemed to be thinking of a reason to back her request. "Father wants money. If Vic dies, he won't be able to make any money at the dump to pay Father back. Maybe you could tell a snake to sleep across his doorway for a day, or something – just... just scare Felirnu...." Her voice trailed off.

Adan chuckled at Soliel's suggestion. He could send a snake too, but it wouldn't get the job done. *She* is *a softy.*

Danjall answered her, "Need more than a snake to scare Felirnu. Making Vic sick should do it. Did you bring a piece of the boy?"

Soliel reached into her pocket and pulled out a folded, dirty scrap of paper. She opened it, revealing a few strands of hair, and handed them to Danjall.

"Your father at least still has some wisdom." Danjall motioned for Adan to take the hair.

Adan added the hair to the other ingredients he had been assembling. Soliel began to pull out some bills to pay Danjall.

Danjall looked at her disdainfully. "Your father will pay me when it's done."

"Of course." Soliel shoved the money back in her pocket and scrambled to stand up. She turned toward the door giving a sidelong glance at Adan. His heart momentarily forgot to beat as she slipped out into the sunlight.

3

Graisia clambered up the mountain of trash after Tayzor, the unofficial leader of their bandhu. The others were already on the far side, and she didn't want to be left without anyone from her bandhu around. The midday sun beat down on her head, making sweat run into her eyes. The meager amount of food she'd found that morning, a few scraps of bread and a half-rotten papaya, hadn't given her much energy.

She'd found a stick to use for sifting through garbage but it served well as a walking stick too. The sack weighed down on her shoulder – half full of cans, plastic bottles and some little knickknacks that might be worth something. She'd already checked the cans for bits of food and soda. They were empty. She loved the mini sugar-rush burst of energy from a half can of soda.

She looked up at Tayzor with his loose cutoffs and thin tank top. His clothes were small in size, but still too big on his lanky frame.

"Tayzor, why do you still hang out with us?" she asked. Most guys his age were either selling drugs or had gotten some job in the city by now. It was usually beneath them to keep digging in trash.

"Who would look after you scrawny rats?" Tayzor replied gruffly.

Kaly poked her head over the top of the pile. "Yeah, right. You care *so* much about us." Then she added, "You just don't want to end up like your brothers." Tayzor's brothers could often be found wasted on drugs and not good for much of anything. Even his youngest brother was a sniffer, carrying around a rag soaked with paint thinner all the time.

Tayzor gave Kaly a dirty look and kept climbing up the pile towards her. He caught up to her, whopped her on the head with the back of his hand and headed down the other side.

Kaly turned back toward Graisia with a piercing look and whispered, "Are you blind? He's too weak to make it into town every day. Don't bring it up again!" She headed down the other side of the pile after Tayzor.

Graisia hadn't thought about that before. She knew he got sick a lot with malaria, and he often took short rests during the day, but it had never occurred to her that was the reason he continued to hang out with their *bandhu*. She hoped he didn't have "slim," a disease that killed lots of people in their town. It was called "slim" because people usually got really skinny before they died. She decided just to be grateful there was someone older around.

Graisia saw an empty soup can just out of reach and to the right. She headed for it on her way to the top. But someone else had seen it too. A girl a few years younger than her grabbed it at the same time.

"I saw it first!" Graisia made a face at the girl and tried to pull it from her hand.

"Let it go, rat!" a boy yelled at her from nearby.

"Yeah, unless you want your face buried," another, younger boy spoke up. The girl's *bandhu* was closing in.

"Or maybe we'll just have to take everything in your sack." An older girl dashed toward her.

Graisia quickly let go of the can and scrambled to the top of the pile. "Tayzor! Kaly!" she yelled. She knew they might not come back to help her, but she wanted to let the other *bandhu* know she wasn't alone. It worked. They stopped pursuing her, and she hurried over to the rest of her *bandhu*, determined not to lose sight of them again for the rest of the day.

Mitina was picking carefully through the trash. Graisia came up alongside her. "You won't find much that way, Teeny. You've got to go like this!" Graisia raised up her stick, jammed it into the pile and then lifted a layer off to see what was underneath. Mitina peered into the hole Graisia had made. Bugs and beetles scurried deeper into the garbage to escape the sweltering heat. Graisia dug her hands in, following the beetles, and sorted through the layer newly revealed.

"Hey Graisia, your friend has come back looking for you," Kaly called out sarcastically.

Graisia jerked her head up and saw Kaly motioning toward one of the paths that led from

Sawtong to the dump. Salim, the crazy, old witch-man, shuffled in their direction. Her heart stopped for a split second. When he reached the edge of the dump he turned onto the dirt road that ringed the mountains of garbage and headed toward Pouyan's shack. Graisia let out the breath she didn't realize she'd been holding.

Kaly snickered. "You're such a roach! Anything'll scare you."

Graisia frowned. They'd seen Salim walk that path hundreds of times before, but today, seeing him just helped keep her nerves on edge. Salim would only be getting items from Pouyan, the man they took their finds to at the end of the day. Pouyan gave all of the kids coins for their finds and then sold their goods to others like Salim, who would put them to use.

Graisia warily turned back to the work at hand, keeping an eye on Pouyan's shack. So far, nothing too bad had actually happened to her today, but the day wasn't finished.

"Maybe we'll find something good today!" Mitina piped up unexpectedly. "Like a gold coin or a pretty dress."

She knew Mitina was trying to make her feel better. She gave Mitina half a smile.

"Yeah, right. People in the city aren't as stupid as they are on the farms, Teeny," Kaly shot out.

"Maybe sometimes they throw things away... accidentally," Mitina said trying to cover up the sting of Kaly's words.

"Believe me, people that live in Kutah, when they

got something good, they are *not* going to let it go."
Everyone saw Kaly as an expert on city life, even
though she'd only spent a few months there.

Mitina looked down at the trash in front of her
dejectedly.

"You never know, Mitina. Maybe we *will* find
something really good." Graisia hated to see her sad.

Mitina poked half heartedly at the trash in front
of her.

"Com' on, *kosa*," Graisia used the term for a
fellow *bandhu* member with Mitina. "Let's look at
what's closer to the top of this pile."

Together, Graisia and Mitina scrambled up a bit
closer to the top of the heap. They dug and poked
around for a while, but didn't really find anything
exceptional – just more of the usual; cans, bottles,
and a pair of halfway decent shoes. They were just
about to move to another spot when a plump trash
bag caught Graisia's eye. It was partially covered by
newspaper pages with pictures of the Prime Minister,
Vivi Sel Luan all over them. Graisia pulled off the
damp, sticky pages and lifted the bag with ease. It
was surprisingly light. Now even more curious, she
tore open the side of the knotted bag. Inside was an
object made of soft, pink material.

"Hey, look Teeny, it's fluffy and pretty," Graisia
called out. She tore the bag wider. The material
turned out to be a puffy rectangle just begging to be
hugged. Graisia pulled it out and squeezed it to
herself. Closing her eyes, she felt like she was
hugging a cloud.

"Mmmmm. It feels *so* good!" Graisia murmured,

completely forgetting she was supposed to be worrying about an omen. "You try, Mitina." Graisia's grimy hands left smudge marks all over the cloud.

Mitina's eyes lit up, and she nuzzled her face into the fabric-covered cloud, adding more filth to the clean surface. "Oooo, it's so soft. Bet you could get a bucket of coins from Pouyan for it!"

Graisia took back the puffy pink object and placed it back into the trash bag. "Pouyan's beady eyes won't even see it!" she told Mitina. The kids rarely kept anything that could be traded for a good sum of money, but this time, it didn't even seem an option. "I wonder what it's for. Bet Kaly would know." Without a second thought, Graisia turned and yelled, "Kaly!" Then yanked her cloud right back out of the bag and bounded over to Kaly and Tayzor.

"Kaly! Look! It's a pink soft, puffy cloud thing! What is it?! Do you know?!" Graisia asked excitedly.

Kaly was bent over, intent on tearing free a can that was caught on an old shoe.

"What are you all wild about?" Kaly stood up and faced Graisia with cool self-assurance, basking in the attention. Kaly seemed to know everything because of the time she spent with her mother in Kutah. Graisia was secretly glad Kaly hadn't liked living with her mother and her mother's boyfriend. After only two weeks, she had returned to Sawtong and moved in with her aunt Lindi. Lindi had taken in a number of kids whose parents had died of "slim," which meant there wasn't much room, but apparently it was better than the city.

"Thought you'd know what this is!" Graisia held

out her cloud with flair.

"Course I do!" Kaly replied instantly – then paused. Graisia wondered if she really did know. Kaly took it roughly from her hands. "Anyone could tell you what it is. They're in movies – only for princesses and queens, though. Haven't you watched anyone's T.V.?"

"Not really...." Graisia murmured, embarrassed. Opana didn't have a television, and Graisia rarely got the chance to hang around someone else's home. She'd only been able to steal glimpses of shows now and then through doorways.

Kaly stood taller. "They call it a... a pillow, and they put them under their feet when they're lying down... or under their head," Kaly added quickly.

"What for? I didn't know there were queens and princesses in the city! Why'd they throw it out?" In awe, Graisia took the pillow back from Kaly and put it into its bag with even more care than before. A thought suddenly struck Graisia, "When they throw these pillow things out, it doesn't bring bad luck to me, does it?"

"'Course not, stupid. A pillow's a pillow." Kaly shook her head, apparently disgusted with Graisia's ignorance.

Graisia relaxed. She fingered the edge of the soft pillow sticking out of the bag. "Wow! I have something that belonged to a queen, or a princess!"

Kaly rolled her eyes and turned back to her digging.

Graisia couldn't wait to get home and try out her new cloud pillow. It was all she could do to keep from suggesting they leave early. Nothing much was added to her sack the rest of the day. Her mind kept drifting to her new treasure. Not once did she think of Opana's dark omen.

The sun had started to fall behind the city skyline and lessen its grip on the waking world when Tayzor, shoulders hunched and looking ready to fall asleep, made a move towards Pouyan's shack. Graisia bounded as fast as she could down the mound of trash, not even thinking of calling to Mitina. Graisia was one of the first kids at Pouyan's shack. She traded everything she had, except the cloud, of course. Pouyan didn't give her as many coins as usual, but she didn't care. She practically danced around the others in her excitement and lack of patience while they got their coins.

"You look like you got worms and need a ditch, girl!" Pouyan hollered out as he watched her from the corner of his eye. "Don't go making any smelly messes around my shack!"

"Nope, I won't," Graisia called back in a sing-songy voice. Mitina had just gotten her coins, and now they could all leave.

"You do look like you've got the runs, but with a stupid smile to go with it," Kaly taunted.

"Yeah, she's an old hunchback with rotten gut!" Tayzor chimed in, laughing.

"Hmph," was all Graisia dared come back with. She tried to wipe the smile off her face, but couldn't help the extra spring still in her step. She still couldn't wait to get home and try out her very own cloud.

Graisia rounded the last bend in the path before Opana's house and stopped suddenly. Opana was talking with Flora and pulling laundry off poles that extended out from the roofline of her shack. Graisia darted back around the corner, out of sight. If Opana saw her sack still full, she would get a beating for sure.

She couldn't go all the way back to Kaly or Mitina's to hide her cloud. They were too close to Adan. She'd have to find a spot nearby. Slipping into a gap between some shacks, she looked for a good hiding place. Cobwebs stuck to her arms and legs as she made her way forward in the narrow, shadowy space. Further in, she spotted a rotting fruit crate covered in more cobwebs. *Nobody's going to use that tonight.* She tugged out her cloud pillow still in its trash bag, lifted up the crate and stuffed her pillow underneath. Satisfied that the black bag helped to conceal her precious package, she cautiously made her way back out onto the path.

Opana was still taking clothes down when Graisia reached the shack. *She looks like a wrinkled, brown elephant, stuffed into an apron.* Graisia managed to stifle a smile as she dropped her coins into Opana's plump, open hand. *She's just missing a trunk....*

Opana went back to working without glancing at Graisia. "Soup's by the door," she said around the clothespin in her mouth.

Isela, Opana's oldest daughter, stood in the doorway smirking at Graisia. "Sorry, it's a bit cold. The flies are enjoying it, though. So you probably will too, trash girl."

Graisia sighed. She was used to Isela's constant berating. *Isela's right, I'll never be more than a trash girl. I wish Opana would make her kids work at the dump too, but no, they're "better than that,"* Graisia mimicked Opana's voice in her head. She dropped her empty sack on the ground and picked up the half-filled bowl of cold, watery mush.

Opana's cynical voice broke into her thoughts, "You know, if Graisia started working harder and bringing more coins home, I might be able to spare the time to teach her the *takra* sticks." Opana was talking to Flora who sat across the way on her own front stoop. Flora looked haggard with her chin in her hands and eyes half closed.

I've heard that before, and nothing's ever come of it. Graisia sat down in the dirt next to their shack and said nothing. She knew Opana was trying to get a rise out of her, but a response wouldn't do any good. Graisia brought home as much as she could.

Opana misread her silence. "She's an ungrateful rat, I tell you."

Flora mumbled something sounding like a condolence.

Opana turned briefly to Graisia. "Fine. Keep digging if that's what you want."

Graisia sighed. It wasn't worth trying to answer back. She looked wearily at her mush. It had a little bit of something resembling rice in it, as well as a dead fly or two. She brushed away some of the still buzzing flies, scooped out the dead ones and took a sip. Helping out with laundry would be nice, or selling peanuts along the side of the road like some of Opana's other kids, but she could earn more at the dump. On the good side, at least she didn't have to hang around Opana all day.

Graisia turned to look at the crude altar made for Harapkan. It had been there for as long as she could remember. A plastic statue of the many legged goddess sat on a simple, homemade table. Harapkan's many legs were supposed to symbolize the various paths one's fate could take.

As one of the lesser spirit gods, she wasn't a threat to Mahalan, so Opana was allowed to worship her as long as she honored Mahalan too. Graisia looked at Harapkan and wondered how the plastic statue helped Opana read omens through tea leaves and *takra* sticks. *Why would she want to teach me how to read the sticks? Why not Isela?* It didn't make any sense. Graisia glanced at the food left for Harapkan – a full bowl of rice and some old fruit. She sighed again. As usual, it was better than hers. She swallowed another mouthful of mush and turned away.

The rest of Opana's kids were in the shack making a ruckus. Graisia heard Isela smack a couple of the younger ones and holler at them to shut up. This only made the commotion worse. Graisia quickly finished her soupy mush and put the bowl back on the doorstep. The flies immediately took over where she left off.

Reluctantly, she made her way around the altar and crawled into her little space. She didn't want to go to sleep. Inevitable nightmares weren't exactly inviting. But she was exhausted from the long sweltering day and her lack of sleep was catching up with her.

Maybe tonight will be different. Maybe if I think about good things I'll sleep better. She tried to think of all the special places her pillow might have lived before. This led to wondering where her mother might be, and if *she'd* ever used a pillow. She tried to draw up the last image she had of her mother. At least she assumed that lady had been her mother.

The only memory she had was of a sad woman with a scarred face, setting her down along the roadside, and then disappearing amongst a crowd of people... forever. Graisia could still see the blurry image of her mother walking away, through tears that flooded her eyes. Graisia had tried to follow, but the crowd engulfed them both mercilessly. She imagined it was like being lost at sea with huge waves pushing them away from each other, threatening to drown them both. Torturous feelings of abandonment filled Graisia's heart with grief and gasping sobs broke through her lips. She covered her mouth, unsuccessfully trying to hold them back. These were anything but the good thoughts she had been looking for.

Adan lay face down, stretched out on the sleeping mat he shared with his father. His father had acted weird and distant all day. He'd hardly said a word. *He's even lying down for the night, before me!*

He usually stayed up late, went out to meet with other *basyo* or spent time down by the river where he could conjure spirits with less interruption. Adan turned to look at his father's dark chiseled features silhouetted in the near darkness. His father was muttering and talking to spirits in a trance-like state.

His mother used to lie there too. But that was years ago and what seemed like another lifetime. He stuffed the feelings that threatened to surface. Rolling over onto his back, he tried to get more comfortable. The air was particularly humid tonight. He wished they could leave the door open and let the occasional breeze dry the sweat that dripped from their bodies, but it wouldn't be safe. Too many people would like to see them dead, and someone else as Spirit Priest.

Adan sensed the numerous spirits hovering in the room around his father. He decided to join his father and see if the spirits might have something to show or tell him as well. He focused on the ethereal beings and began to draw their *lakás* into himself.

4

Graisia panicked. She was standing just inside the doorway of the Spirit Priest's shack, looking down at Adan and Danjall. How did she get here? They were both staring blankly toward the ceiling and murmuring strange words she couldn't understand. Shadowy spirits swirled around the room. Graisia wondered if she was dreaming – but it felt so real. Before she could figure out what had happened, two shimmering gray spirits swooshed past her right arm. They went straight for Adan and circled his head twice before coiling over his face, pulsating.

She had seen enough. She didn't know how she had arrived, but she wanted to leave. This was the worst possible place she could be. Even if the ones she feared were lying down, even if it was a dream – that did not make them safe. She tried turning her body. She couldn't move.

As Adan chanted to conjure more power from the spirits, a startling image appeared. The chant caught in his throat. The spirits had never given a picture of her before. His mother's loving face hovered faintly in front of him. Her chocolaty brown hair flowed softly around her cinnamon features. She spoke, in a barely audible voice, of ancient legends and goddesses. He was so caught up in looking at her that he hardly heard what she was saying. He did hear her say something about Ivah though, a rival goddess of Mahalan.

"Ivah... love... superior to Mahalan..." Her words floated in and out of his hearing range.

Ivah was the goddess whom the Spirit Priests had worshiped generations before on this land. Before the dump was established, farmers used to own the land where Sawtong stood. They were known for being fairly peaceful and worshipping Ivah faithfully. Adan's ancestors, however, had been among the first to settle Sawtong as a town, and they had pledged allegiance to Mahalan. His grandfather and father had forbidden any in the town to worship Ivah. As the town grew and swallowed up the farms, worship of Ivah disappeared as well. The last known prophetess of Ivah had promised that one day Ivah would return and reclaim her territory.

Danjall allowed families to worship spirits of lesser power, as long as they also pledged allegiance to Mahalan and did whatever they were told. But Ivah was a different matter. Mahalan and Ivah were sworn rivals with almost equal power. Someone who served Ivah was a threat to the current Spirit Priest and would have to be dealt with.

Adan looked at his mother's face, memorizing

afresh the soft markings and lines around her eyes and mouth. She stirred in him a long buried yearning for love, softness, and sacrificial kindness. She'd been gone since he was about four years old, but still his heart ached for her – something he would never admit to in waking hours. Her image, however, was like a key that opened a room full of sorrow and desire. She had abandoned them, though – disappeared without any note or goodbye. One day, she was there as the brightest source of love and joy in his life, and the next day, she had taken his heart away. His father had never offered an explanation.

Adan rarely let himself miss her this much. A single tear slipped down his cheek, stirring him from his trancelike state.

Why would the spirits show him his mother? Was she trying to reach him? A twinge of fear and guilt troubled him when he thought of his mother mentioning Ivah. He wondered if the spirits loyal to Mahalan would tell his father of this encounter. His father always reacted swiftly and harshly to anyone who mentioned Ivah favorably. *Maybe he drove my mother away... or killed her!* The thought hit his chest with a suffocating blow. His unwavering trust in his father was suddenly on shaking stilts. *Could he have? Did he kill her? Could she still be alive? Did she really worship Ivah? She never said anything about Ivah to me when she was here. Are the spirits lying?*

The image completely blurred and dissipated. He was left with the feeling of the coursing *lakás* fading to a distant thrum in the recesses of his muscles. He lay stunned, shaken to the core by the thought that maybe his father took the only love he'd ever known. He closed his eyes and tried to re-imagine his mother's face. He felt the spirits weigh down on him. He sighed deeply as they drew him into another trance.

What Graisia saw contradicted all reason. Danjall stood up, walked woodenly over to a shelf in the corner of the shack, picked up an old knife and some rope, returned and stood over Adan. One moment his eyes were intense and focused, the next he looked shaken and uncertain. This rock of a man almost seemed unable to control his own actions. He was sweating profusely and took no notice of Graisia, whose fear was mounting by the second. She really wanted to run now. It looked like he wanted to use the knife on Adan, but she would be an easy target too, especially with a body that wouldn't move.

Sinister shadows shrieked and swirled around Danjall, swiping at him, begging for blood. One of the shadowy forms hovered around Danjall's head like a green vapor of mist. Graisia cringed at the smell of death. The power of the spirits grew stronger within the shack. She covered her face with her hands and arms. Everything in her told her to run and flee....

A muddle of images took shape before Adan's eyes, clarifying and forming into distinguishable figures and pictures. Jagged shadows danced slowly around a fire, the pace quickening until their movements became a frenetic war dance, like one that might be done just before a sacrifice. The largest spirit leapt out of the circle and swept around menacingly in front of Adan's face. A knife hovered in the air nearby. Adan pressed himself further back into the floorboards beneath him. He couldn't see a distinct face of the shadowy spirit, but he could see wafts of green vapor drifting from its face and smell the putrid stench of death on its breath. Suddenly his father's face flashed through the vapor. Adan cried out in alarm.

Danjall's eyes were filled with greed for power, but at Adan's cry, they widened in agony and despair. Then his father's face disappeared, and he was left staring into a shadowy green mist. In a low husky voice that sounded like grating metal, the spirit spoke to Adan, "You are mine... all mine... from the blood of your ancestors. I will do with you as I wish."

Adan tried to roll away but couldn't. A good dose of fear was to be expected when working with the spirits, but did this have to do with the vision of his mother and the mention of Ivah?

Then as quickly as the images had come, they disappeared. Sleep pulled at him. He tried to cling to consciousness, but it pulled away from him like the helpless unwinding of a yo-yo.

Graisia watched Danjall wrestling internally with what the spirits seemed to be telling him to do.

Suddenly he lurched toward her, trembling violently. He leapt over Adan and proceeded to run right through her, pushing the door open and staggering outside. He dropped the knife and rope in a clatter on the doorstep.

Graisia spun around in shock to watch him – her feet now free to move. He dragged and wrestled his way down the path with the murky tormentors shrieking all around him. After zigzagging a few steps, he turned around to look behind him and apparently saw something Graisia couldn't see. Eyes wide-open in terror, he stumbled towards the darkness of riverbank.

She glanced down at Adan, who lay motionless on his back. His eyes were closed, and he appeared to be sleeping deeply, completely unaware of everything going on around him.

Then everything went black.

She blinked her eyes and found herself staring up at the roof of her little cubbyhole in the dull blackness of after-midnight. Everything around her was so still and quiet she could hear the termites in their rhythmic nibbling, eating slowly away at her home.

She took a deep breath as her pulse attempted to return to normal. *Why would Danjall want to kill Adan? Is that what he was going to do? Or was he after me? Did he even see me?* It had all seemed so vivid, like she'd actually been in their shack. She lay trembling in confusion, relieved that at least she seemed safe for now.

A yell of anguish jolted Adan from his slumber. He rolled over in the still darkness of early morning to look for his father and see if he had heard the same cry. The floor next to him was vacant. He turned the other way and saw the door ajar. Glinting in the moonlight, his father's sacrificial knife lay by the door next to a piece of rope. Both were angled awkwardly, as if dropped in a hurry.

He jumped up, confused by the scene. He wondered if the yell he'd heard had even been real. Not knowing what he'd find outside, he grabbed the knife and rope and staggered out the door. He made his way down a path behind their row of shacks. The path led to the river below in the direction he thought the yell had come from. *Maybe he's gone to put a spell on someone. Maybe his own spell over Felirnu's son wasn't good enough, and he had to do something more.* But even as Adan thought this, he doubted it was true. Worry crept over him. *Dad never gets up this early in the morning. And he never leaves the door open. Why didn't he wake me? Why didn't I wake up?*

As Spirit Priest, Danjall would often go at the darkest point of the night to the water's edge to offer sacrifices, cast spells, or conjure spirits. It was quieter there, with fewer prying eyes, a place dedicated to and empowered by sacrifices. But he rarely went at this time of the morning. Adan almost slipped and fell a couple of times in his nervous haste to climb down through the slime, weeds and mud. His hair clung to his neck and forehead in the humidity. He looked uneasily in all directions.

It took a few minutes before he reached the flat area by the river, frequented by Danjall and hidden from the main view of Sawtong. His father was not there, but dirt and ash left from previous sacrifices were scattered as if a fight had occurred in the center of the clearing. *What happened?*

"Dad!" Adan whispered as loudly as he dared, squinting into the darkness around him, hoping that whoever fought with his dad wasn't still there. No answer. He lifted the knife tentatively, ready to attack just in case.

The only sounds he heard were the rush of water, the occasional truck rumbling by in the distance, and his own blood pounding in his ears. He walked cautiously farther down the path to the water's edge. A shadow to his right caught his eye. He did not want to go see what it was, but his feet kept moving.

Adan made his way to the shadowy mass amongst the weeds. *Maybe it's Dad in a trance,* he thought hopefully, *or –* but the sight of his father's mangled body sprawled on the ground cut his thoughts short. The knife slipped from his hand, thudding to the ground. His mouth went dry. He felt like someone had thrown a bucket of ice at him. Blood drained from his face. He stood frozen, staring. His father, mentor and only friend stared up at him blankly, locked in a permanent contortion of pain. *This can't be happening.*

"Dad," he whispered. Slowly he knelt down by

his father's face. Adan's mind wanted to refuse what he was seeing. He looked up and down his father's body and cringed at the deep scratch marks torn across his father's chest, shredding through his clothes, almost as if from the inside out. Danjall's arms and legs were covered with bruises.

No, this can't happen. How could he be beaten in the ultimate battle? Everyone knew there was no greater battle than for one's life. *How? No one's more powerful than him! No one!* Adan quickly thought through the names of all the other *basyo* who might have wanted to see him dead. There were none powerful enough to win against his father. *How could this happen?*

It seemed impossible. As long as his family had lived here, they had been the invincible guardians of Mahalan's worship. No one could be the cause of this horror. There was no one more powerful than his father.

No one must know! Adan's mind raced like a freight train heading downhill with broken brakes. *I can't let anyone know he was beaten, they'll stop fearing us. Me. We'll lose control. I'll lose control. I've got to find out who's behind this before anyone else finds out what's happened. They're going to pay.... They will pay....*

In the eerie pre-dawn light he came up with one coherent thought. He had to get rid of his father's body. The murky light brown river, the river that carried the refuse of the city, as well as the run-off from the distant mountains to the waiting ocean, was the only place he could think of. It served both as source of life and sewer for their town, and now it would serve as grave. He knew that it would go against all protocol, especially for the Spirit Priest. According to tradition, his father's soul could be kept from joining the ancestors if the body wasn't disposed of properly. But what would it matter if Adan lost all his father had worked for?

He tried to hold onto his sanity and not give in to feeling like he was on a drug trip gone wrong. How could he think of getting rid of his father's body like this? He wrestled with himself. *There's no other way,* he finally decided, *the spirits will understand. Mahalan will understand. They'll allow Dad's soul through. They have to. He's served Mahalan faithfully. They would all want it this way so I can keep control of the town.*

He had to do it quickly before daylight brought exposure and stripped away the fear he and his father demanded of others. Adan looked around again to make sure no one was watching. Trying to ignore his screaming emotions, he picked up a long piece of wood that lay nearby. He grimaced as he pulled his father's mangled body onto the board and then dragged it towards the river's edge where an ever-present band of garbage lapped along with the water. He scoured the shore until he found the largest rock he could carry, tied the rope around it, and carried it back to his father's body. After tying the other end of the rope around his father's waist, he set the rock gently on his father's shredded chest.

He couldn't believe what he was doing. *It's not right! He deserves more than this.* Yet he continued.

With trembling hands, he slid the piece of wood, supporting his father, into the water. The wood kept his father and the rock afloat. Muddy, trash-filled water splashed against the wood as he sloshed alongside it. Shadowy clouds covered the partial moon, aiding in his grisly task.

Soon the water got too deep, and he had to swim as he continued to push his father further toward the center of the river. The board threatened to tip over, but he held it firm. Finally, when he was about midway across the river, he paused and began to tread water. Awkwardly reaching across the motionless body, he grabbed the bracelet on his father's right wrist. It was the one worn only by the Spirit Priest, made of two metal bands: one copper and one silver. Each of the bands had been twisted alone and then placed side by side. At its clasp, a round copper seal of the *dusanays* symbol was surrounded by an inscription. For as many generations as Adan knew, the Spirit Priests of his family had worn this bracelet. It was a symbol of power in his family, and also an object they believed contained power itself.

He deftly slid it on his own wrist, and then with his face set, slowly tipped the board, rolling his father's lifeless body into the shadowy grave. Half stifling a sob, he let the empty board float away down the river. With his fingertips, he touched his forehead and next his heart. He could at least half try to honor the river god. He hoped Mahalan, the other spirits, the river god, and his father would understand. With the bracelet transferred to his own wrist, a chilling thought dawned on him.

Whoever killed my dad will want me dead too.

He slowly swam back to the river bank and dragged himself out onto the shore. He sat at the water's edge staring at the swirling, drifting water that had now become a partner to his secret. He stayed until the sun spread its long fingers over the horizon. He tried not to think, hoping it was all a dream.

5

The rest of the night went too quickly for Graisia. Morning light stole through the cracks of her splintered walls, forcing her from the longest period of dreamless sleep she'd had in a long time. *Couldn't the sun forget to come out for one morning?* Graisia rolled over, but the walls of her shack were like a sieve, and the sun found her yet again. In rebellion she shut her eyes even tighter, but it didn't help.

Why do I even try? Reluctantly, she stretched her thin frame as much as she could in her little space, opened her eyes and sat up. She stared absently for a few moments at a spider that had made its new home in the corner.

Her mind flitted back to the experience she'd had earlier in the night, and she was instantly jarred from her reverie, shivering at the thought of Danjall's knife and the faceless spirit of green vapor. She didn't want to think about that anymore. *My cloud!* She scrambled out her hole. Maybe she could bring it back to her little space before going off for the day. But Opana's bucket hit the wall behind her.

"Get moving! And don't forget to bring something for Harapkan!" Opana yelled.

"Aye, *lakás*," Graisia whispered to herself. She snatched up her worn sack. Getting the cloud would have to wait.

"What was that, trash girl?"

"Yes, Opana, I won't forget," this time louder. She sighed. *Another thing to worry about today – extra food for the goddess of fate. I don't want my fate made worse.*

She passed numerous other shacks, built haphazardly; some, on top of each other, out of whatever the inhabitants had found. Each home was a single room where the whole family lived and slept, if you could call them families. Some were lucky enough to actually be families, but most were only parts of families, or made-up families. Graisia allowed her mind to daydream momentarily about how wonderful it would be to have family to live with, or even just a mom who loved her.

She stopped herself. It was too painful to think about. She shifted her focus again to one of the shacks nearby.

Someone was hacking and coughing inside. It was Felirnu's shack. Felirnu stood at the door, giving a wad of bills to Soliel.

"That's half of it, right?" Felirnu asked.

Soliel looked uncomfortably at the bills in her hand and rifled through them nervously, then nodded.

Felirnu pulled a few more bills out of his pocket and stuffed them in Soliel's hands. "This is something extra for Jandro to break the curse off Vic.... And I'll pay the other half of what I owe him in a few days." Felirnu's voice then dropped to a harsh whisper, but Graisia could still hear what he said. "Make sure your father knows my allegiance is still with him."

Soliel nodded again and then turned and darted down the street. Her black braid flew behind her like the tail of a kite whipping in the wind.

Graisia wondered what that whole exchange was about. *Why would Felirnu give allegiance to Jandro? That's weird.*

Graisia finally drew closer to Kaly's home. Her steps slowed, and she stared at Adan's door. It was wide open. Her heart pounded in her ears, making her feel like one big beating heart. Kaly appeared and surprised her with a shove. Graisia let out a startled cry.

"No one's seen him or his dad all morning. The door's been like that since before the sun came up," Kaly informed her. "Nothing for you to worry about today."

"Really?" Graisia asked in surprise. "It's been open like that?" She thought of her dream and how she had seen Danjall flee out the door. "Maybe my dream's true, then."

"What, you dreamt of an open door? Aye, Graisia, you and your imagination. You worry too much! You need to loosen up. Want to look inside?" Kaly asked excitedly. Without waiting for an answer, she grabbed Graisia's hand and dragged her towards Adan's shack.

Graisia panicked and yanked her hand out of Kaly's grip.

Kaly just laughed. "Roach!" Kaly taunted. Then with a sly smile, she headed away from Adan's shack and toward Mitina's.

Graisia didn't appreciate Kaly's idea of a joke.

Kaly went on as if nothing had happened and began telling Graisia the latest gossip about whose parent had taken off and the newest families that had arrived from Kutah or the struggling farms in the countryside. Then there was her neighbor's wife who had turned up dead a few days ago. No one knew how, but rumors flew – an angry neighbor, some sort of spell, maybe a jealous old boyfriend, or husband for that matter. No one would really bother to find out the truth.

Graisia let Kaly ramble on, not really listening. In spite of herself, Graisia peered across the path and through Adan's open doorway as they passed. She couldn't see everything from this far away, but she did see that Adan wasn't on the floor, and the knife and rope weren't near the door where Danjall had left them in her dream. *Did Adan get them? Is he going to use them on me?* She remembered the dark omen from yesterday and shivered involuntarily in the heat. She drew closer to Kaly who continued on with her monologue of rumors.

Mitina joined in as the girls passed her shack. Down the road a bit more, and across an open sewer ditch, was Tayzor's home. Tayzor's youngest brother was leaning against the outside of the shack with a friend, fighting over a small bottle of paint thinner.

Tayzor wasn't out yet though, so Kaly stuck her head in his doorway. Graisia could see Tayzor lying on the floor. Beyond him, his mother sat squatting on the ground stirring something in a pot and staring vacantly off into space. The woman seemed to have no emotion. Her face was as smooth as dirt after someone had drawn a picture in it then wiped it away, wanting to forget what they had drawn.

"Get up, you miserable lump of rat!" Kaly yelled as she knocked Tayzor on the head. His mother didn't even blink but continued stirring.

Tayzor reached up and tried to grab Kaly's hand, but Kaly was too quick and had jumped back out the door. Moments later, Tayzor appeared in the doorway, pulling his grubby and torn t-shirt over his head. The shirt had a faded picture of their country's largest building on it. He gave Kaly a quick smack to her head. "No wonder your mom kicked you out. Who'd want to live with your annoying voice?" He walked on ahead.

"She didn't kick me out. I left!" Kaly called after him. She actually looked like she was sulking for a moment or two afterward.

The four of them walked together, continuing toward the dump. When they rounded the final bend they were greeted by the familiar stench of trash cooking in the sun, and they were just in time to see a garbage truck unloading its latest delivery.

"Hey! Fresh pickings!" Tayzor shouted and took off running in spite of his chronic weakness.

Kaly raced after him. The truck rumbled off in a cloud of dust. As an afterthought, Graisia turned and grabbed Mitina's hand to make sure they didn't get separated. *Bandhu* was family, after all.

Adan had dried off sufficiently as to not appear suspicious when he returned to his shack. It *was* his now. He stumbled at the thought, and his stomach twisted with acid. He still had to appear as if everything was okay. He could not let anyone know someone had defeated his father. And he had to find out who was behind the murder... before they found him.

Just as he reached his shack, he spotted Soliel heading his way. *Not now,* he groaned inwardly. He wasn't ready to deal with whatever Jandro was up to, especially with Soliel in the middle of it.

"I have the money for your father." She kept her head lowered and showed him the few bills in her hand.

Adan cleared his throat. "I'll give it to him."

He reached for the money, but she withdrew it and quietly, apologetically replied, "My father said to give it directly to Danjall... so he knows."

A flash of terror streaked through Adan. He wondered if Jandro's instructions were so specific because he wanted to let Adan know he knew Danjall was dead. Jandro *had* come to mind first as being responsible for his father's death.

Adan snatched the money out of her hand and turned to go in his shack. "He's out.... I'll give it to him." And he bolted indoors.

The muscles of his jaw were clenching and unclenching, expressing the range of his assaulting emotions. Fear, grief, anguish and loneliness wrestled for prominence. He closed the rickety door quickly before Soliel could protest and the darkness of the room engulfed him. He wished everything would just disappear, and he'd find himself waking up from a dream. He opened the window a crack to let in some light and then turned and made his way to the shelf. His hands shook as he put together a mixture of herbs and various other substances. He stuffed them into an old metal can and dropped in a lit match to set the ingredients smoldering.

He closed the window again, placed the can on the floor and sat down next to it. He let the smoke waft over his senses, hoping it would help numb his pain. But in the blackness, his memories of the pre-dawn hours flooded in like a vortex threatening to suck him into its depths. It took everything within him to hold back the cries straining at his throat, wanting release.

He struggled to focus his thinking on the biggest problem at hand. If he wanted to keep his family's power in Sawtong, he had to find out who killed his father, and why. Yet, at the same time, he didn't want to even face the fact that his father was gone. The sun beat down on the tin roof above him mercilessly and made the smoky air almost unbearably stifling. Sweat from both the heat and his fear trickled down the side of his face.

He began centering down into the absence of thought, breathing deeply, eyes closed, preparing himself to try to commune with the spirits. Maybe they would have information that would help him. It took longer than usual to empty his mind completely. If not for his years of discipline, it would have been impossible. When his mind finally became blank, he started chanting softly, summoning the spirits.

In a hushed voice, he uttered their names... over and over... but received only silence in response. In frustration he chanted their names stronger and with more urgency. The spirits seemed sworn to secrecy. Exasperated, he cursed and stood up; knocking over the smoldering can in the process. Not even their whispers could be wakened.

Adan couldn't stand the shack's empty darkness. Cursing at the smoldering ashes strewn across the floor, he tried not to step on them with his bare feet as he made his way to the door. He shoved his feet into his shoes and yanked the door open.

Cursed spirits! Why wouldn't they say anything? Have to find out who did it. How could this happen? What would Dad do? Dad –

In the midst of his anguish, a subtle thought arose. As painful as it was to admit, it was also freeing – he didn't have to do things exactly the way his Dad wanted anymore. *Maybe there is someone who could help me find out.* He strode out into the blaring sun and headed down the dirt path.

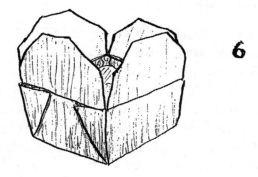

6

The noonday sun beat down on Graisia's back as she and her *bandhu* climbed and searched through the small mountains of garbage. Her sack was partly full and beginning to weigh her down.

"Anybody got food?" Kaly yelled out to the others.

"Some," Tayzor replied. "The usual."

He and Kaly headed over to the edge of the dump, where they could sit on the dirt to eat their midday scroungings. Graisia and Mitina took their cue and followed after them, digging out their saved food from the bottom of their sacks. Tayzor plopped himself down in the sparse weeds and scattered trash – one could never totally get away from garbage – and swigged the last few drops of soda from a can.

"Hey! We're supposed to share!" Graisia called out.

"There *were* only a few drops. Can't share that," Tayzor replied dryly.

Graisia dropped her argument and sullenly plunked down on the ground. She would have loved even one sugary drop. She pulled out half a piece of fruit and bits of a sandwich, placing them in the center for everyone to share. Mitina, Kaly and Tayzor put their scraps in too.

They were just about to dig in when a young boy, of about nine or ten, came up and stood beside them. Graisia had never seen him before, which was odd. All the kids in Sawtong pretty much knew each other, at least by sight. His sandy hair, naturally bleached by malnutrition, was tussled and sticking out awkwardly. The light color was a stark contrast next to his tanned skin. "Have any room for me in your *bandhu*?"

Kaly let out a hiss, scoffing at the boy.

Tayzor, more practical, asked, "What've you got for food?"

The boy pulled out a restaurant take-away box with a mischievous smile as if he had just won the lottery and was about to be everybody's favorite friend. Graisia leaned in with the others at the sight of the box. Without saying a word, the boy opened it and showed what was inside – half of a roasted chicken, plump and golden.

"Yippee!" Mitina let out in a squeal.

"Shhh! Don't announce it to the world!" Kaly whispered, cuffing Mitina on the shoulder. They all knew other kids would descend on them if it was known what a goldmine they had.

"You're in," Tayzor stated simply and moved aside slightly to give him room. "Name?"

"And where'd you come from?" Kaly asked with her eyes narrowed.

The boy sat down next to Tayzor. "Lio. I used to live in Trakston, but my mom and I had to move here 'cause she said my *bandhu* there was getting too violent."

Tayzor seemed satisfied with the answer and motioned for Lio to put the box in the center of the circle.

Ferociously hungry, Graisia couldn't keep her eyes off the box of chicken. As soon as Lio set it on the ground, she shoved her hand in the box along with everyone else and ripped off chunks of meet as fast as she could. There might be benefits to having another *bandhu* member. When the meat was gone, and she was sucking on one of the bones, she allowed herself to look around. No one unusual was milling nearby.

"Your friends aren't going to follow you, are they?" Graisia asked hesitantly.

Lio wiped his mouth with the back of his hand. "Nah, they've got more important things to worry about."

She hoped he was right. She studied the surface of his face as if she might be able to detect some residue of his violent *bandhu's* past. Maybe some of their cruelty had rubbed off on him. His face seemed unreadable, though. She wanted to convince herself he was harmless, but so far, she wasn't succeeding.

Adan walked all the way to the far side of the dump and now stood just a few shacks away from Jandro's. He rarely got over to this side of Sawtong, but he knew his way around well enough. Most of the *basyo* lived on this side. They liked to have their own space to work in, a little ways away from the Spirit Priest – still in his area of control, but not under his nose – though they knew he had ways of watching them anyway.

Trying to catch Soliel alone and scope out the possibility of gaining her help was a huge risk. But if it worked, it could be well worth it – and not just for the information he would gather. He continued on towards their home hoping the spirits were helping him and Jandro wasn't there.

"Hey! *Kaibigan*!" Adan cringed and cursed inwardly as he heard Jandro call the typical word for family friend through their open window. The spirits had let him down again. He couldn't turn back now. If you saw a good friend and did not invite them for a drink, it was considered a great offense. And if you refused the invitation, it was even worse. Though Adan was hardly friends with other *basyo,* they treated him as such because they wanted to keep in good favor with his father. If Adan ignored him and kept walking, Jandro would be shamed and angered. There was no way out of this.

Adan made his way to Jandro's door. *Must appear in control.... Must show nothing is wrong.* Jandro was a short, sinewy man, with skin darkly tanned and hardened by work in the sun. Adan knew Jandro was calculating and could be both congenial and lethal at the same time. A person wouldn't know Jandro was twisting a knife in his back until he or she was on the ground dying. As a result, Jandro was both feared and well liked among the other *basyo.*

Adan set his jaw firm and with every ounce of energy, tried to appear aloof as he greeted Jandro. "Hello, Jandro, *Kaibigan.*"

"Sit down, sit down, *Kaibigan.* The daughter is getting us a drink."

Adan sat down on the doorstep, and Jandro joined him with a welcoming grin as he wiped the sweat from his forehead.

"Tell me how your father is doing," Jandro continued, turning to Adan.

Adan swallowed hard. He wasn't sure if Jandro was bluffing, or if he really did not know anything about what had happened to his father and was just going through formalities of conversation. "He's good thanks, but, um, he had to go away for a while, business in the city." Adan figured that was the safest he could be.

"Hmm..." Jandro looked off at the hazy sky, yellowed and tanned from pollution and the burning sun. "I felt something early this morning, like something had broken or shifted in the spirit world, but I couldn't sense what." Jandro looked back at Adan curiously. "I wanted to ask your father about it."

Adan gave him a sidelong glance, Jandro seemed genuine enough, but Adan knew as well as Jandro that in these parts, deception went with friendship like rice with water. Soliel appeared with clay cups full of weak tea. She looked beautiful even with sweat glistening on her cheeks.

Jandro took the cups and handed one to Adan.

"Soliel said she gave the money to him this morning, so I thought he'd still be around."

Is he bluffing? Is he trying to catch me? Or did she lie to him to protect herself? Soliel left quickly, before Adan could read her face. He watched her leave and took a sip of tea, buying time to come up with a good answer. He decided to try and ignore the comment about the money. "I suppose," he said cautiously and then paused to take another sip, "the shift could have been from him going into Kutah.... You know the spirits he works with have an effect wherever he goes."

"Maybe." Jandro didn't look convinced. "But I felt it early this morning, while I was still lying down. And he didn't leave that early, if Soliel saw him."

Sweat beaded on Adan's temple. He felt trapped.

Suddenly Jandro's attention was drawn to Adan's wrist. "Hey, isn't that Danjall's bracelet?" Jandro narrowed his eyebrows. "What are *you* doing with it on?"

Think fast! "Yes, it's his." Adan sat up straighter to at least seem more confident. "The business he has in Kutah, he doesn't know how long it will take, and he wanted to make sure his authority continued here. I'm taking his place 'til he comes back."

Jandro's eyebrows rose. "He didn't tell any of *us* about it. He wouldn't do something that significant without letting at least one of us know."

"He didn't have time. It came up suddenly... and he thought the only way everyone would trust me was if he left the bracelet with me." Adan knew he was walking a fine line. For his father to take off the bracelet it would have had to be because of something incredibly momentous. Danjall hadn't taken it off since the day he had become Spirit Priest.

Jandro's shrewd eyes locked with Adan's. They both knew that socially it would be unacceptable for Jandro to accuse Adan outright of lying. Adan was counting on this. Jandro would have to find out what he wanted to know some other way.

Holding Jandro's gaze, Adan stood up, leaving the tea cup on the step. "I will see you at the next ring gathering." Before Jandro could answer or challenge him, Adan turned and headed back towards his side of town, hoping Jandro didn't notice his trembling hands. *So much for seeing Soliel alone.*

He walked briskly past the shacks towards the mountains of garbage, planning to skirt the edge of the dump. As he reached an area where hardly anyone was working amongst the trash, he began to slow down. The ones that were working there quickly left as they saw him approaching. He was glad to be alone. It was easier to think without others staring at him.

Behind him, running footsteps caught his attention. Annoyed, he turned around. When he saw it was Soliel heading straight toward him, though, he couldn't help but allow a smile to play at his lips.

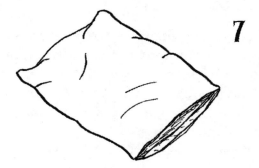

7

Adan wiped the smile off his face and waited for Soliel to catch up. Who knew what her reason was for coming after him? But still, he couldn't believe his luck. Maybe the spirits were helping him after all.

She slowed down to a walk and then stopped at a respectful distance in front of him and stared at the ground. Adan waited patiently to see what she would say.

"I... I'm... thank you. Thank you for covering for me," she finally said. "I'm sorry it got you into trouble with my dad."

This was better than Adan could have hoped. He hadn't even been trying to let her know he cared for her. He frowned though. *Maybe her father sent her out here to try and catch me. But why would Jandro go through all this trouble of playing this charade if he was the one that killed my father? If he'd really killed him, wouldn't he just try to take his place? Maybe he's waiting till he gets more basyo behind him.... Maybe he's buying time or trying to get me to slip to prove to everyone Dad's gone. Maybe all the basyo know already, and they're just playing with me...* His thoughts were spinning out of control. *This is craz –*

"I'm really sorry, please don't tell my father. I'll do anything." Soliel's plea brought him back to the present situation. She must have taken his frown and long silence as anger.

He decided to resort to his first idea of trying to befriend her for help. He tried to soften his face and not appear threatening. "Don't worry about it. I'm glad you didn't get in trouble."

Soliel lifted her head slowly and looked into his eyes. Her eyes were wide in astonishment. They were also entrancing, and a rich, earthy brown. She looked quickly away.

"How were you able to come to me right now? Didn't he see you?" Adan asked and stepped closer to her.

"He sent me on an errand. I should go now and do it." She started to edge away.

"Wait." Adan reached out and took her arm to stop her, then let go like it was on fire. "I... I wanted to ask you something. I could use your help." She *had* offered to do anything.

Soliel glanced up at him again. Asking her for help was probably the last thing she expected.

Adan glanced around to make sure everyone else had truly cleared the area. No one was close enough to hear. Even so, he lowered his voice, "Our... fathers," he stumbled over the word, "we know they don't get along. I know that your father wants to be Spirit Priest."

Soliel looked at the ground and bit her lower lip.

"But that doesn't mean that *we* have to be against each other." Adan wondered if he'd gone too far. He'd never dared to have a conversation with her like this.

Soliel's face looked worried. She whispered harshly, "Aren't you afraid of what our fathers will do to us if they find out?"

Adan thought a moment. "My father can't do anything to me except forbid me to see you anymore. He won't disown me. I'm his only child. And if your father finds out, well... I guess we'll figure out what to do when, or if, that happens. We can't live in fear of them all our lives."

"Maybe *you* can't," she said barely loud enough to be heard, "but I might not even live if he finds out."

His desire to protect her rose up in his heart. "I'd help you any way I could."

"How do I know I can I trust you?" she answered back quickly, looking incredulous. She did have sufficient reason to be skeptical.

Adan sighed. "Good question. Guess you'll just have to take a risk, like I did in asking you for help."

She stood silently for a moment. "What kind of help did you have in mind? I do owe you."

Adan smiled and took a deep breath. "I need your help finding out who's against my father, and who's actually planning something against him."

"You're asking me to betray my own father and his friends?" Soliel asked. "They really *would* kill me if they found out." As if to prove her point she looked around to make sure no one had come near them.

Adan backpedaled. "Okay, just tell me if you hear of any plots against him, anything that sounds like they're going to make a move."

"And I wouldn't get killed for that? Doesn't your dad find out stuff like that from the spirits?"

"Yeah, lots of it, but the spirits can't be everywhere at once. I don't have to know all the details, just hints are enough." She looked a little more willing. "Have you heard anything like that lately?" Adan tried.

She appeared to be thinking. "They're always talking about wanting to do something, but I can't think of anything specific I've heard lately. Sorry."

"No, that's good. Your father hasn't been gone at strange times or for long periods recently?"

She shook her head and a few strands of raven colored hair fell across her eye.

Adan resisted the urge to brush them away. "Will you let me know if you see or hear of anything strange? I mean, just give me hints about it?"

She nodded once in consent, then looked around nervously again. "How do I tell you?"

"You could use a spirit to summon me, or if it's easier, just leave a note crumpled up behind my –" Adan caught himself, "our shack."

She nodded again.

He could tell she was anxious to leave so he nodded his dismissal, and she quickly took her leave.

Wow. I did it. How that turns out is in the hands of the spirits now. He watched her run down the path, off to carry out her father's bidding.

He started walking thoughtfully back towards

his shack. *If she's telling the truth, maybe her father's not behind dad's death. But then who is? And why are the spirits quiet?* He knew he couldn't hold onto his power without them. If he was going to be acting as Spirit Priest while his father was "gone" he'd have to back it up with power, or whoever had killed his father would have no problem coming after him.

Even if Jandro didn't kill his father, he wouldn't put it past Jandro to take this opportunity to try and get rid of him so he could become Spirit Priest. He thought of Yantir too, the Spirit Priest of the neighboring slum, Trakston. Trakston had earned its name because it bordered and was crossed by numerous train tracks. If Yantir heard Danjall was "out of town" maybe he would try and move in on Adan too. Maybe *Yantir* had killed his father. Adan decided to make one more stop before going home.

Graisia dashed away from Kaly's home, glad to be free of a long day's work. She also wanted to get as far as possible from Adan's home, where the door was now shut. She raced along the twisted pathways, finding her way back to where she'd left her cloud pillow the night before. She had thought of her pillow off and on all day, wondering, hoping, her treasure would still be there. Her chest tightened at the thought that it might be gone.

Panting hard, she skidded to a stop at the opening between two shacks. She'd never dared to keep anything like this for herself. Opana might kick her out if she found it. At the very least, she'd get a beating for not selling it. But she was drawn to the cloud pillow like an ant to sugar. There was something special about it, something she couldn't explain.

She made her way into the shadows and slowly lifted the crate. Her body filled with relief. The soft, puffy trash bag was still there. She didn't care if Opana was at home already or not. Tonight, she'd figure out some way to sneak it into her space. She reached down in awe toward the bag. She was the owner of something that once belonged to a queen or princess. With utmost care, she pushed it down into her rice sack. She couldn't contain the huge smile that burst upon her lips when she slipped the sack over her shoulder. Something good was going to happen. She could feel it.

Graisia came out from between the shacks and looked down the path. Opana was taking a basket of laundry inside her shack. Now was the time! Graisia darted down the path, around their shack and threw her sack inside her cubbyhole. Then she raced back to give Opana her money.

"Here, Opana." Graisia held out her earnings.

Without turning, Opana opened her hand for the coins. Graisia plopped the coins on Opana's palm and left as fast as she could.

She was ducking into her hole when Opana yelled after her, "Hey! What's this?! You've hardly given me anything! You good-for-nothing trash girl!"

Graisia scooted all the way in, just in case Opana aimed something hard at her backside.

Opana railed on, "The landlord comes in a few

days. You'd better bring me more than this tomorrow! And where's the food for Harapkan? Don't expect any food for this kind of work!"

Aye, I forgot about Harapkan! She'd have to get it tomorrow. She didn't even want to think about the fat-bellied, rich-looking landlord who was going to come soon with his huge thugs and demand however much money he felt he could get – she was sure they were friends of Danjall's.

She was safe for now though, Opana hadn't come after her. With her heart still thumping, Graisia carefully pulled her cloud out of the sack. Fear and tension began to melt off her. The pillow was somehow sweetly soothing. It seemed to take her outside of the world she knew. She sat on her cardboard-box mat and turned the pillow over and over as if one side or another might reveal a secret.

Something that belonged to a queen. She buried her face in its softness. Fears of dark omens, no food, mean landlords and angry gods faded into the recesses of her mind.

How did Kaly say they used it? I'll try it under my feet.... I think that's what she said. Slowly and reluctantly she pulled the pillow away from her face and placed it at her feet. She leaned back and gently plopped her filthy ankles onto her cloud. She lay there for a few moments with her arms straight at her side. *This is not very comfortable. I guess I could learn to sleep like this though, but...* She wanted to snuggle her face in the pillow again. She reached down and snatched it up, drawing it against her cheek.

"Mmmmm…" she murmured, leaning back again. She turned on her side, hugging the bottom of the pillow and resting her head on the top half. She barely had time to think that this was a much better position before she fell sound asleep.

It was almost dark when Adan found Efrin feeding his favorite rooster – the rooster he competed with in local cock fights. Efrin had been Danjall's most trusted messenger and *basyo* since before Adan was born. If there was anyone in this town Adan could trust, it would be Efrin.

"*Kaibigan*, come walk with me," Adan called through the open window.

Efrin looked up, immediately closed his rooster's cage and came outside. They both knew that walls had ears in Sawtong. They walked silently toward Adan's home and the bank of the river behind it. As they walked, Adan strategized how he would approach the situation.

When they finished descending the muddy path to the river's edge, Adan spoke, "My father told you yesterday about having to go into town, right?" He watched Efrin's face closely for any unspoken clues.

Efrin looked confused. "Kutah? No, he said nothing."

"Really? You didn't come when he called?"

Efrin looked momentarily mortified and then quickly regained his composure.

That was all Adan needed. Usually, Danjall

would send a spirit to Efrin as an alert that he wanted to talk with him. Efrin would then immediately come to a prearranged location to talk. If Efrin had missed it, it meant he was slipping in his spiritual powers of perception.

Adan was counting on Efrin wanting to prove himself after being shamed by not hearing Danjall send for him. Adan pretended to show grace and did not force an answer. "He had to go into town," Adan continued, "for some urgent business... snake eye suppliers are giving problems... threats, bribes, you know..."

Efrin nodded understandingly.

Snake eye was a mixture of local herbs and drugs that played an integral part in their spiritual rituals. It was not unusual to have an occasional problem with suppliers in the city who wanted more money or favors.

Adan glanced around to make sure no one else was listening. His eyes stopped momentarily on the river's edge, and the memory of pushing his father into the river flashed in his mind. "Um... he may be looking at some new suppliers, but he doesn't want the regulars to know.... You know how suppliers like faithful customers."

So far, Adan's plans were working. If no one could find Danjall with the regular contacts in the city, there would be a believable story out there that Danjall just might be with unknown people. And if Danjall didn't return, a murder story wouldn't seem too unlikely an ending.

Adan took a deep breath; it was hard to be back

by the river. They were nearing the spot where he had found his father amongst the weeds. His chest tightened, and his head felt light. He wanted to turn and run. Instead, he steered their course in a different direction. *I've got to find out if he knows anything more.* "What have you heard about Jandro stirring up his loyal *basyo*?"

"Just the usual... he keeps a close circle. I have a friend in his circle now and there's nothing new." Efrin looked thoughtful. "But I have seen Yantir around a few times lately."

The hairs on the back of Adan's neck bristled. Maybe his suspicion had been correct. Yantir served Verhor, another ancient spirit god of the area, and of course a rival of Mahalan. His thoughts about Yantir were cut short by Efrin breaking in.

"You have Danjall's bracelet!" Efrin stared at the bracelet on his wrist with unmasked surprise.

"You never know about these suppliers. It's just in case something happens to him... he wants to make sure I rule the town."

"But wouldn't he be safer wearing it than without it?" Efrin asked incredulously.

Adan hadn't thought of that. "Yeah, well... he cares more about the town... keeping it in the family, than himself." *That's enough*, thought Adan.

Efrin did not seem totally convinced. "And why didn't he send..." His voice trailed off as he realized that Danjall had probably wanted to send him instead. "Oh."

If it wasn't for all that he was trying to cover up, Adan could almost have smiled. His plan had worked perfectly. Again he feigned graciousness and did not comment on Efrin's seeming failure. Adan stopped walking. He didn't want any more questions and he wanted to get away from the river. "I have to go. Let me know if anything changes or if you see Yantir around again."

"Sure." Efrin stopped also, looking slightly perplexed.

Adan made an about face and started jogging back the other way. He may have succeeded in convincing Efrin with lies, but he had stirred up memories and images he wanted to escape.

The images would not be outrun. Pictures of his dead father came coursing through him afresh. He could feel his emotions about to spill over. He ran hard to get out of Efrin's eyesight. Then from the back side of the river bank, he snuck between two shacks just in time to hide an onset of silent convulsions of grief.

How can I go on without you, Dad? What do I do? I can't do this without you! His body heaved again and again, the pain flooding continually over him like unceasing waves as the depths of his grief and loneliness refused to be held back any longer.

Adan stayed between the shacks, trapped with the heat until the waves of sorrow and loneliness receded. Black night had engulfed the town, but a small glimmer of hope had lodged itself deeper into a corner of his heart. Maybe one good result, one new alliance, would come out of all of this – a relationship with Soliel. Perhaps together they could figure out how to rule this town without their fathers.

He crawled out of his hiding place, weak and spent, blinking his swollen eyes, now empty of tears. Only faint slivers of moonlight slicing through the clouds, and the shafts of light creeping out of homes, helped him find his way. Arguments and murmurings wafted from doorways mixed with the smells of food. A hungry child cried, and another yelled in response to some abuse. He almost stumbled over a group of men sitting in the darkness drinking. He cursed at them all.

Suddenly he heard the sound of familiar voices murmuring in an unintelligible conversation. He did not hear the voices with his physical ears, but ricocheting inside his head. A surge of adrenaline shot through his body. He changed his mind about going home, and instead, quickened his pace, passed his shack and headed back down toward the river. The muffled conversation continued, audible only in his mind, yet he knew it was taking place somewhere in actuality. Half jogging, half stumbling, he reached his father's deserted clearing hoping the spirits would answer his summon for help.

8

Graisia awoke to the feeling of radiantly warm light. She couldn't figure out where she was or where the light was coming from, but she didn't care. She didn't see anything except light. But it wasn't a normal light. It came from nowhere in particular, but from everywhere at once. It was warm and gentle, yellow and white, filling her with a satisfying thrill of love, flowing over her like ripples of pure liquid gold. She felt like the light was kissing her all over her face. She breathed in and out, filling herself with the radiance around her.

On the shoals of the river, the spirits had indeed assisted and changed Adan into the form of a crow. As he took off, soaring into the night air he felt controlled more than in control. The spirits were in charge now. They took him towards the far end of Sawtong, finally landing him silently on a window sill where the weak light from the oil lamp at the center of the room could not reach. Numerous voices broke in on one another in anxious and hushed tones. Though he couldn't make out the faces, he recognized a number of the voices.

"You said *he* was wearing the bracelet? How could he be? Why would he do that?"

"Maybe he finally surpassed his father and got rid of him!"

"Hardly likely, they were like rice that sticks, and no one could beat the Priest anyway."

"I don't know; the boy's pretty powerful."

"The boy's weak, and he doesn't know how to rule! We could take him." That was Jandro.

"Careful what you say, Father!" Adan recognized Soliel's voice too.

"I think the Priest had some problem and he left, maybe just as the boy said – didn't his wife leave him some years back? Maybe it's some trouble with her."

"Someone said his suppliers were giving him problems... that he's looking for new ones."

"He'd leave the bracelet for that? Doubt it. Wherever Danjall is, I think now's our time to have a new leader." Jandro made his opinion clear. "That boy can't lead us, I don't care how powerful he is; he's not smart enough to beat us if we all pull together."

"I don't think we should talk like that! You know Danjall can know what's going on," Soliel spoke with a slight tremble in her voice and started to get up. Her long black hair covered her face.

A man hidden by shadows beside her, who must have been Jandro, reached up and roughly grabbed her arm to pull her back. He spoke firmly, "I'm telling you, I felt a shift last night and it wasn't small. We don't need to be afraid of Danjall right now."

"What about the boy? Shouldn't we fear him? He

did take his father's place, it seems. He wears the bracelet!" another man said.

Jandro replied, "I think we should try and find out what happened to Danjall, ask our contacts in Kutah. If he is there, other *basyo* will know it. Of course we can ask the spirits as well, but so far that's turned up nothing...."

That was all Adan needed to know. His wings flapped silently, lifting him from the hovel into the night sky. He circled around once and found himself letting out a long caw. He hoped it sent shivers down the spines of those left inside. The voices did indeed go silent, and soon thereafter, he watched the people slip out of the shack like scared cats hunkered to the ground, except for one. Jandro stood in the doorway, looking into the sky with his head stubbornly high.

Adan returned swiftly to his father's clearing and landed. Shuddering momentarily, he stood back up stiffly, returned to his human form.

Soliel lay curled up on the floor at one end of their shack. She listened to the sounds of her parents sleeping. Her mom's breathing was steady, and her father snored irregularly in his usual low rumble. Only late at night did she feel like her thoughts were truly her own. She wondered what Danjall and Adan would do as a result of the meeting tonight. One of them had obviously been there. *How can Dad be so stupid? He's going to get us killed!*

Adan's words from earlier in the day flitted through her mind, tantalizing her with hope, *"I'm glad you didn't get in trouble."* He had seemed so genuine. Could she dare to believe him? Was there someone who really did care for her in this town?

She glanced at the walls around her and realized it didn't really matter. Adan couldn't protect her inside this flimsy shack. The walls might as well be made of cement. It was stupid to think she could have any existence out from under her father's prison grip. He'd kill her himself if she tried to do something without him. She rolled onto her stomach and tried to convince herself that maybe her father did know what he was doing. *Maybe he and his friends are stronger.*

Her questions refused to be squelched completely, though. *Why do I have to be a basyo? They just go around threatening people and using the spirits to enforce the Spirit Priest's rule! It's all about power. Power and hate.* She hated her life. Hated feeling like a balloon, filled with someone else's stale, suffocating breath, that could explode irreparably at any moment.

Graisia basked in the soothing light of her dream for hours, wishing she never had to leave. But a swift kick to her spine instantly shattered her state of bliss.

She let out a yelp and opened her eyes. The cloud still lay underneath her head, but she could hear Opana's foot receding from her doorway.

"You're wasting my precious time! I want more coins than yesterday!" Opana demanded from somewhere up above. "And don't bother to come back unless you've got something for the landlord and Harapkan! There won't be a place to come home to soon if you don't!"

"Aye, *lakás*! The elephant never stops!" Graisia exclaimed to herself. Graisia sat up and took her "door" of loose boards that Opana had moved and pulled them inside. In the far end of her cubbyhole, she nervously hid her cloud pillow behind the planks. She hoped no one would look behind them while she was gone.

Adan lay awake on the floor of his shack looking up at the ceiling. He could barely make out the ridges of the corrugated metal in these early morning hours. A smile played at his lips as he remembered how Soliel tried to get Jandro not to make any plans. *She's a smart girl. Maybe it'll be easier than I thought to win her over.*

No matter how smart she was though, he knew she couldn't stop Jandro for him. The only thing he could think of doing to find out more about his father's death and keep power over Sawtong was to summon Mahalan himself.

He'd been trying to put this off as long as possible. If Mahalan hadn't protected his dad, maybe he wouldn't be able to protect him. There didn't seem to be any alternative though, and time was of the essence. If he didn't do something quick, Jandro or someone else would be happy to rid him of his duties and take his place as Spirit Priest. Adan had to, at the very least, summon Mahalan and speak to him.

He had Efrin get him a good supply of snake eye for the encounter. It would open him up more fully to receive from the spirits. When Efrin had delivered it and left, Adan quickly took some. After an initial wave of nausea, the worries of his life slipped one by one into oblivion. The momentary respite, however, was not long lasting.

Adan's pulse raced as his roof split open with a burst of fireworks, revealing a sky of orange with blue stars streaking beyond. Red waterfalls poured down the walls, disappearing into nothingness as they hit the floor of the shack. Then the enjoyment was over – the spirits had taken over; spiders came out from the bottom of the waterfalls, crawling and stinging as they scuttled. He tried to move and scream, but it felt like there was some gooey web-like substance that had filled his mouth and stuck him to the floor. Only moans and muffled shrieks could escape his throat.

He could only watch as the waterfalls evaporated to reveal vast canyons on all sides of his shack. Then thankfully, the spiders and the webs vanished. He thought the worst was over, but spirits replaced the spiders; dark shadows with hideous faces, taunting, mocking his weakness and swiping at him with their claws. The spirits were definitely not silent now.

He crawled over to one edge of his shack floor and stuck his head over the edge to look down into one of the canyons. The bottom was so far down he couldn't see it. A rush of wind came from behind, knocking his can of ashes off the floor and into the canyon below. He watched it fall with growing alarm. There was no way out of this dream, or trip, or whatever it was.

Spirits swirled around his head, swooping in with torturous shrieks, claws scraping along his scalp and back. Adan curled up in a ball in the middle of his floor with his arms over his head and ears, moaning and screaming as they left marks all over his body.

Finally, in desperation, Adan cried out to Mahalan.

Nothing happened.

Adan called again. After his fourth attempt the atmosphere began to tremble. The spirits screamed and fled in all directions. With the spirits gone, Adan uncurled and painfully pushed himself up onto his elbows. There were still only canyons surrounding his shack, not walls. The sky was dusky shades of orange-brown along the horizon and grayish blue higher in the sky.

Then he saw him – a tall, muscular man on the horizon, who Adan knew must be Mahalan. Mahalan headed straight toward him, walking regally in midair above the vast canyon.

He wore a brilliant flowing robe of orange and gold silk reaching to his ankles. The gold was in a swirling pattern adorning the lower half, gradually blending into orange from the waist up. The robe flared and billowed as he walked, as if the robe itself were alive and full of power. However, instead of reflecting light, as one would expect from something so brilliant, it seemed to absorb it, leaving the surrounding space dull and shadowy.

Under his robe he wore a tailored, dusky brown suit. At his neck, in place of a tie, a gold glimmering swath puffed out slightly and then disappeared under his vest. His face was handsome, but hard and shrewd, like a prince who was not used to being out-maneuvered by his enemies. Each step he took made the ground shake and sent waves of power rippling in all directions.

Adan wondered if calling Mahalan had really been the wisest choice. Mahalan was obviously not the kind of spirit one could control. Instinctively, Adan knew he should not speak first, but wait to be spoken to.

Mahalan drew nearer, slowing his steps until he came to a complete stop at the edge of the floor where Adan sat, yet still Mahalan stood above the crevasse.

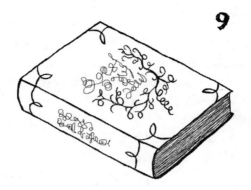

9

"You called rightly," Mahalan's voice rang rich and smooth, but also sent piercing needles through Adan's spine. The air filled with the stench of death. "I am the *only* one who can help you keep control over Sawtong. With me, you will even increase your power and rule over more towns."

Adan swallowed. He was glad for a momentary reprieve from the needles in his spine. But his fear didn't dissipate.

"However, I am not your servant, Adan. Remember this. You will regularly have to please me and do as I say." Mahalan looked down into one of the canyons at his side. "Your father was not able to keep me pleased. He had a weakness that became his downfall." He turned back to look at Adan. "But I have hope in you."

Adan's mind was spinning. *What weakness? Why don't I have it?*

"I will tell you your father's weakness in my own time," Mahalan continued, the sound of his voice continuing to shoot pain through Adan's back. "You have six days until the full moon, when you will have to decide if you want my help. If you do, you know how to summon me for the re-sealing of the contract." Mahalan turned to go, his fiery orange cloak billowing behind him. Almost as an afterthought, he turned back toward Adan, "Jandro is a calculating man and would make a good Spirit Priest... if you don't think you can handle it." His lips turned up at the corner with a smirk. He swung around and took a few steps over the vast emptiness. Then in a flash of light, he was gone.

Each night, Graisia's dreams and times of sleep were more radiantly wonderful than the last, better than any amount of soda-sugar rushes she could find at the dump. She raced home at the end of every day (and she finally did remember food for Harapkan), with hopes that her pillow was still there, and that once again she would be able to get lost in her dream world. There were no words to describe the calmness that would settle over her as she leaned back into the pillow. The moment she drifted off to sleep, she became lost, in the best kind of way, as feelings of love and delight washed over her senses.

There was always light to begin with, that wonderful light. But as the nights progressed, and her eyes adjusted more to the light, she was able to better perceive her surroundings. Eventually, she came to realize she was lying on a huge cushion with a cloud pillow, like her own, behind her head, and what seemed like a huge cloud-like, blankety thing covering her body up to her shoulders. She sat up to get a better look at the puffy blanket.

Her own dirty skin and ragged dress looked desperately out of place. A longing to be clean and to fit in with her surroundings flitted through her heart, but her attention quickly returned to the unusual blanket. Its colors were vivid but softened by the golden light that exuded from it. Later, Graisia had a hard time finding words to name the colors, they included all of the colors in the rainbow, and more; colors she had never seen, all interwoven with golden threads of light.

When she touched the various colors on the billowing blanket, she experienced different feelings. She ran her finger along a green line and felt like a fresh spring of water was spraying lightly over her body, but leaving a deeper thirst for more. She tried a blue color and watched pictures appear out of thin air in front of her, but obscured by the light and too faint to make out. For quite a while, she experimented with the different colors. She tried two fingers on two different colors, then her whole hands on lots of colors, and all the combinations in between. It was hard to keep this experience all to herself.

"Mitina, it was amazing! It's like nothing here! It's another world." She paused from picking through the trash and stared off into the distance, bringing back to mind the images of the night before and the longings they left in her heart.

Mitina let out a sigh. Her eyes were wide and attentive to all of Graisia's "seemed likes" and efforts at descriptions.

Graisia didn't trust Tayzor, Kaly and Lio enough to share her dreams with them. They'd just accuse her of trying to get attention, or going crazy with her imagination. Or maybe they'd try to steal her cloud. She didn't think they would, but they might demand to use it for a while to see if it was magical. She wasn't going to take that chance. She shared her dreams each day only with Mitina. The days went by much faster as they talked together about Graisia's dreams. Mitina stuck with Graisia like a gnat on flypaper, hanging on her every word.

The next night when Graisia awoke into the room of light, her vision was clearer still, and she could see the edge of the platform she was sleeping on. All around the edges of the cushion hung beautiful, sheer, white curtains with luminous imprints of birds and flowers that shimmered as the curtain moved. Graisia saw a division in the curtains and crawled over to it. When she pulled one of the curtains to the side, blinding light burst through the opening. It knocked her onto her back, making her laugh with all that was in her. In the dump town nothing had given her this much joy. She lay on the bed, rolling and laughing, enjoying the delightful feeling of being tickled in love.

The next instant, she was waking up to Opana's short-tempered bellow.

"*What* are you doing in there? I'm trying to read

the sticks for someone. Go make yourself useful!"

Graisia could barely stifle her laughter. Opana didn't seem scary right now, just ridiculously funny. She grabbed her sack and scrambled out into the growing sunlight. Bowing her head quickly at the altar to Harapkan, which now seemed absurd, she ran, covering her mouth and trying to hold her laughter back. Finally, she couldn't contain it anymore. A couple of shacks down, she burst out laughing and giggling as she went.

Between the effects of the snake eye, a lack of food and the intensity of the spiritual experience with Mahalan, it was taking Adan days to recover his emotional and physical strength; days that gave him plenty of time to think. Too much time, actually. His thoughts swung back and forth from wishing his father was still around, to cursing his mother for leaving, to wishing she were back again, and then blaming his dad for chasing her away. Seeing her in that vision had really messed with his emotions and left more questions than answers. *Why did she talk about Ivah? Did she know something I don't know? Would Ivah be better than Mahalan?*

Adan thought as he walked. It was the first time he'd been out walking around Sawtong since his encounter with Mahalan.

Someone's laughter stopped him in his tracks. It reminded him of his mother's laughter... an attribute he had loved about her. It had always made him feel like everything was going to be alright. He remembered how before she left, her times of laughter had been less frequent and more forced.

What he heard now though, was clear, unrestrained, and music to his ears – not like the course laughter one usually heard in Sawtong. He stood and waited at a crossroads among the maze of paths, half expecting his mother to pass in front of him at any moment. Instead, he was shocked to see Graisia appear, laughing, tripping and giggling her way down the path that intersected his.

She didn't see him at first. But when she did, she immediately froze up, the laughter caught in her throat.

They just stared at each other for a moment – Graisia paralyzed, and Adan caught in a memory. Then she dashed up the path and was out of sight before Adan could call after her. He almost felt sorry that he had scared her. He wanted to hear her laugh again. He wanted to feel like everything was going to be okay.

It was a few nights before she could handle the light outside of the bed without being blinded and overcome with giggles and laughter. It was strong and powerful, but so much fun. When she finally was able to step out of the curtained bed, she found herself in a room. The brightness farther out in the room kept her from knowing how big the place actually was.

She looked down at her toes on the cool stone

slabs. In stark contrast to the almost glowing and luminescent floor, her grimy feet and dress looked horribly out of place. It bothered her. If someone happened to find her, would they let her stay? She really didn't seem to fit in with the beauty around her. She felt colorless in the midst of a rainbow.

Looking around the room, she could only see a long, low, narrow cabinet set against a wall. The rest of the room was hidden in light. The cabinet had lots of fascinating, different-sized drawers and compartments that beckoned to be investigated. Her thoughts about her clothes and grime faded, and her curiosity got the better of her.

She made her way over to the cabinet, admiring the chestnut-colored wood. It looked ancient and had a noble air about it. When she ran her hand across its top, she was startled by an impression of its long history and that it held many secrets.

She quickly pulled back her hand. "How weird!" she whispered to herself.

But it wasn't weird enough to stop her from wanting to find out what was inside. The same feelings came when she tugged on the handle of one of the compartment doors. It opened easily enough, and when it did, a little breath of air rushed out from inside. She bent down and peered in. The only thing there was a huge ancient book.

The sound of someone's whispered voice swirled around her head, "Tells how... you may defeat Mahalan...."

Stunned, Graisia looked around, but no one was there. She turned back to the book with her eyes wide in anticipation. Could this really have secrets of power? She reached in to pull out the book. *"Lakás!* This thing's heavy." She had never seen a book this beautiful; the closest thing had been a water-stained hard-backed book in the garbage with a blurred picture of their stately and elegant Prime Minister, Vivi Sel Luan, on the cover. But this... this was a *real* book and the Prime Minister's beauty couldn't even compare to this.

She ran her hand over the smooth cover. Just looking at the book she had to squint – there was so much light coming from it. Intricate designs and words were etched into the cover and glowed with golden light. She didn't recognize the words, though. They could have been in any language, for all she knew. The only word she knew how to read was her own name. Across the spine of the book were more glowing words and stripes sparkling and pulsating. The light seemed alive.

She sat down cross-legged on the floor with the book on her lap and slowly opened the cover. When blinding light shone from the pages, she instinctively lifted her right arm to shield her eyes. This time, though, there were sounds too – melodies and harmonies, swirling out of the book, along with bright colored lights streaming off the pages like a theatrical dance.

The lights circled and twirled with the music, first around her head and body, and then around the room. She watched them play and dance until at the height of the music's crescendo, the colored lights gathered together into a white ball and burst into multicolored fireworks glittering down upon her.

"Oooo! Wow!" Graisia exclaimed, stunned by their beauty.

After the colors settled, she turned back to the first page. She could tolerate the light a little better now. The lights and song continued to come, but she looked at what else was there.

"That's my name!" Graisia leaned closer to make sure. There it was, the first word on the page, written in gold and embellished with unusual and beautiful little pictures. *My name is in a book that has secrets for defeating Mahalan?*

10

Mitina's eyes were open wide in rapt attention as Graisia described the images. "There were these weird looking animals... or creatures, drawn around my name, some looked like balls of fire with wings, and there was a stone house, a man, and lights sparkling and colors and..." Graisia turned and in frustration dropped her arms to her side. "Oh, I wish I knew how to read! Then I could find out what it says about me!" She lowered her voice to a whisper, "and about defeating Mahalan.... Can you imagine?" Graisia could hardly picture herself standing up to Adan, let alone Mahalan. The thought had never crossed her mind to stand up to Mahalan.

"How do you know it was about you?" Lio called up, his voice taunting from behind her.

Graisia hadn't realized he was listening. She hoped he hadn't heard what she said about Mahalan. What else *had* he heard?

"There *are* other Graisias in this world," he pointed out.

"Who asked *your* opinion?" Graisia snapped back. She gave him a nasty look that covered her momentary doubt.

Lio ignored her and turned back to digging.

"You'd never understand, anyway," she retorted.

She turned back to Mitina, and her excitement returned, though she continued in a voice only just above a whisper, "I haven't told you the best part yet! I was sitting and looking at the book, and I heard someone say my name. I looked, but no one was there! The voice said it again. But it wasn't a regular voice, it sounded like the whoosh of the river... and... and thunder, and..." Graisia scrunched up her face as she wracked her brain, trying to think how to describe something that wasn't normal, "and like the singing of a pretty voice, all mixed together."

"All together?" Mitina asked, her face tilted to the side.

"Yeah, it was really weird, but beautiful! There was power in it, but a pretty sound too. Anyway, I asked 'who's there?' And this voice, the really weird one, said, 'I am Uri, the one who dreamed of you and sang you into being. I wrote the book you are holding.' Then this feeling washed over me, *lakás*, I don't know how to describe it... kind of like eating a huge chunk of chocolate, only better.... It felt soooo good." Once, she had tasted a piece of chocolate she found in the dump, and the way it coated her mouth with rich sweetness was something she'd never forgotten.

"Did you see who it was?" Mitina asked quietly.

"Nope, but I could feel him... her, Uri, whatever... it. Anyway, the voice was coming from the light all around, and Uri said more. It told me that the book was part of its dreams for me that it had dreamed up before this world was sung into existence! Uri said there were amazing things for me to do, but I'd have to obey and trust what he, she, whatever, says if I want to do the amazing things. Can you imagine, *kosa*? I wonder what kinds of things Uri has planned for *me* to do! And how could *I* defeat Mahalan?"

Graisia suddenly realized her voice had gotten significantly louder.

Lio's warning yell from nearby affirmed it, "What are you, insane? You're starting to sound like Rawiya, the crazy legend master. If you keep talking like that, you're going to get us all killed!" Lio stomped on a soda can. "Mahalan'll send his *basyo* after us! Then he'll crush *you* like a can." He tossed the can in his sack and shook his head as if he couldn't believe how stupid Graisia was, but he didn't walk away.

Lio was right; she'd gotten so carried away with the beauty of her dreams she'd forgotten how dangerous it was to talk against Mahalan. But for some reason, Mahalan didn't scare her as much as he used to. Her dream had been so real. Uri had felt so wonderful... so different than anything related to spirits she'd felt before. *Maybe I should be a bit quieter, though... especially about defeating Mahalan.*

They silently picked through the trash.

"Who's Uri? I've never heard of that god before," Mitina asked.

"I don't know. Some sort of spirit god, I guess, but a kind one, I think. Opana's never mentioned Uri before, either."

Lio came running over to them and dropped his sack at their feet. "Hey, watch my sack for a sec, I gotta find a ditch." He ran off to take care of business before they could answer.

It was almost the end of the day, and as Graisia looked down at Lio's sack she thought about the coins she'd have to take home to an angry Opana. *Didn't Opana say this morning if I didn't bring back enough coins she'd kick me out?* She'd been so enraptured with telling about her dreams, she'd forgotten, and her bag was not very full.

She looked closer at Lio's bulging sack. There were some valuable glass jars near the top that would bring in a few extra coins. She wrestled with herself. Lio needed the money too, but he wouldn't get kicked out for bringing home less. And he had plenty to take care of him and his mom for today, even if she did take one or two jars. *I'll just do it once... and pay him back tomorrow,* she told herself. Quickly, Graisia reached in and grabbed a couple, switching them to her sack.

"He won't notice. He's got so much in here anyway. And I'll pay him back tomorrow," Graisia told Mitina. "I mean, we are family, and we've got to watch out for each other, right?" Graisia pushed back the twinge of guilt and tried to convince herself as much as Mitina. "If I don't, Opana's going to kick me out! He's just helping me, like any *kosa* would do. He just won't know he's helping me."

When Graisia reached home, almost all of Opana's kids were playing outside. *Opana must be reading sticks for someone.* She peered in the door and found Flora, from across the path, sitting opposite Opana with an overturned crate between them. Opana's back was to Graisia, so Graisia stood at the door and watched over Opana's shoulder as Opana worked. Opana held the sticks in her large leathery hand with the bottoms of the sticks touching the makeshift table. She let go and they gently clattered into a pile. Opana leaned her huge frame forward to examine their pattern.

Opana mumbled a few times as she worked at discerning their message, "Not good... same as always for your husband." Opana continued peering at the *takras.*

I could have told her that. Graisia thought as she looked at poor Flora. Her husband had been a drunk for as long as Graisia could remember. *Why does she even come to Opana?*

"Hmmm... but it seems something about your daughter... maybe something good coming." Abruptly Opana looked up at Flora. "That's all."

Flora's shoulders relaxed a bit. "Maybe it's the job she asked for in the city. She goes in tomorrow to see if they'll take her."

"She'll get it," Opana stated matter-of-factly as she stood up. She turned and saw Graisia standing at the doorway. "What have you got for me today, trash girl?"

Graisia gave her the coins.

"That's a little more like it." Opana counted the coins. "If you bring in more than this tomorrow, maybe I'll show you how it's done." Opana snapped her hand shut and dropped the coins in her pocket. Then she stooped down to deftly squash a cockroach and brush it aside out of her toddler's reach. "Soup's in the corner."

Graisia wondered again if Opana would ever really get around to showing her how to use the *takras*. She got her bowl of cold watery soup and plopped down in the dirt outside to enjoy the last of the fading light. Glancing at the altar to Harapkan, she noticed that yet again, the goddess had been served a much better meal. *At least Opana and Harapkan are happy.*

Graisia thought about how her dreams had made her feel and wondered if Harapkan ever gave good dreams to Opana. *She'd probably tell them to go away.* Graisia chuckled and tipped the bowl up to get the last swallow, then turned to put it inside.

As she lay in her little space that night with her cloud beneath her head, she thought about how nice it was to have someone to talk to about her dreams, someone who liked to listen. *Maybe I should let Mitina borrow my cloud sometime.... Maybe not borrow.... Maybe she could come over here and we could both use it the same night. If she had dreams, then maybe at least Lio would believe; probably not, but maybe. I wonder if Lio figured out I took some jars....*

The prick of guilt she had felt earlier returned and nagged her. It was also confusing. She wasn't used to feeling guilty for taking something from someone. She'd taken things from Opana's kids before, and it never bothered her. Why now? *He was just helping me. I'll pay him back tomorrow,* she told herself, trying to rationalize the guilt away. It wasn't working very well. She turned over on her side and tried not to think about it. It didn't take long for her tired and hungry body to drift off into sleep.

Over the last few days, Soliel had left two crumpled notes for Adan behind his shack. One of them acknowledged the meeting he already knew about. The other simply said her father had been going off to talk to lots of people. She didn't know who or what they were deciding, though. Adan smiled. At least she seemed to want to help him. She was taking a huge risk leaving the notes for him, even if they weren't very helpful... yet.

The moon was a night away from being full and he had made his decision. Wanting to carry on the legacy of his father and keep control over the town won out over his fears of Mahalan. If his father had been able to rule with Mahalan, he should be able to as well. And besides, he wasn't trained for anything else.

Then there was his new hope. He wanted to rule with Soliel by his side. Maybe if they were together Jandro would quiet down. But Adan knew he had to have the power of Mahalan backing him before he could even have a chance at earning Jandro's respect.

The more he thought about it, the more he wondered why his dad hadn't agreed to arranging their marriage in the first place. It might have appeased Jandro from the beginning.

 When Graisia awoke this time, it was not to Uri's light and warmth, but rather to a dreary and muted world. She could tell it was supposed to be day, but everything looked dull and colorless. The sky was a slightly darker shade of their smoggy air back home, but that's where the similarities stopped. All around her were tall shadowy trees, probably once beautiful in ages past, but now suffocated by cruel, thorny vines. The air felt thick and stifling, like it had been breathed by violent people and never cleansed. Everything was oppressive and still.

Graisia coughed a couple times and realized her chest felt tight.

What happened? How did I end up here? Where's the light? Where's Uri? She heard a bird screech and looked up at the only patch of hazy sky visible between the trees. A hawk circled, watching her. Goose bumps spread over her neck as fear rose from the pit of her stomach. *How can I wake myself up?* she wondered desperately. *Maybe if I pinch my arm or hold my breath.* She tried these, but only ended up with sore spots and taking huge gulps of the wretched air to catch her breath. She tried closing her eyes and imagining herself in a different place, but a coughing fit forced her to open her eyes again. It was no use.

Okay, there has to be something I can do. Call for help? No. Who knew what, or who, would answer her in a place like this? Maybe she could walk out of here. But looking around at the forest floor she saw that the thorny vines covered the entire forest. She stood on the only bare patch of ground in sight. She couldn't walk anywhere unless it was over thorns and her bare feet put an end to that idea.

"Guess I'm going to just stay here until I wake up again," Graisia said tentatively, fighting the tears welling up in her eyes. She looked down at the ground and slowly sat down, pulling her knees up under her chin. She hugged them tightly, trying not to shiver with fear.

She sat for what seemed like hours, even dozing a little, only to wake up in the same place. She began to think she might be trapped here forever. Maybe it wasn't a dream after all. Tears dripped off her face, leaving track marks on her dirty knees and legs.

Something brushed against her ankle. She looked down to see what it was and gasped. A thorny vine was growing before her eyes, wrapping itself around her ankle. In spite of herself, Graisia screamed. She jumped up, pulled her ankle from the vine and inched away from it. The tightness in her chest now felt like a thorn piercing her heart. Other tendrils of the vine reached toward her and started wrapping themselves around both her ankles.

"Somebody, help! I want to leave! Please, somebody, help!" she screamed out in desperation. The air was so thick it sounded like her voice didn't carry beyond the closest tree.

"I see you have discovered where you really belong," said a smooth rich voice from behind her; it was a beautiful voice. The vines clinging to her ankles stopped moving.

Graisia spun around as best she could while tangled in the vines. She was startled to see a handsome man who looked like a prince from one of the torn up movie magazines she'd found. He was dressed in orange and brown with a swath of gold at his neck.

"What do you mean? I want to be home, or where there's light... with Uri...." Her voice trailed off.

The man flinched when she mentioned Uri, and then seemed to force a laugh. "That being only lives in your imagination and cannot help you here. You dreamt it all up just to make yourself feel better. Look at you! You're a filthy scavenger. Of course you want a beautiful place. What you haven't seen yet is the beauty in this place, the place you belong; the place where I rule." The man stood taller and swept his arm out broadly toward the forest.

For a moment, Graisia thought she saw the town of Sawtong, and Kahitsa'an beyond it, overlaid on her view of the woods. But it quickly faded and she was left only looking at the dingy forest surroundings.

The man smiled sickeningly sweet. "I think you will learn to enjoy living under my rule here and working with me."

Graisia did *not* want to be here, wherever she was, and she definitely did not want to be under this man's rule, or work with him. She bit her upper lip nervously. As it looked right now, she didn't seem to have much choice. *Did I really only imagine Uri's place?* Maybe she *had* only dreamt it up to make herself feel beautiful. But she was still filthy. Even in her dreams she couldn't make herself beautiful. *Am I just imagining this place too then?* It certainly felt real.

The man continued, "If you want to learn how to live in this sacred forest, how to have the vines obey you, you'll have to do it my way." He paused and his smile grew bigger. "I'd be glad to show you how."

"What... are your ways?" Graisia asked tentatively. At the very least, she needed to know how to survive right now... and maybe in some weird way, it would help her at home too, if she ever woke up.

The man laughed, putting her slightly at ease this time. "You only need to do what comes naturally, look out for yourself, love yourself... and don't try to be something you're not. You'll hardly even notice the prickly little nuisances around you."

Guilt for taking Lio's glass jars flitted across her mind. She shrugged it off.

"There was nothing wrong with taking something from Lio. You are *bandhu*, you are family. It is his obligation to help you."

That's what she had thought! It made sense. Opana would've kicked her out if she hadn't brought home more money. What was so wrong with that?

She'd done things like that before – taken some of Cuni's food or even kept a few coins for herself now and then. Cuni and Opana were still alive and so was she. What was the big deal? Everyone did it.

"You were totally justified in what you did," the man's smooth voice washed over her, "you are supposed to look out for yourself. It's only natural." He bent down and gently unwound the vines from around her ankles. Though they yielded to his hand as he pulled them off, it still felt like they were wrapped there. "You'd be surprised how you can actually use these vines to help you," he commented, distracting her.

He stood straight again and placed a reassuring hand on her shoulder. The radiance of his cloak got brighter. She noticed his thick brown boots protecting his feet from the thorns. The ends of a few vines swayed around his feet in a hypnotic dance.

It all started making sense. Coldness was creeping from where his hand touched her shoulder and spread over her mind as she realized the truth. This is where she felt at home – a dark, dirty place, bereft of color. How could she have thought she really belonged in all that beautiful light? *It must have been my imagination. It's just because Kaly told me that pillow came from a queen. How stupid to think I could be like a queen.*

"You have a gift for being sly and tricking people." The man drew his hand away from her shoulder. "You are very good at it. You keep a straight face so well."

"I do?" she asked surprised. She hadn't thought

she was *that* good at it. *Maybe that's my gift! It sure would come in handy. Maybe I could start getting enough to make Opana happy all the time... and then she'd teach me the takras... then I could make even more money!*

The man chuckled. "Come, I will show you how to live here. Soon, the thorns won't be able to bother you. You will be enjoying it immensely." He held out his hand to her.

One last twinge of guilt flickered in her mind. She quickly dismissed it. With a mix of anticipation and excitement, as well as a faintly sick feeling in her stomach, she reached out and took his hand. Instantly, a stab of pain shot up her arm and through her heart, jolting her awake.

"So what happened last night?" Mitina whispered eagerly when she joined the morning procession next to Graisia.

"Nothing." Graisia gazed off to the side, trying to distract herself.

"What do you mean, 'nothing'?"

Without looking, Graisia knew Mitina's eyes would be wide in shock. "I mean, nothing. The stuff before was all just my imagination. It wasn't real. It's not worth talking about. We have real life to deal with and we have to learn to live in it." She looked at Mitina briefly. "C'mon, we've got a lot to do today." She quickened her steps to catch up with Kaly and didn't look back to see if Mitina followed.

The full moon had finally come, and Adan was ready. He left his shack shortly before midnight, pulling the door closed behind him with a slightly trembling hand. He looked up and down the row of shacks to make sure no one was watching and then slung a large sack over his shoulder. It contained all he would need for the sacrifice.

He quietly slipped into the shadows and down the path. The mixture he had taken a couple hours ago to calm his nerves also made him a little unsure in his footing. He moved on however, with determination and a face set hard towards a goal and prize. *The cost will be worth it. Whatever he asks me, I can do it. He said I'm not weak like my... father....* Adan was passing the area where he'd found his father that night, over a week ago. He shook his head in an effort to clear the horrific images that sprang into his mind. *Mahalan will give me power, I'll be able to defeat anyone who tries to kill me....* His thoughts trailed off.

Adan arrived at his father's clearing. He set his bag down with mustered defiance against any fear that might try to stop him. He laid out all that he needed, sat down cross-legged next to his supplies and began to chant. He centered down into himself, breathing deeply, eyes closed. Without opening his eyes, and yet seeing clearly, he used a rock to deftly and methodically draw an angular symbol on the ground in front of him. Next, he drew a circle around the first shape, feeling the *lakás* coursing through his body as he drew it to perfection. With eyes still closed he placed the candles at the points where the symbol touched the edge of the circle. His father had been careful to teach him that the circle was important in order to contain the summoned spirit. Adan waved his hands over the candles while chanting, and they lit.

As he offered the sacrifice in the center of the circle, he kept his eyes closed and continued chanting, first without emotion, but then with determination tinged with anger and hatred. All of the people he would take down and be able to rule over passed before his mind. The sacrifice burned and Adan continued to chant intermittently calling on Mahalan and trying to ignore the unsettledness of the spirits within him.

Graisia spent the night tossing and turning, drifting between dreams of the sordid forest and a state of being semi-awake. She'd woken up a number of times to find she had pushed the pillow away from her head. Finally, she threw it down beyond her feet where it stayed till dawn.

She was beginning to hate herself and despise all that she was. Who did she think she was that someone would like her so much there would be a book written about her? She couldn't even treat the others in her *bandhu* good. What kind of spirit god would love her? Only one she could imagine. *Opana's right, I am a "trash girl." My fate is to lie, steal and search in the trash. My gift is stealing. I don't deserve*

a room full of light or a pillow belonging to a queen....
I'm nobody.... I'm nothing.

She drifted off into the vine covered forest, where words from a smooth, rich voice brought little comfort, and a screeching crow taunted in the distance.

Adan's eyes remained closed, but he could still see the sacrifice burning in the circle in front of him as clearly as he could smell it. Without warning, Mahalan suddenly materialized above the sacrifice. His presence sent shock waves of power through Adan. He reflexively pulled back and opened his eyes wide. Mahalan was really there, standing in the middle of the fire. Mahalan locked eyes with him. Adan held his breath and remained still, trying to maintain his composure. Both were silent, almost challenging the other to speak first.

Adan finally took a shaky breath and cleared his throat, "I've decided I want your help." His lips felt dry. He tried to sound confident, but his voice cracked nonetheless. All of his previous thoughts of bravado were dissipating with the smoke. Adan knew Mahalan would help him gain respect, but... the cost was returning to haunt him. *Must keep a brave face.* His other option – to hide from Jandro for the rest of his life and sell gum or shine shoes along some roadside – was not really an option. *I have to do this.... It will be worth it.*

Mahalan closed his eyes, smiled and inhaled the

smoke deeply through his nostrils. He towered above Adan. "Not a bad sacrifice," he said, turning his attention back to Adan and opening his eyes again, "you do well to take me seriously." Mahalan took a step off of the sacrifice toward the edge of the circle.

Adan was glad he had drawn the circle to contain Mahalan. An arm's length away was close enough.

"So you want my help," Mahalan continued slowly, "I'm glad to hear that. You will not be disappointed. I am a vice regent and not used to being deposed. My power will be at your disposal... as long as you do what I command." Mahalan lifted his chin yet kept his eyes on Adan. Adan felt even smaller. Mahalan continued, "Shall we re-seal the contract of your fathers?"

Adan swallowed hard. *This is what I've been waiting for. It's all or nothing now.* He willed his mouth to cooperate and finally forced out, "Yes." As the word left his mouth, he picked up the knife he had used for the sacrifice and scrambled to his feet. Quickly, he made a shallow cut on his arm to draw some blood. He walked toward the other side of the circle, around Mahalan who was watching him intently. Adan reached his arm out, letting the blood drip slowly over the sacrifice. Adan glanced furtively back and forth between his arm and Mahalan's sly, heartless face, wondering how much blood was enough. Mahalan's smile grew wider, even as Adan struggled not to show pain.

"It is finished!" Mahalan suddenly cried out, lifting his fist in triumph. "You are mine!"

12

Adan backed away from the candle-lit circle, out of Mahalan's reach. He was unsure what to expect next and was grateful for the circular boundary.

But suddenly distance and the drawn circle didn't matter. The candles went out and Mahalan stepped easily out of the circle, heading straight for Adan.

Bewildered, Adan just stared. *Mahalan's supposed to stay in the circle! I drew the circle! Why is he walking out of it!* He tried to turn and run, but he couldn't move. Adan's eyes only got wider and wider as Mahalan laughed and kept walking.

Mahalan slammed with full force into Adan's body.

Their bodies merged. Adan screamed in agony and terror, trying to recoil from something that suddenly was inside of him, inescapable. The pain was beyond excruciating. Every fiber of his being felt as though it were being burned with a hot iron. A huge claw scratched the inside of his scalp then traveled painfully slowly, the length of his chest.

"Just letting you know I'm here, my friend,"

came Mahalan's low and wicked whisper, not from the outside this time, but from inside Adan's own head. This was a whole lot more than he had bargained for. Of course, he knew Mahalan would have to indwell him, but somehow, he hadn't been expecting it quite like this.

"I... I..." Adan didn't know what to say. It was useless to protest. Lesser spirits who lived with him would harass and bother him, but this – this was going beyond what he'd ever experienced.

"Remember, you have given me your life and sealed that gift with your blood. Your life is in the blood you offered. You are now mine. You will do as I say... and soon, I will show you who killed your father." Mahalan's voice turned to a wicked laugh and took over Adan's throat, spilling out involuntarily from his lips and tasting like bile.

"We have to go to the ring gathering," Mahalan then commanded. "They're meeting without you."

How could he forget the ring gathering? Adan tried to swallow and keep from choking. It was the practice of the *basyo* to meet at midnight on the full moons. Besides their sacred days, these were the times of strongest power. Adan had been so wrapped up thinking about his decision regarding Mahalan that the gathering had slipped his mind, and he was supposed to lead the ceremonies as the Spirit Priest! *They're meeting without me! No!* He took off running towards the gathering.

The other *basyo* had gathered at their usual place, farther down the river, under the large cement bridge that led in to Kutah. At this time of night, there was not much car traffic and even fewer people, especially on the night of a full moon. People were not foolish enough to hang out around a gathering of *basyo* on a full-mooned night. Who knew what consequences they would receive if they were found watching or interfering?

Adan made his way toward the gathering. They had already begun the rituals and started the fire *he* was supposed to light. Someone else had taken his role as leader. Adan's anger boiled. *Who would dare to do this? We should kill him. We'll kill him. I bet it's Jandro, that double-faced rat.*

"Yes, Jandro has tried to take your role," came Mahalan's voice in a deviously soothing way, "but you are my priest, and after he sees your power tonight, he will back away. We will not kill him, though. He is useful."

Adan raged, *Jandro is nothing but a knife waiting to stab my back! We have to take him out!*

"No!" Mahalan's voice rose, dwarfing Adan's anger. "You do what I say, or I will help someone else more willing!"

Adan clenched and unclenched his fists as he strode toward the group. Mahalan's power rippled through his body. He felt like he could fly, walk on water, or kill someone with a glance. It seemed he had the power to do almost anything. Yet he had to obey.

He could tell someone had seen him. One after the other, the *basyo* looked his direction then turned back to whisper in voices too low for Adan to hear. They stopped their ritual. Some backed away from where Jandro was standing, others stood taller.

Adan stepped into the clearing. The light from the fire, and the shadows of the surrounding beastly spirits, played with the feature of those around him. "*Who* is responsible for starting this gathering without me?" he demanded. He wanted to see if Jandro would stand up for what he'd done.

Everyone was silent. Adan looked around at the gathering. All of Sawtong's thirty or so *basyo* had shown up for this occasion; mostly men, but a few women, including Soliel were there too. He spotted Efrin near the back staring nervously in Adan's direction. *Is that...?* Adan couldn't be sure, but it looked like Yantir's spirit hovering in the air behind Efrin.

Spirit Priests were known to occasionally leave their body in order to travel to other places, but he'd never seen the neighboring Spirit Priest from Trakston dare to come to their gatherings. *How dare he think he could barge in on us!* Then a thought flew into his mind that made him shudder. *Maybe he did kill Dad... and he's come to plan how to take over Sawtong. Why is he behind Efrin, though? Has Efrin sided with him?*

Rage stirred up anew in Adan. *Never! He will* never *take this town from me!* Adan was about to move in the direction of Yantir's spirit when Felirnu stepped out from among the others to speak, drawing his attention away from Yantir.

"We figured you were probably too afraid to do your duties." He was so patronizing Adan wanted to silence him. Felirnu looked around at the others with a smirk on his face. "Since you're so young, we figured we'd help you out and take care of your responsibilities until your father came back. We asked Jandro to start for us. We wouldn't have wanted you to –"

Adan stepped forward, too furious to let him finish the sentence. Mahalan's *lakás* coursed through him and out of him. Felirnu's face contorted. Adan was vaguely aware of the gasps around him as Felirnu's body arched then flew backward through the air, slamming into one of the bridge supports. The man dropped to the ground with a soft thud.

Everyone turned and stared at Adan as though they were seeing someone they hadn't known. Adan opened his mouth to speak, but out came Mahalan's deep voice, full of power and demanding allegiance, "I am the Spirit Priest! You think I am weak! You fools! I killed Danjall."

I didn't kill my dad! Adan yelled in his head, *No, I didn't do it! How could you make them think I did it?* He wanted to take back what Mahalan said through him, but he couldn't control his mouth.

Mahalan continued talking through him, "I killed Felirnu, and I will kill the next person who wants to oppose me! Do not forget this... I rule Sawtong!"

With this last sentence, Adan turned to look where Yantir's spirit had been. He was gone, but Efrin's face was one of horror. Whether it was horror that Adan had apparently killed Danjall, or Felirnu, Adan wasn't sure. Adan turned to Jandro whose mouth was slightly agape and eyes were as large as *donya* coins. Adan knew there was no question now in Jandro's mind who had the upper hand.

Adan, however, was at a loss. He was out of control. He may have gained the respect and fear of all of his *basyo*, but he was no longer the master of his own body, his *basyo* thought *he* killed his dad, and he still didn't know who really did it.

Another crazy thought occurred to him. *Did Mahalan kill him? He did say he killed him... through me anyway. But how could he, and why? That's not part of the deal of being Spirit Priest. Would Mahalan really do that? No, he must have said it only to get me more respect.*

It seemed to have work. The *basyo* stood silent. Mouths hung open around the circle and Soliel stepped back further into the shadows.

Jandro finally spoke up, his voice as smooth as melted butter, "The people obviously were not aware that you were as powerful as you are, and more than qualified to be our Spirit Priest. I tried to convince them to wait, but..." He bowed his head deferentially, ever so slightly, touching his hand to his forehead then heart as he faced Adan. "The center is yours. We await your leadership."

Adan half smiled, despite the circumstances. Jandro had *never* treated him with such respect. If Jandro had killed his father, he obviously didn't feel the courage to challenge Adan now. Adan would be free to rule the town, at least for a while, and maybe have some leverage to pursue Soliel.

He stepped forward to complete the night's rituals. Yet even as he did so, he couldn't help but feel like the rock holding his father at the bottom of the river was beginning to pull him down as well.

Early the next morning, Adan lay on the mat in the middle of his floor, trying to fall back to sleep. Over and over, the experience of Mahalan slamming into his body, taking residence and then speaking a confession of murder through him, replayed in his head. *How am I supposed to live like this? What am I going to do? I don't even know if I have my thoughts to myself anymore!* Even though he had the power he wanted, it was going to take some getting used to the conditions that came along with it.

"You're going to work with me," Mahalan answered back inside his head. *"We'll have fun ruling Sawtong. Just trust me. I'll watch your back. I have some things in mind I think you'll enjoy."*

Adan could only hope.

Now that he didn't have to worry about people finding out his dad was dead, he was free to take on the full role of Spirit Priest; as free as one could be as a prisoner in one's own body.

He wondered if anyone would come to him for his services today. He doubted it. He had shaken up the *basyo* pretty good last night, and by now, word had probably spread throughout town. But maybe it would be a good time to talk to Jandro about Soliel, or at least try and see her. Would she still be interested after his confession last night? Maybe he could explain it all to her. She might understand. His heart ached. He desperately wanted her to understand, wanted someone to understand.

Then he remembered Yantir and made a mental note to summon Efrin to try and find out more. But he'd do that later, after some more sleep.

He finally drifted off into a fitful sleep and dreamt he was dragging his father's body to the river over and over again. Each time, he wasn't able to pull his father completely into the river.

When Graisia came to meet Kaly in the morning, Kaly was practically bursting with the news. "Did you hear what happened with the Spirit Priest?" Her aunt, Lindi, whom she lived with, thrived on finding out what was going on in everybody's life, and really, the people in their dump town didn't need a telephone system – everybody's business was passed from window to door quicker than the river could rise during a monsoon. If her aunt was the first to know everybody's business, Kaly was usually the second.

Graisia eyed Adan's doorway. "No. What?"

"Adan..." Kaly paused for dramatic effect, "killed his father!"

Graisia whipped her head around to look at her friend. "What? I knew it! I knew he was dangerous! I told you!"

"And... that makes *him* the new Spirit Priest," Kaly said smugly.

Graisia groaned. She thought about Danjall holding a knife over Adan. *Maybe Adan had to kill him in self-defense.* She turned back to stare at Adan's shack. She really wanted to get out of here fast. "Can't we go another way?" Graisia pleaded. She pictured his dark, cold eyes staring at her with hatred. Her skin crawled at the thought of what he might do in the town as Spirit Priest. She'd never be safe now.

Kaly just laughed. "Why, are you a threat to him? Are you planning to take over Sawtong sometime soon?"

Graisia was unnerved by the accusation. She thought of the voice telling her about secrets for defeating Mahalan. She thought she'd convinced herself those dreams weren't real.

"Stupid roach." Kaly laughed again. "Come on, let's go tell the others." She grabbed Graisia's hand and dragged her past Adan's place, off to find the rest of their *bandhu.*

13

Soliel walked tentatively down the path, keeping her eyes open for any *basyo* that were loyal to Adan. She had to tell a message to one of her father's co-conspirators, and she did not want to get caught. She'd thought a lot about what Adan had said to her over the past few days. She had almost believed he was genuinely interested in her. But what happened last night totally confused, and scared her. She couldn't understand why he would be so concerned with who would be after his dad when he had actually killed him. It didn't make sense. *Maybe he was trying to find out who might come after him in the future.* She hoped she didn't run into him today.

She turned a corner and found her path almost completely blocked by a group of kids sitting on the ground. They had found an amusing break from the heat – listening to the crazy legend lady, Rawiya. Rawiya wasn't her real name, but it meant 'storyteller' and she'd been called that so long no one remembered her original name anymore. Soliel wished she could turn and go another way, but that would mean taking a longer route by homes loyal to Adan. So she began to make her way through the puzzle of children.

Rawiya was in the middle of a legend about Ivah. Soliel's skin began to prickle. She hadn't heard Ivah mentioned for a long time, by anybody. It was as good as treason to be talking about her, especially in such a favorable way.

She tried not to listen, just thinking about her seemed like betrayal to her father and Mahalan. Although, when she had first heard of Ivah, she had secretly admired her. The legends spoke of her as a gracious and benevolent goddess whose Spirit Priests actually tried to help people. When Ramél, Adan's grandfather, had introduced worship of Mahalan to the area, Ivah had been furious. It was said she had sworn to return and depose his descendants when the time was right and a new ruler had arisen worthy of the position, one who wanted the good of the people.

Soliel had been fascinated with the story and thought it would be wonderful if the Spirit Priest and *basyo* were actually trying to do good rather than always intimidating, killing or cursing people with their power. She couldn't believe she was thinking about this! The spirits would tell on her for sure. She focused again on not stepping on any children's toes or fingers and wondered why no adults were stopping Rawiya in her talking.

She had just made her way to the other side of

the little gathering when Rawiya's words seized her attention.

"She came to me last night!" Rawiya's voice was intense.

Soliel looked back cautiously at Rawiya. The woman was leaning forward, peering into the children's eyes. *Ivah appeared to her?*

"How do you know it was her?" a little boy whispered with wide eyes.

Rawiya held out her hands over her head and drew them down as she spoke, "She had white long hair, and skin as smooth as a baby's bottom."

A girl in the group giggled. Soliel ignored her and kept watching Rawiya.

"And her eyes," Rawiya continued boring her own wild eyes into the girl's who had laughed, "shone with the light of the gods, piercing through her golden tiger eyes... eyes that watch you, holding all that you do... and do not forget."

The kids were silent now, not daring to speak. Soliel knew she should leave. If another *basyo* caught her listening, she would be turned over to the Spirit Priest for sure.

"And on her legs I saw the stripes of a tiger, showing her quickness and strength." Rawiya pulled back, sat up straight and placed her hands on her knees. She closed her eyes and dropped her voice, "She told me the time was near... the new leader was arising, one who would live sacrificially and pass the test... who knew what it was like to be treated badly and be oppressed, who desired freedom and the good of the people, and one who longed to restore the old ways." With that, her eyes flung open and she was staring directly into Soliel's eyes.

Soliel felt a momentary jolt and stepped back to stabilize herself. *What is she talking about? Could she mean me?!* The thought came as a shock. Yes, she was definitely oppressed by her father, and she would love to be free from that. She would also love to see the power of the *basyo* and Spirit Priest used for good. *But who am I? Pass what test? My father will kill me if I try to do something without him, especially if it has to do with Ivah! Adan would kill me. I can't do anything! I'm nobody! I'm weak!*

Rawiya spoke again, still looking at Soliel, "Don't fight fate my dear, you are destined to be who you are destined to be. If you fight your fate, the imbalance will continue and we will all suffer."

Startled speechless, Soliel turned and stumbled away as fast as she could. Everything seemed to spin around her.

Even as she delivered the message and then was beaten by her dad for being late, Rawiya's words haunted her. *Don't fight fate... if you fight your fate... we will all suffer... one who knew oppression and desired freedom... live sacrificially... pass the test... restore the old ways,* the words echoed and replayed. *Could it really be true? Did Ivah choose me? Am I destined to restore the old ways?*

It was the end of another long, hot, sweat-dripping day and the kids were gathered around Pouyan's hut with their collections. Graisia kept at a distance from those in her *basyo* until they had all exchanged their finds with Pouyan. She didn't want them to see any of their treasures coming out of her sack. She had let them 'help' her more and more over the last few days. *I'll just do it until Opana's happy enough to teach me the takra sticks. Then I'll be able to make more money, and pay my friends back.*

She hadn't talked with Mitina much lately. Every time Mitina had attempted to ask about the pillow, Graisia had snapped back at her. Mitina didn't say much to her at all anymore. Graisia hadn't wanted to drive Mitina away, but she didn't want to think about the wonderful dreams that weren't coming anymore. It hurt to be reminded of how awful she felt since they stopped.

As she trudged home with the rest of her *bandhu*, Mitina came up alongside Graisia, frowning. "I liked you better when you had those dreams, even if they weren't about real things." And as quickly as she had come up next to Graisia, she dropped back again.

Something in Mitina's words stung and struck at the core of Graisia's heart. Her thoughts wouldn't form quick enough to come up with a response. What Mitina said was true. Graisia liked herself better then too, even if she didn't fit into her dreams very well. She walked the rest of the way home in a haze, trying to keep from crying and not sure what to say.

After giving her coins to Opana, she went to be alone in her little space. She looked down at the end where her cloud was pushed against the planks.

Opana calling to her from outside, "Never thought you could do it Graisia. If you bring back this much tomorrow, we'll start your lessons tomorrow evening."

Tears welled in her eyes. She didn't care about the *takras* anymore, she just wanted her friend back and she wanted to feel the love she'd felt in her dreams. She grabbed the pillow and buried her face in it as the sobs came and tears began to flow.

Adan sensed Efrin coming. He opened the door and looked out at the town shrouded in dusk, and waited. Sure enough, moments later, Efrin appeared down the path. Adan held the door open for him then quickly shut the door behind them both. The solitary candle in the corner would be enough light for their business. Adan simply needed information.

Efrin's words, however, were not comforting. The more Efrin talked, the more Adan wanted to choke a confession out of him, but he thought better of it. Efrin might just be the only trustworthy *basyo* he could count on. He had to earn Efrin's trust. He had tried to convince Efrin that it had only been Mahalan talking through him about his father being killed, that it was meant to make the people afraid, and be a cover up for his father being killed in town through a drug deal gone wrong. Adan knew he walked a fine line telling this story. But even if Efrin tried to spread the rumor, after his display of power the other night, he doubted if anyone would believe Efrin. He wanted to keep Efrin's loyalty, though, especially if Efrin was innocent.

Still, as Adan questioned Efrin about Yantir, the lesser spirits wrestled inside of him for action.

"I didn't even sense him there." Efrin told Adan.

Efrin's face was absent of any telltale signs of lying, but Adan had a hard time believing him. Efrin was not a spiritually dull person. *Of course he could have been distracted by my confession. I hope he'll still be loyal out of fear.* "When you've seen him in Sawtong, what has he been doing, who was he talking to?"

Efrin looked worried and then pensive for a moment. "He's always been on the far side of Sawtong, by the tracks. Couple of times I've seen him just buying small items of food or something from people along the paths. But it's always just on the border of our towns, and he heads the other direction as soon as he sees me."

Is he trying to mislead me? Adan wondered. It was so infuriating to not know if he was being given the full truth or not. Jandro could be trying to work out some deal with Yantir. *Or is Yantir just trying to feel out our strength and taunt us? If he is, why didn't my dad know about this? Or maybe he did and just didn't tell me.* Adan closed his eyes in frustration. *I guess I'll just have to pay Yantir a visit.*

He opened his eyes again. "Find out all you can about Yantir and what he wants."

Efrin nodded his acknowledgement and turned to go.

"And Efrin..." Adan paused as Efrin turned back.

He made sure he caught Efrin's eyes so Efrin would feel the *lakás* coming from him. "I do take note of what you do." He left the comment ambiguous enough that Efrin could interpret it however he needed to.

Efrin nodded again, his face emotionless, and disappeared into the darkness.

Graisia didn't remember falling asleep but she awoke in the forest crying, just like she had been at home, except here, her chest seemed tight and there was no soft pillow in her arms. The ache and longing for the love she had once felt seemed about to burst her heart. She looked up at her forest surroundings, tears streaming down her face. She was hoping to see something or someone new who would help her, but there was no one. The forest was as dreary and creepy as ever.

She looked down at herself and cried out. Wound around her chest, in numerous loops, was a prickly vine like the ones that covered the forest floor. It seemed alive, like it was trying to constrict her when she wanted to breathe.

Tingly panic rose from the pit of her stomach toward her heart and down her arms. She fought to keep the hopelessness from reaching her mind. *There has to be a way back to Uri.* She tried to pull off the vine from around her chest. Thorns cut and scratched at her as she pulled, but she couldn't loosen its grip. Frantically, she searched for the end and attempted to unwind it from around her chest.

She succeeded in unwrapping two layers, with numerous more to go, but then the free end of the vine began to wind itself around her left arm. She stared at it in alarm and tried to tug at it with her right hand. From there it only got worse.

A shoot darted out from the vine on her chest and wound itself around her right arm. Now both her arms were captive and immobilized. And to make their point and squelch any lingering hope, the vines tightened even more around her limbs in willful resistance. That's when she noticed it. In a way only possible in dreams, she saw that the vine wrapped around her was actually growing out of her chest – out of her heart.

She slumped to her knees on the hard ground, crying out with the tears returning in earnest, "Uri, please! Get me out of here!" Her voice bounced off the rancid air and came right back to taunt her. But even with that sensation, a spark of light pulsed in her heart.

Emboldened, she decided to try again. She leaned her head back and cried out with abandon, "Uri! I want to be with you!" This time her voice shot straight up into the sky like an arrow. Then all was silent.

14

Still looking toward the sky, Graisia waited. Nothing happened. But something felt different. She couldn't explain it, but something had changed. Suddenly a faintly cool breeze came from behind her – a waft of fresh air brushing against her neck and face, reminding her of the air from Uri's room – like from a forest of new growth. She tried to take a deep breath of the sweet air, but was stopped by the thorny vine digging into her chest. She attempted to stand up – which was quite difficult with her arms still bound – and turned to see if someone was there. No one.

But she did hear something new. In the distance, a man's voice singing clear notes that cut the air like a crystalline knife. She wondered if it was the man who had come to her before. That man certainly hadn't helped her tame these vines. Listening to the man singing, her fears slowly ebbed away. If it was the same man, maybe he was good after all, and he'd really teach her how to survive this time.

She strained to see the singing man between the

vine-covered trees and finally caught a brief glimpse of him. He was average looking, and definitely *not* the one she'd met before. This man had on well worn blue jeans, and a faded blue, long-sleeve, button-down shirt with the sleeves rolled up. His skin was dark like her own, and he looked strong enough to have worked as a builder. She didn't want to interrupt his singing, but she wasn't about to let him pass her by.

"Hello! Over here! Can you help me?" she called out in his direction.

He kept singing in his incredibly rich and pure voice, gradually coming closer. She could hear the words of his song now.

The keeper sees
In and beyond time
Heart of sorrows rent
The key to golden paths

    Mine for yours
    Yours in mine
    Love forever wins

The beggars come
Dropping cherished coins
Bowing to the fountain,
Where wishes all came true

    Mine for yours
    Yours in mine
    Love forever wins

The song was beautiful. His voice seemed to reverberate through the forest, creating a breeze that ruffled the trees. As he got closer she could see the trees around him were actually changing. For a moment their grayness was gone. She even thought she felt the trees smile. Music was not the only thing emanating from him; he seemed to glow with the same loving warmth that had been in Uri's room. Graisia was starting to get excited. Maybe this man could really help her!

He walked straight toward her now, only a few trees away. His soft dark chocolaty curls framed his tanned face and made him look like he needed a haircut, almost. Even though he looked like an average man, she was intensely drawn by his face. He had a smile that was like the sun itself, full of laughter.

Then he was in front of her, and his eyes... she was riveted by them. They were a dark earthy brown, and yet, every now and again, they would momentarily shimmer, becoming like the purest core of a flame – a ring of brilliant blue fading to a deep-water navy and punctuated with a calm, black, pupil heart. The strangeness didn't scare her; rather, when his eyes shimmered, she felt somehow safer. She wasn't sure why.

But it was the depth in his eyes that was most striking. They seemed to encompass the whole of the world, and more. She saw in them a knowledge of all the pain of history, a hope stronger than any storm, and a deep love that left her breathless.

She immediately knew that he knew all about

her, every last thing she did and felt, more than even she knew, and yet loved her still. It was amazing. She couldn't help the tears that came to her eyes over this astonishing and foreign love.

She could barely tear her gaze away from his, but she noticed from the corner of her eyes that he was barefoot and his feet were bloody. Behind him, lay a trail of blood on the vines. He had walked barefoot on the thorns to get to her, but it didn't seem to bother him.

He had stopped just in front of her with a gentle smile on his face.

Graisia smiled back.

"You wanted help to get back to Uri's place?"

Graisia felt that if she could eat the sound of his voice, it was sure to taste like the richest kind of chocolate there could be.

"Uh-huh," she barely squeezed out the words, nodding slowly.

He reached out and offered her a hand. She strained to take hold of it even while the vine continued to hold her in its grip. His grasp felt strong and sure around her tiny hand.

The vine on her arm had started to grow again and reached out for his arm.

Graisia screamed and tried to pull back, but the man held tight. How was he going to help her get out if the vine got him too? As soon as it touched his hand the vine became energized. It grew faster, climbing his arm and quicker than she could think, it had spread over his entire body.

There was no way she could pull back now. Even

then, the man continued to hold her hand and look into her face with quiet confidence. The vines tore holes in his clothes as they wrapped themselves around his legs, arms and chest. Blood stained his clothes. He winced in pain, but still, his eyes remained filled with tenderness.

The vines finally pulled them both to the ground. Graisia cried out in pain as thorns gashed her knees and legs. She was helpless beside this man who was quickly becoming a part of the forest floor.

"Can't you do something?" she asked in desperation.

Blood flowed on his arms, head, chest and feet. "Everything that can be done... is being done," he whispered.

Then it was hopeless. His attempt to rescue her had failed. They were both doomed.

The vines continued their merciless mission, and in one final attack, a tendril of the vine wrapped itself around his chest, pierced viciously through his body, and tightened like a noose around his heart. The man gasped one last time, and all was silent. The vines even ceased to move.

Graisia stared in despair. She had only just met this man and didn't even know his name, but she had liked him. He'd come to help her and put his life in danger because of her. Tears slipped down her face. *If he hadn't taken my hand, if I hadn't asked for help, if I didn't deserve to be here, he wouldn't have tried to help me... and now... now he's gone.*

Her tears turned to deep, convulsing sobs.

Though she'd known him for only a few minutes, she felt he knew and loved her intensely. She lifted her head and watched his dark red blood flow freely from the places his now pale skin was pierced. The silent vines now pulsed, seeming to feed on the blood of his lifeless body. Shame and sorrow set in further. *Why'd he do this? He couldn't even fight the thorns!*

She wanted to hug him and show her gratitude even though his life was gone. The vines did not allow her to move very far, but she managed to somewhat awkwardly lay her head on his chest and lean against his frame. She rested her hand gently against his cool and silent face. Thorns pricked and jabbed at her, but she didn't care. The love he showed lingered in the air around him, and that was enough. She hoped that somehow, wherever he was, he would understand she was sorry, and grateful he had tried to help her.

Adan woke an hour or so before sunrise. Unable to sleep any more, he got up to go for a walk through his territory. At this time of the morning he'd have most of it to himself. He grabbed some dried rice from a jar and jammed it in his pocket before he went out, then slammed his door. He didn't care if he woke anyone else up. If he had to suffer from lack of sleep, they did too. It was hot and muggy even without the sun; the sweat started dripping from his face immediately. He headed through the sleeping town towards the path leading to where the lady with the shrine to Harapkan lived. He could use some good fate at this point in time. What could it hurt to try and get help from any spirit who would give it?

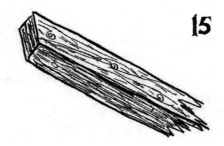

15

Graisia lay with her head upon his chest for what seemed like hours, simply waiting for the vines to determine when it was time for her own death. Suddenly, a waft of a breeze startled her. She barely lifted her head to look around when a surge of power jolted through the man and leapt from his chest into her own ribcage, shocking her heart with a dazzling rush of kaleidoscopic light. The man took in a quick, deep breath. Color flooded instantly into his cheeks even as the stunning power quickly spread throughout her own body.

In its wake, the rainbow light left a warm, love-filled trail of energy and life, as thick and smooth as golden honey, and bursting with the sun. It was just like the light and love she'd felt in Uri's room! But this time it was deeper. Instead of feeling like a shower of rain on the outside, the light of Uri was at once a multicolored refreshing stream as well as a molten gold river rushing inside her. Closing her eyes, she savored the feeling as it made its way to the ends of her fingertips and toes.

There was something else about this powerful love. She felt changed in the very ingredients of who she was. It was like love and laughter bubbling in her veins. At the core of her being, she felt a connection to this man in some way, like they were spinning in unison or somehow their very breath was linked together. She had the impression that if she exhaled, he would inhale, and visa versa.

When she looked up into the man's face, brilliant eyes filled with laughter greeted her. His arms, neck and even his legs were completely free of vines! She pulled back to look at herself. There were no vines on her either! And to top it off, she was wearing an extraordinarily lovely dress, and there was not a smudge or mark on her skin.

"Where'd they go? What happened?" She had never seen herself so clean. Overwhelmed with joy and relief, she jumped up and twirled once around. She then stood swishing the folds of the dress over the tops of her clean toes, entranced by its beauty. It was made of fuzzy, purple flower petals, hinted with shades of red one moment, and blue the next, depending on how she moved. It felt softer than even her cloud pillow, and was sewn together with golden thread that sparkled when she moved, like fireflies at dusk. She gazed at the man who now sat cross-legged in front of her.

"*Lakás!* What happened?" she asked in wonderment.

"You just moved from only being in time to also being in eternity."

"What?" He wasn't making any sense. "What happened to *us*? Who are you?" She noticed his clothes had changed too. Now he was wearing green pants and a loose clean white shirt that shimmered as he moved, like the bed curtains in Uri's room!

"Questions, questions, questions... and all of forever to answer. What if I start with a name. I'm Jarón, Graisia."

Graisia didn't ask how he knew her name. Of course he knew it, he knew everything!

"Jarón, what happened!"

The man's grin turned to laughter. He looked up to the sky and let out a yell of triumph.

Despite her bewilderment, she found herself laughing along with him.

He stood up and took her by the hand. "Come. Walk with me. We have much to be in this forest." They began to walk together back the way he had come.

She couldn't keep her eyes off his kind face. *Much to be?* she thought. *That's a strange thing to say.* "Are we going to Uri's place?" she asked aloud.

"Yes, and no. We'll go there often because you are there, but we'll also get there." He seemed to know what he was talking about, but it was as clear as the muddy river to her.

Then she got distracted by something else. She noticed that everywhere the thorns had drawn Jarón's blood earlier, whether it was where he had walked, or where they had bound and killed him, the vines had disappeared. In their place was a path of translucent gold, and beneath the gold, she could see the dark rich earth of the forest floor, strewn with the occasional pebble or exposed root. On either side there were still miles and miles of vine-covered forest, but where Jarón had laid and walked, it was now pure gold – at least what she assumed was gold.

"I didn't know gold was so beautiful," she said looking at Jarón again, waiting and wondering if he was going to explain anything.

"What do you want to know most?" One corner of his mouth turned up, she guessed in amusement.

"How come we're alive?" she practically blurted out. And she really did mean *alive*. She'd never felt so invigorated.

"We had to die to live, 'love forever wins... mine for yours, yours in mine, love forever wins,'" he said, repeating part of his song.

"But I didn't die. Only *you* did."

"It seems that way, doesn't it? But is the vine coming out of your heart?"

She looked down to make sure again, and shook her head.

"The thorn seed isn't in your heart anymore because that part of you died along with me. The thorns don't have power over you now. You don't belong here anymore. You belong with Uri. You can go back to Uri's place, and well, you are in Uri's place too."

Graisia wasn't sure how she was there now, but she certainly felt like she belonged there, she even *looked* like she belonged there.

"In fact," Jarón continued, "you are in Uri and Uri is in you. The light that leapt into you, took the seed's place and will keep growing until you shine with all the light of Uri you can hold."

"Really? That's great! But... how did you know

that would happen? How did it work? Why did you let the thorns get you?" She still didn't understand it.

"You know how the Spirit Priest and *basyo* offer sacrifices to gain more power and appease the spirits?"

A shiver went down her spine and she nodded. She knew that they often sacrificed animals if they wanted more power or wanted to win back the favor of the spirits and gods. Sometimes they would even sacrifice a baby or a person. Opana had told her she should be grateful that a *basyo* or the Spirit Priest hadn't found her first.

"You needed a powerful sacrifice, one that would release Uri's power into you and destroy the seed. A sacrifice who has never had any thorn seeds, one who could really win over the vines."

"But you died. Do you have the strongest power?" It wouldn't surprise her if he did.

"There's no more powerful love than to willingly give your life for someone." He stopped and turned to look searchingly into her eyes. His eyes pierced into hers with a depth of love almost incomprehensible and caused her to gasp. She felt like she was melting inside. She *knew* he was perfect love in human form.

He continued, almost in a whisper, "They can't keep love down. Love is the strongest power there is, that's the power of Uri."

"That *was* Uri's power... that came through you," Graisia said softly, almost to herself.

"One and the same. 'Love forever wins.'"

He gazed into her eyes for a moment more, and then straightened up.

As they started walking again, hand in hand, Jarón resumed his song. His rich, resonant voice carried among the trees, cleansing the air around them in ever widening circles.

> Shadows cover
> 'Round olden fountain
> Treasures buried wait
> Ancient locks young broken
>
> > Mine for yours
> > Yours in –

Before he could finish, Graisia stopped in the middle of the path, pulling Jarón to a halt. The deep pleasure of his love had been cruelly interrupted by another, very unpleasant yet familiar sensation. She knew they weren't alone anymore. She could sense Adan, and he wasn't far away.

As Adan reached the lady's shack where the altar to Harapkan was, he dug into his pocket for the rice. He knelt down and placed the rice in front of the shrine. Bowing his head, he touched his fingers to his forehead then heart. He could feel the goddess hovering ominously. She was a volatile and unpredictable personality, but he could hope to catch her favor. Mahalan didn't bother him about coming by this altar. She wasn't in competition for the town's allegiance. He made a quick prayer and then got up to move on.

He started to head off down the path, continuing the direction he had been going, but just as he reached the edge of the shack, it was like walking through an electrified sheet that sent his veins coursing with rage. Mahalan seethed in agitation inside him. Adan glanced down and saw a little addition to the shack. The makeshift addition wasn't much higher than his knees. He had no idea why, but he was filled with such powerful hatred that he despised whatever or whomever was in there. He had an overwhelming desire to smash the place to smithereens and immediately glanced around for some sort of stick or pipe.

Graisia looked up into Jarón's eyes imploringly. His eyes held her gaze in steady confidence.

"Why have you stopped?" he asked.

"He's... here..." she whispered.

"Yes, he is."

Graisia wondered how he could agree with her and not seem worried. A crow cawed angrily from somewhere over her left shoulder. She kept looking at Jarón, hoping he would offer some suggestion for escape.

"Do you trust me?"

The crow cawed louder and closer this time.

"Ye... yes," she replied hesitantly, still staring into his deep eyes.

"Then walk with me. Ignore the crow."

Easy for you to say, she thought but didn't say.

Jarón smiled as if he heard her anyway.

Adan didn't have to go far to find a thick plank of wood leaning against someone's shack. He came back fuming. There was something inside that little space that was wrong. He swung the wood to test its weight in his arms. It would be perfect.

Graisia heard the crow squawking loudly behind her now. She could hear its wings flapping, flying straight toward her. She looked up at Jarón in anguish.

"Continue walking... keep your eyes on me... he cannot hurt you."

Although her panic was mounting, she obediently kept her eyes on Jarón who walked backwards so they could look into each others' eyes. His eyes momentarily flickered in their shades of blue.

Adan swung the beam like a baseball bat, straight towards the little addition to the shack with all his might.

The crow screeched in Graisia's ear. She was sure her eyes were as wide as chicken eggs, but still, she kept them focused on Jarón. Then came a flash of light swiping across her vision... and quiet.

Adan let out a yell as the beam slipped from his hands and thudded to the ground, missing the little addition completely. He cursed and held his hand close to his face in the dim morning light. Three huge splinters had lodged themselves deep into the palm of his right hand. There was no thought of picking up the beam again. He took off cursing and running down the path.

16

"What happened?" Graisia looked around, stunned. The crow was flying off squawking miserably.

"You trusted me. He's gone... for now. "

Graisia blinked and thought about home. She wished it was that easy walking the paths of Sawtong. "What's going to happen when I go back?"

"You are already back and you're already in Uri's place, even as you're here. You're in all places at once, Graisia, just as Uri and I are. We are with you here in the forest, Sawtong and eternity, all at once... and eternity is in you."

She looked down at her velvety dress and sparkling clean skin. "Will I still be pretty and clean in Sawtong too?"

The tenderness in his expression melted the edges of her fear. "Our love will always be in you, no matter what you or your surroundings look like." He stopped. Holding both her hands, he looked her in the eye. "Our love isn't just to feel and keep to yourself – then it wouldn't be love at all – love is for everyone." Looking deeper into her eyes, he continued gently, "You need to tell your friends you stole from them, and pay them back."

Graisia's heart dropped as the guilt returned. *I guess he really does know everything.*

"I do...." His voice surprised her because it wasn't aloud this time, he was answering back in her own thoughts. *"And it doesn't make me love you any less."*

Had he really talked to her in her thoughts?

He smiled and nodded at her.

"But I needed coins to give to Opana..." she stammered, starting to explain out loud, "and the landlord was coming... and Opana was going to kick me out, and..." Her voice trailed off. The excuses seemed empty when she voiced them aloud.

"We would have taken care of you if you trusted us," Jarón replied softly.

Graisia looked down the path ahead of them, avoiding Jarón's penetrating gaze.

The next morning, while walking with her *bandhu* to the dump, Graisia was still thinking about how she had escaped from Adan, or the crow... and Jarón's instructions to confess to her friends. She kicked at little pebbles and bits of trash as they walked.

I don't want to tell them. What if they don't want me as part of the bandhu anymore, what if they beat me up? What if they turn me over to Adan? What if they tell him I've found another god? She argued back and forth in her head. What if her dream had been nothing more than a dream, her own imagination gone crazy like that other man in her dreams had said? What if Jarón didn't come through for her here, and she couldn't earn enough coins to pay them all back and have some for Opana? *And Opana said she was going to teach me the takras if I bring home a lot today!*

Silence looked like the best option. *They don't have to know what I did, I just won't do it anymore. That's it; I'll make it up to them without them knowing it.... I'll just be extra kind to them.*

Then scenes from her dream began popping into her mind. She pictured Jarón's eyes looking into hers. How could she deny that? It had been *so* real. She had wanted to feel love while she was awake, and this was part of it; if she wanted to receive it, she'd best be able to live its results. *Help me, Jarón. I want to do it your way.* Instantly, it was as if she could feel his hands on her back, giving encouragement and a gentle push, showing her he was with her.

She cleared her throat. "Umm... I have something I need to tell you." The others turned to look at her curiously. "The last couple days... I... uh..." She looked down at her feet. "I took some of your things... to get more coins." She tilted her head up nervously to look at them.

Kaly narrowed her eyes as if she could spit venom from them.

"I'm sorry. I won't do it again.... I'll pay you back," Graisia added quickly. "Can we call it cleared?"

"You stole from our stash? You weren't just comparing our goods!" Kaly yelled. The ties of a *bandhu* were almost sacred. You could steal from others, but never from your own *bandhu*. "How do you expect us to trust you again, rat? You think just because you tell us you did it, everything's okay?" Kaly looked as hurt as she sounded. She spun around and strode away in a huff.

Graisia hadn't thought about how much it would hurt Kaly to find out she'd stolen from her. She ran after Kaly. "I'll pay you back! I'm sorry! Opana was going to kick me out!"

The others walked slowly behind them in silence. Graisia glanced back at them. They looked stunned. She didn't know if it was because she had stolen from them or because she told them she did. Kaly kept walking, ignoring Graisia.

"Com' on Kaly, please..." Graisia pleaded.

Kaly turned to her. "I thought I could trust you Graisia; that we were family. I was wrong. As far as I'm concerned, you're not a part of this *bandhu* anymore."

Graisia's feet stopped moving and everything around her seemed to flow in slow motion. She stood open-mouthed trying to catch her breath. Kaly might as well have socked her in the stomach. She couldn't imagine life without her *bandhu*.

She didn't notice Mitina coming up alongside her until she spoke. "I'll call it cleared, *kosa*." Mitina slipped her small hand into Graisia's with a smile.

Kaly walked away.

"Com' on, roach." Tayzor punched Graisia on the shoulder lightly. "She'll get over it."

Graisia wasn't so sure. She staggered under the weight of Kaly's words. Kaly had *never* told her anything like that before.

"Why'd you do it anyway?" Tayzor asked. He shook his head, showing how stupid he thought she was.

"I... needed money for Opana. She was getting angry at me because I wasn't bringing back enough," Graisia replied ashamed.

"No, I don't mean that, idiot. Why'd you even tell us you stole from us? That's *stupid*!"

"Oh. Uh..." She wasn't sure she wanted to give the reason. "I had a dream last night...." She paused to see if Tayzor would think she was a nutcase for mentioning this, but he was looking at her with eyebrows raised in interest. Lio stood behind him, unreadable. Mitina seemed to be holding her breath. Graisia decided to continue. "And there was this guy in the dream, he did something for me that was so much love, and he... he showed me I was wrong to take things from you, and that I could trust him to take care of me. He told me I needed to tell you what I did and pay you back, 'cause that would be the love thing to do." She felt her cheeks burn in embarrassment. She wasn't sure what they would think of her explanation. No one talked about love in this town – at least not this kind of love.

"All I know is Lio's right, you really are going a bit crazy. Harmless for now, but crazy," Tayzor said as he scrutinized her. "Just make sure you pay me back." He turned and headed on toward the dump.

Lio glared at her, sending a shiver down her spine, then he turned away as well. Graisia guessed Lio was almost as mad as Kaly but simply let the others do his talking.

But Mitina smiled at her, the Graisia she liked was back again. Mitina squeezed Graisia's hand comfortingly and started walking, tugging Graisia along. At least one person was happy to be with her and didn't think she was crazy like old Rawiya.

I'm trusting you to help me get enough to pay them and Opana, she said in her head, hoping Jarón could hear her still. *And please help Kaly take me back.*

Soliel had made her decision. She would at least try summoning Ivah to see if anything happened. Her father was out visiting someone, so right now was as good a time as any. Her heart pounded and skipped uncontrollably. She had never attempted anything like this before; going against her father. He had beaten her when she tried to please him. What would he do if he found her going against him? *"Don't fight fate,"* Rawiya had said. It seemed crazy... but Rawiya's words gave her just enough hope to keep her moving forward.

She looked up at the tall walls around the little roofless room, fearing that somehow, someone was staring through them at her. Her father, Jandro, had built the little room to keep out spying eyes and give them a place to perform sacrifices without having to travel far. It was just big enough for two people and the small altar she now sat before. She was alone this time, though.

Sitting cross-legged, she whispered chants to

Ivah as the hen on the altar burned. She hoped Ivah would think it a worthy sacrifice. It was the only thing she could get her hands on at such short notice, and she'd had to swipe some money from her mom to be able to buy it. She wiped the sweat that dripped down her chin and continued chanting, hoping her mother wouldn't hear. Her mother would tell her father and he would want to know why she was offering a sacrifice without his direction, and to whom. To hear it was Ivah would absolutely enrage him. He might not like the Spirit Priest, but he was absolutely devoted to Mahalan. She couldn't believe she was summoning Mahalan's sworn enemy in the middle of his territory. She should have at least tried to go outside Sawtong. What if Mahalan showed up!

As she chanted, she could hear her father's threats playing through her head. Maybe he would sell her off to someone in the city where she'd be nothing more than a slave to the first person with enough money. Her father constantly reminded her of how much he could make if he sold her. The fear of being beaten or sold always hung just above her head like an ax ready to fall.

Her whole body trembled while she still tried to conjure up the goddess. Ivah didn't seem to be responding, though. This was looking more and more like a huge, foolish mistake. She continued chanting as long as she dared. *Just one more minute, I have to keep trying.*

Suddenly the door to the little room flew open. Soliel pulled back against the wall in dread. Efrin stared down at her through the doorway, looking as surprised as she felt.

Efrin backed away and made room for Jandro, who pushed through to see what was there. When he saw Soliel and what she was doing, his face became like a bloated, dead pig along the roadside – pale and about ready to burst.

"What do you think you're doing?" There was an unmistakable quiver in his voice.

Soliel instinctively recoiled, lifting an arm to block the coming blows.

"You think you can get away with something without my permission?" His nostrils flared. He seized one of her arms and began dragging her through the doorway.

The rough wooden doorframe scratched her back as he hauled her out, but she knew better than to yell. It would only make matters worse. Efrin moved aside to make room for their passing and then turned away. Soliel's heart sank.

Jandro pulled her in to the main room of their shack, where he threw her against the far wall, cursing. The flimsy shack shuddered at her impact. She cowered in the corner. Inside the confines of his house Jandro always released his emotions more freely.

"Who were you sacrificing to? Who were you trying to curse without my permission? Why are you betraying me?" He seemed to only expect the worst motives from her, petrified she would use his training against him. It would be something he would do.

Soliel tried to hide her face again with her arms.

Jandro grabbed her arms away from her face and slapped her hard, leaving her cheek stinging. "Are you so ungrateful for all I do? You're hiding something! You're trying to ruin me!"

"No," she replied softly, earnestly, but barely audible.

"Then tell me!" Jandro demanded, twisting her arm till she felt like it might pop from its socket, "Who were you summoning?"

"I..." Her shoulder throbbed. "I was trying to... to summon Ivah."

Jandro looked like he'd been shot with a bullet. Everything went quiet, and seemed to slow down. He dropped her arm. Soliel tired to hurry and curl into a ball to shield herself from the blows sure to follow, but she felt like she was moving through water.

"You would dare..." he even spoke each word slowly, "you would dare to upset all, all we have worked for in this town!" Then everything sped up again. He grabbed an old wooden chair next to him. "Who do you think you are?!"

The last thing Soliel remembered that day was the crash of the chair coming down on her head.

17

Truly determined, Graisia set herself to working as hard as she could to make the extra money for Opana and her friends. At least she had done what Jarón had asked her to do. *I'll show him. I can be as good as he wants me to be.*

By mid-day she could feel the sun trying to drain every ounce of energy from her body. Mitina had been working alongside her, never leaving her side, looking up at her from time to time with expectant eyes.

"What was the dream like last night?" Mitina finally asked.

"Hmm?" As Graisia turned around from the pile she'd been focused on, she replayed in her mind what Mitina had asked her. "Oh, there was this man I met." She couldn't help the smile that came to her lips. She closed her eyes momentarily to recapture the feelings of Jarón's love. "He was wonderful, really loving and –" Then she remembered what she was trying to do and why. "I'll have to tell you about it later, I've got to get enough coins." She turned back towards her pile. She couldn't really concentrate on telling her stories while she was searching.

Graisia heard Mitina behind her, "Stories are better than coins. Don't pay me."

"Thanks, *kosa,* but I still have to pay the others. I'll pay you back too. Don't worry."

When the day was over and Graisia turned in her finds, she stared down at what Pouyan handed her. "I don't believe it! I hardly got anything! I worked all day, hard." The small coins barely filled her palm. She checked her sack to make sure she hadn't missed anything. It was as empty as it was when she came in the morning.

"He said he'd help!" Then turning to the others in her *bandhu,* she told them, "I tried, but I barely got enough to give Opana tonight. I promise, I'm trying. I *will* pay you back."

Tayzor lifted one eyebrow questioningly. "You'd better." He then glanced in Kaly's direction. Kaly stood off to the side, looking away. She had ignored Graisia all day and didn't appear to be changing her attitude now.

Lio leaned in. "Maybe Kaly's gonna have Adan put a curse on you if you don't pay us back!" Was that a gleam in his eye?

Graisia took in a shaky breath, hoping Kaly could never afford to have her cursed – or would want to. She liked Lio less and less these days.

He smirked at her and walked over to join Kaly.

Mitina just kept her head down and moved around a piece of broken glass with her toe.

Graisia started towards home, determined to show them she could be trusted.

Soliel woke up in the middle of the night with a throbbing head. She wondered why she was lying huddled in the corner of their shack – then it all flooded back. Remorse came with the memories. *I knew I shouldn't have done something so stupid. Father will never trust me again. He'll sell me off for sure now... or keep me locked up forever in this shack. It's what I deserve anyway.* She tried to sit up. Every movement made the throbbing feel like someone was hitting her head with a hammer. She moaned and leaned back against the wall, closing her eyes. By morning she'd probably know what her father had decided to do with her.

Slowly she opened her eyes to look around the room, squinting in the darkness to make sure she was seeing right – her father wasn't lying on the floor in his usual place. Her mom lay sleeping soundly. *He's probably off arranging to sell me right now.* She couldn't imagine her life getting any worse, but it probably would.

She tried not to groan and wake her mother as she turned to lay the unbruised side of her head against the wall. It would be useless to ask her mom for help. Her father had purposefully chosen a wife who would do anything he wanted. Soliel didn't hold it against her mom. She felt almost sorry for her – always obedient, never objecting, like a scrap of paper blown through life by whatever breeze was the strongest around her.

Soliel reached up to the low table nearby where her father kept his supply of snake eye. She managed to find it by touch without moving from her spot. Never had she dared to take any without her father's permission, which was usually only given just before a ceremony with all of the other *basyo*. This time, she didn't care. She just wanted something to dull the pain and help her forget. She'd already infuriated him beyond his limits anyway.

She doubled what they usually took. A wave of nausea swept through her before she drifted into a hazy state somewhere between sleep and wakefulness. Half-dreams and images floated through her mind, the pain in her head completely forgotten.

Then she heard someone call her name.

"Soliel... Soliel..." The voice was beautiful and gentle, soothing to her mind. She almost drifted into complete sleep. "Soliel, chosen one, I have come to help you."

Soliel realized she should pay closer attention, so in a dreamlike way she put more effort into focusing on the voice. As she did, the image of a beautiful lady appeared before her, one with flowing white hair and smooth ageless skin that seemed to be alive with moonlight – it was Ivah! She had on a fluid, flowing gown that turned sheer below her knees, where Soliel could see the tiger markings on her legs, just as Rawiya had described them. Soliel looked into Ivah's yellow tiger eyes. Ivah did not seem ready to lunge, but definitely made Soliel want to be cautious.

Soliel stared in awe.

"Soliel, you were chosen for a very special

purpose." Ivah's voice washed over her leaving her skin tingling in its wake. "You are here to bring change to Sawtong and the surrounding towns... changes that will last for all eternity."

"But who am I?" Soliel stammered. "I can't do anything...."

"You are a chosen one and can do more than you ever thought possible." Ivah paused, giving Soliel time to let her words to sink in. "You have lived many lives before this one, and in each of them you have lived sacrificially, trying to make life better for others."

"Other lives?" Soliel asked in wonder. She had no recollection of anything other than living in Sawtong!

"Let me unlock the histories you have lost," Ivah answered softly. She reached out and placed both of her hands gently but firmly on either side of Soliel's head and whispered in a language Soliel did not understand... at first.

Suddenly, Soliel felt like something in her mind exploded. She heard multitudes of languages and understood them all at once. Lifetimes of people from around the world and different times in history burst through her thoughts like movies, speeding hundreds of times faster than normal. Memories of lives lived long ago seemed to come rushing back, lives where she had acted sacrificially for the benefit of others.

She also saw the stories of struggling people all over the world. There were castles and nomads, river tribes and peasants, camels and kangaroos, pyramids, coliseums and high-rises, ships and tanks, and so much more – most of which, as Soliel, she had never seen and had no way of knowing about, unless... unless what Ivah said was true, and she *had* lived other lives before this one.

"The centuries of life you have lived before now were times of preparation and testing," Ivah's voice drew her back to the present.

Soliel focused on Ivah's shimmering form before her.

"As a human, you have continually chosen to live for others. This has let your true *aysh* nature emerge and allowed you to advance to the next level. All are called to be *aysh* but few are able to pass successfully through the trials that burn away their selfish desires. You risked your life for the sake of this town by summoning me and have shown yourself once again. The *aysh* within you has been cultivated and released in greater measure. I am here to be your guide for the next part of your journey."

Soliel reeled at the implications. Her thoughts were so jumbled she fought to keep from feeling dizzy. Snatches of legends she'd heard about Ivah mixed in to her thinking. She remembered hearing words like 'emerging nature,' 'trials' and 'sacrificial' sprinkled throughout, but she'd never known what they really referred to. Could this really be true? But she had seen it – she had seen her past lives. She *did* want to help others – she always had... and she was talking with Ivah now, who seemed to understand her deeper than anyone ever had....

Ivah spoke quietly, "If you are successful in this

journey, in your next life you will be completely free of your body and able to fulfill your ultimate destiny in the universe as a perfected *aysh*."

"But... how?" Soliel asked daring to believe that maybe what Ivah was telling her was really the truth.

Ivah reached out her hand and caressed Soliel's head, lovingly like a mother. "Embrace your destiny, bind yourself to me, and together, we will see the change in this town you desire to see."

Tears slipped down Soliel's cheek. Ivah touched her deepest longings – to be significant and make a difference. It *must* be real. Ivah's hand now rested on her cheek. Soliel lifted her hand to place it on top of Ivah's as a sign of acceptance. At the instant she touched Ivah's silken hand it was as if a bolt of light and fire surged through her whole body. For a single moment, Soliel felt like a living ball of flames, full of power and splendor, able to conquer anything that might stand in her way. She heard Ivah's voice declare, "Your true *aysh* name is Nala!"

Then in a flash, she was back looking into Ivah's face, their hands still touching.

Ivah's eyes glowed piercingly bright. "You *will* fulfill Uri's destiny for your life... and become like us, a perfected *aysh*."

Graisia crawled out of her cubbyhole as the sun was barely climbing over the horizon to start its cruel journey. She glanced at Flora's shack across the way. Her husband was slouched in front of the door as usual, and her daughter was stepping over him to leave.

"Tell Opana she was right!" the daughter whispered cheerfully. "I got the job!"

Graisia gave a half-smile and nod of acknowledgement and then headed off toward her own job. She had decided to leave extra early so she could work as much as possible. She ran off down a different path, one that would get her to the dump quicker. She figured the rest of her *bandhu* would go on without her when she didn't show up. And she really didn't want to see Kaly's reaction if she arrived at her door. She *had* to get enough to pay them back today, and she was determined not to steal.

When the others in her *bandhu* did finally show up, Kaly simply ignored her.

But Mitina looked pleasantly surprised. "I thought you skipped on us."

"No, just want to get extra money," Graisia said with some satisfaction, noticing Tayzor's slight nod of approval.

Kaly walked over to Tayzor and suggested they scrounge somewhere else, "...away from the rat."

Tayzor nodded again, but only shifted over a few feet. Kaly gave him a dirty look and moved as far away as possible from Graisia while still being near enough to the others for protection.

Mitina stuck close by Graisia but remained silent.

At one point Lio came over with an air of superiority. "Just checking to see if there's anything of mine in your sack...." He peeked inside Graisia's sack. "Nope. And not bad for half a day," he added, lifting his head so he could look down his nose at her. Age was usually taken as a serious marker of seniority in a *bandhu,* deserving of respect. Apparently Lio thought it didn't matter anymore with her in disfavor.

"Shut up, Lio." Graisia sighed. "You'll get your money back."

Lio frowned at her. "If I don't get my money back by tomorrow, maybe I should tell them more about your dreams. More about this new god you worship and how you're going to go against Mahalan. You know, it's not safe for us to be around someone who worships someone other than Mahalan."

Graisia felt her cheeks get hot. *How could he?* She wanted to knock him over. She probably could – he was still smaller than her.

"Love, Graisia. My power is love," Jarón's voice floated through her mind.

Graisia picked up her sack and turned away before she did something she would regret. She fumed inwardly, though. She had been a faithful member of this *bandhu* since she was younger than Mitina. And he had just joined the group. Sure, she'd made a mistake, but who was he to treat her this way?

Graisia worked in silence the rest of the morning. Only once did Mitina start to ask if she'd had any dreams the night before. Graisia cut her off and snapped, "I don't remember."

When the scorching heat and humidity had made her clothes as damp as her skin, Tayzor called out to them to stop and eat.

Graisia turned to Mitina. "Don't wait for me, Teeny – I'm just going to keep working."

Mitina stared. "You're going to kill yourself!"

Graisia shrugged in indifference even though she was exhausted and hungry and had never in her life given up an opportunity to stop and eat.

Mitina finally wandered away with the others.

Graisia hadn't focused on picking up any food during her searching. She had been concentrating only on finding things that would bring in the most coins, including a lot of cans. With this many cans, maybe she'd be able to almost pay everyone off by the end of the day. She thought of Kaly welcoming her back, and how Lio wouldn't have anything to hold over her. It still made her mad to think he would use her dreams against her. She was just coming up with some choice words to call him when she felt a tap on her shoulder.

She turned and found herself looking up into the face of "The Mop." At least that's what she called him in her head whenever she saw him. He was a tall lanky boy with dark curly hair that almost completely covered his mocking eyes. Behind him were some of his *bandhu*; a shorter, stockier boy and the lanky mop's younger sister.

When Graisia had decided to work through lunch, she'd forgotten one thing: she'd be alone, without protectors, on the mountains of garbage.

She took a step backward and tightened her grip on her bulging sack.

"What you got in that sack?" the Mop asked smiling.

Graisia wished she'd at least tried to stay in sight of her *bandhu*. There was no way they'd even hear her if she yelled now. The dump trucks, coming and going, made sure of that.

The shorter boy leaned forward, pulling the sack slowly from her grip. He opened it up and peeked in.

Graisia let out a slight whimper.

The boy smiled at what he saw inside.

Graisia could only see all her hard work evaporating like a cloud. Without thinking, she swung her digging stick at the shorter boy and then lunged to grab her sack back.

It was the wrong thing to do. The Mop wrenched the stick out of her hand and punched her on the side of her face, knocking her down into the garbage. The Mop's sister grabbed Graisia's sack and clambered over the mound.

The two boys stood laughing down at her. Graisia hoped they wouldn't do anything more to her. *Please...* she pleaded in her mind to whoever might be listening, *make them leave.*

The younger boy stepped closer and gave her a strong kick in the ribs. "That'll teach you not to give us trouble next time." They laughed again and took off after the girl.

Graisia sat up, aching and in disbelief. All she'd worked for that day was gone. She didn't even have a sack anymore. She lay back on the garbage and cried silently, wishing this part of her life was just a dream too.

18

Sitting on the floor of his shack, Adan leaned against the wall and popped the last bit of a beans and sticky rice mixture into his mouth from its leaf wrapper. The movement stretched the splinter wounds on his hand. "That's the last time I'm asking Harapkan for better fate," he grumbled to himself.

Before he could set the leaf on the ground, he felt Mahalan's squeezing, suffocating presence press in on his soul and push it up out of his body toward the ceiling. Mahalan was taking him somewhere. It was a bit disconcerting and wasn't the most pleasant feeling, but he still liked the experience of being out of his body. He rose through the roof and flew over Sawtong. Spirits swirled around him. He could almost forget all of his troubles back on the ground – almost. But the heaviness of Mahalan seemed to keep him grounded even in the sky.

He sensed Mahalan's desire to go to Trakston so he headed that way. He'd traveled many places this way, but never to another priest's territory. It was basically a sign of war to do such a thing, and Yantir had made his move, so now, why couldn't he?

Apparently it was time to return the visit.

Flying over the dump, he saw Pouyan leaning against his shack, and swarms of kids picking through garbage like overgrown ants devouring mounds of grainy custard. He skimmed above Jandro's rooftop, seeing nothing unusual, and continued on toward Trakston.

At that moment, trains were running on two of the three tracks that divided the towns. Men and a few women and children were hanging out of the crowded rail car doors as they sped along. A few people had even climbed on the roofs of the trains to hitch rides.

Though the tracks divided the two towns, they also brought people together. Between the tracks were patches of weeds and dirt where people sat and talked or sold goods. As soon as the trains passed, people returned to spread out themselves and their wares into the open space. A group of men settled in on one of the tracks to continue a conversation. Older kids ran after younger kids darting this way and that. The one track not in use by trains currently served as a place to dry laundry.

He flew even lower now, over the heads of people walking on a narrow dirt lane. No one looked up or seemed to feel his presence. He liked that. He wasn't sure where Mahalan had for him to go, but following his leading, he slowed down, slipped through the wall of a nondescript shack, and hovered near the ceiling. Sitting on the floor were two men with their heads near each other, talking quietly. One probably in his twenties and the other in his late thirties or forties.

"What do you think of Yantir's plans?" the younger asked. "Do you think he could really take over Sawtong?"

"It would seem very possible," the older replied. "After all, he says *he* is the one who killed Danjall, not the son. He says the boy priest is bluffing."

"But do you think Yantir really killed Danjall? Is he that powerful?"

"Why not? For nearly twenty years, he has grown in strength. The boy priest will fall easily to him."

If it were possible for a spirit to shudder, Adan would have. He did not like the direction this conversation was going.

Just then, the older man looked straight up in Adan's direction and narrowed his eyes as if to see into the shadows. Before Adan could tell if the man recognized him, he felt himself yanked out of the shack and flying back towards his own home.

Graisia lay on the garbage mound staring up at the sky until the others returned. What else could she do?

Kaly hung behind the others, but Mitina ran up and placed a hand on Graisia's shoulder. "What happened?"

Tears slipped down Graisia's cheeks. She quietly told them her story.

Now Lio would have all the ammunition he needed to drive a final wedge between her and the two older kids.

Sure enough, he took the opportunity.

"Yeah, right, Graisia," he began sarcastically. "Maybe you *really* went down to Pouyan's shack, traded it all in, then hit yourself with something so we'd believe you. It's not going to work! We're not going to feel sorry for you."

Tayzor shoved Lio roughly, but spoke sternly to Graisia, "You got one more day, Graisia. Or you're out."

She knew he was right. If Lio and Kaly didn't like her, the *bandhu* couldn't function as a group, and she'd have to leave. She didn't blame Tayzor. She blamed herself.

Opana was not happy to see Graisia come home empty-handed either. She slapped Graisia's face hard on top of an already growing bruise. "If you don't bring home enough money tomorrow, you'll be out on your own! You're not worth it anymore. You're bringing bad luck to my whole family!"

Graisia had no idea how she was bringing bad luck... and didn't ask. She tumbled into her little home, sore and completely spent. She lay down in a daze knowing it was useless to think of getting any food. She'd eaten nothing all day and had never felt so completely exhausted in her life. She thought of other kids she knew who had slowly died of starvation. It wasn't hard to starve in this town.

I thought I was doing what he wanted me to do. What'd I do wrong? I worked as hard as I could, and look what it got me. When she closed her eyes, tears squeezed from under her eyelids and slipped down onto her cloud.

Graisia awoke stumbling on the forest path, holding Jarón's hand. She was so exhausted she could barely keep her eyes open. *Why are we even in this forest? I want Uri's place.* Beneath drooping eyelids, she watched the vines hanging from the trees wave slowly and patiently as if knowing she couldn't last long. The air was thick, humid and foul for breathing.

Jarón was with her, but she wondered how this could be the right path. No longer golden, it was simply dirt. Tree roots broke through it, and rocks and pebbles lay scattered around. Even Jarón seemed far away, though he walked just slightly ahead and still held her hand. She worried the vines might swing out and latch on to her. Her hand slipped from Jarón's. She tripped over a root and went sprawling. As she lay still on the hard dirt, fear and panic rose in her throat. Her eyesight grew darker.

Where'd he go? "Jarón, where are you?"

Graisia woke in her cubbyhole to the pitch black of night. A dog howled somewhere outside. Her cloud pillow lay at her feet. She reached down and slowly pulled it up to hug it. It didn't take her long to drift back to sleep.

Graisia found herself back in the forest, awaking just where she'd left off – lying on her face in the dirt surrounded by the dark and oppressive forest.

Hadn't Jarón said he and Uri would be with her, even in the darkest places?

"Jarón, help.... Uri, help.... Please," her weak voice hardly traveled.

The haze cleared a little. Jarón's green pant leg appeared in front of her eyes, and his hand reached down in front of her.

She grabbed onto it and he pulled her up with his strong arm.

She stumbled on, holding his hand, barely able to stand. He guided her around more roots and rocks. Gradually strength was flowing from his hand to hers, and her steps became more sure and confident. Finally she smiled at Jarón in gratefulness.

Then she turned to look around her again. The forest was still so dark and intimidating.

What if I fall again? What if he doesn't reappear and the vines get a hold of me? The very thought drained energy from her. She stubbed her toe on a rock and cried out both in surprise and pain. She let go of Jarón's hand and used both of her hands to rub her eyes, trying to get rid of the darkness that plagued her. When she uncovered her eyes, she saw no one, and it was deathly silent.

Jarón! She started to run down the dim path, hoping she'd catch up to him, but her dress snagged on a vine. She lurched and tried to catch a tree branch for balance, but a thorny vine was wrapped around it. She screamed, lost her balance completely and fell in a despairing heap.

Crying quietly, she held her torn and bleeding hand. "Jarón, I can't do this."

Immediately, he stood in front of her, brighter

than ever. Her overwhelming relief lasted only momentarily. She felt weak and humiliated. She couldn't even walk straight without him.

"I can't do this," she mumbled again.

"I know," he said gently, "that's why I haven't asked you to do it. I've only asked you to trust me, to *be* with me."

She couldn't even lift her hand to take his. She felt like a wet newspaper as his strong arms easily hoisted her onto his back. He draped her arms around his neck and tied a cloth sling strapping her onto his back like she'd seen mothers do for their babies who couldn't yet walk. She felt so ashamed... she couldn't even walk on her own.

She didn't know where they were going – or "being," as Jarón would say – except that it had to do with Uri's place. She laid her head against his shoulder and felt his deep peace seep into her. Her breathing began to match the steady rhythm of his, soothing her into sleep.

Groggy from fatigue and hunger, Graisia struggled to wake up the next morning. Then she remembered she still had to get enough money for everyone. She didn't want to get kicked out of the *bandhu* or her home. Adrenaline rushed through her body, sending her pulse running, somehow giving her the energy to crawl out her doorway.

Soliel's father had been gone for two days. She'd spent most of that time drifting in and out of consciousness, talking with Ivah, learning secrets and being given instructions about her future. Now, she sat wide awake against the wall at the back of their shack. Her head didn't hurt anymore, and she felt ready for what Ivah had told her would come next.

As if on cue, Jandro walked through the door. A tall, burly man stood behind him blocking all the light from outside. Crooked teeth showed under his dark mustache when he smiled. Soliel cringed, but only momentarily.

"Get up!" her father commanded. "I've sold you to this man. You're going to live in the city and get what you deserve. I'm done with you!" Jandro leaned over and stretched out his arm toward her.

She got up before he reached her. With a foreign, yet familiar boldness she looked Jandro in the eye. "I'm not going anywhere with this man. I am no longer your daughter, and you have no right to sell me."

Jandro stared at her with his mouth wide open until he finally found his voice. "You have no choice! I have *sold* you!" Turning to the large man he said, "She's all yours."

The man stepped forward, delighted to take the girl off Jandro's hands. She was beautiful, appeared healthy, and not big enough to cause much trouble. He wrapped his huge hand around her delicate wrist to pull her out the door.

But she wouldn't move; it was as if she was a beam of steel imbedded in cement! "She's... she's so small!" he stuttered. No matter how hard he pulled he couldn't move her. Finally he dropped her wrist.

The girl looked at her father and then at him. He felt a momentary jolt as she bored her eyes into his. Then she spoke evenly, "I will only go where I want to go and when I want to go, and it's not with either of you."

She walked straight toward him and he found himself, without thinking, moving out of her way. She stepped out the door and headed down the path.

He turned back to the girl's father. "You can *keep* that one. I want my money back." He held out his hand to Jandro. "She's got some strange power with her that I want no part of."

Ivah appeared to Soliel again as she walked away from the shack. Over the next hour or so, Ivah led Soliel around Sawtong to various obscure places. Everywhere Ivah led, Soliel found money, sometimes a few coins, and other times a bill or two. Eventually, Ivah led her to one particular shack and told her that the family living inside was just about to move into the city, but hadn't found anyone to buy their shack yet.

Soliel knocked, paid the surprised family exactly what they had asked for, and then waited as they moved their meager belongings outside.

She stood in the center of her empty one room home, complete with two windows and a door. She smiled. *Home. Now I can begin to do what I was born to do.*

19

Graisia made sure she found things to eat today, and Mitina was nice enough to share food with her – even though no one else did.

As the day wore on, Graisia knew no matter how hard she was working, she was not finding enough. "He said he'd help me!" she complained to herself. "I can't do this on my own." She slumped down on the pile where she'd been working.

One of the numerous stray, mangy dogs that scrounged through the dump with the kids came over and tried to nose through her bag. She made half an effort to pull her bag away from the boney creature, but he kept digging his nose in deeper. She waved at the flies buzzing around her face.

"I can't do this!" she yelled into the air. A sudden peace came over her with that admission. The kids nearby turned to stare. The dog even looked up at her. She didn't care.

Very softly, she heard the words, *"Trust me,"* float through her mind.

Tayzor stopped digging and headed off towards

Pouyan's shack. *It can't be that late already! We have to go now? Lakás!*

"*Trust me,*" came the words again.

I can't! We're gonna leave right now!

"*Trust me.*" The voice was softer this time. Graisia knew it was fading and she'd lose her chance at this offer for help if she didn't take it now.

"Okay, okay," she said desperately. "I'll trust you." What other choice did she have?

The annoying dog pushed at her leg, wanting to dig beneath her. "Go away!" She pushed the dog aside and stood up. The dog dove into the pile where she'd been sitting. Despite her resolution to trust only a moment ago, her heart started sinking again. She lifted her digging stick to take out her frustration on the dog. "Stupid –" She stopped, stick raised in midair. Something silver glinted under one of the dog's paws. She plunged into the pile alongside the dog and pulled out a shiny object.

She couldn't believe it – she was holding a beautiful pocket watch with only a few dents in it. She held it to her ear. It was still ticking! Tears sprang to her eyes. *He* does *love me.* She held it tightly in the palm of her hand and whispered a quick, "Thank you," then dashed off after Tayzor.

After Pouyan had gone through the contents of Graisia's bag, she confidently placed the pocket watch on his counter.

His eyes got big, and then just as quickly he made his face appear calm, almost sullen. "I'll give you one and a half *donyas* for that." A *donya* was the biggest coin there was. Each one was worth about a day or so's work at the dump.

"What! That's nothing! It's worth at least five." She had figured she owed the others a little over two. If she could get five for it she'd be able to pay her friends back and have some left over to make Opana more than happy.

"My offer is two, and that's final." Pouyan spit on the ground. "Unless you want me to pass on your name to police, for *stealing* this nice watch."

Graisia stood there with her mouth open. *He knows I didn't steal it!* Maybe he was bluffing about informing the police, but she didn't want to risk finding out.

Other kids were beginning to push and shove around her to get a look at her big find. "Fine. Two," she mumbled quickly with tight lips.

"Glad we can agree on business." Pouyan swiped the watch off the counter, shoved it into his pocket and dropped a little over two *donyas* worth of small coins into her waiting hand. Pouyan moved on to the next kid haggling for his attention.

Graisia turned away. There was only enough to pay her friends back. She'd have none for Opana. She couldn't explain it, but she knew she had to pay her friends first, even though she would have nothing left.

She distributed the coins to her friends.

Kaly raised an eyebrow. "Who'd you steal from this time?" Without waiting for an answer she spun around and left.

Tayzor and Lio simply took their money and followed Kaly.

As Graisia and Mitina followed behind, Lio turned and taunted, "Guess you're safe for now."

Graisia couldn't tell if his voice still held a hint of a threat. At least he looked happy. He should be. He had money to take home. She didn't.

Mitina patted Graisia's pocket that was empty of coins and frowned. She tried to hand Graisia some coins back.

"Don't worry about it, Teeny." Graisia smiled weakly. "Even if I took it, Opana'd still think it wasn't enough." Mitina's family needed it as much as she did. Graisia took Mitina's hand as they walked. "Everything'll work out somehow."

It didn't take long for Adan to hear what had happened with Soliel and her father. Efrin filled Adan in on as many details as he knew, including Soliel's new location. Adan's heart sank. Any chance of romance with Soliel would be just about impossible now. But that was the least of his worries. *Now I've got to deal with Ivah too?* It felt like everything was unraveling; like a knit shirt caught on a fence. The more he tried to hold on to his power and pull it to himself, the more everything came apart.

"You sure it's Soliel, Jandro's daughter?" Adan asked, incredulous. "How? How did she even summon Ivah?" He paced in front of Efrin.

"I saw her with my own eyes, making the sacrifice... and all of Jandro's neighbors heard what she said when she stormed out of the shack." Efrin shifted his weight from one foot to the other.

"How did you see her making the sacrifice?" Adan stopped pacing.

Efrin's mouth was half open as if unsure of what to say.

"Never mind. It doesn't matter." Adan started pacing again. "I've got three people to deal with now, and who knows how many others." *I wish,* Adan added to himself, *Mahalan would just let me get rid of Jandro. Then I'd only have two to worry about.*

Adan was beginning to be glad he *had* made his alliance with Mahalan. *Ivah, of all spirits.* He thought about his mother talking about Ivah. What was the true strength of Ivah? Could she really be more powerful than Mahalan? *I guess we'll find out.*

He desperately wished his father was here now; he would know what to do. *That's it!* Adan couldn't believe he hadn't thought about it earlier.

He dismissed Efrin and headed off to get what he needed to attempt a séance. He could try it at his shack, but his father's clearing was a greater spiritual portal. He'd go just after dark.

To Graisia's relief, Opana wasn't home when she arrived. She slipped into her space and lay motionless on the cardboard, utterly exhausted. After a moment she reached down for her cloud pillow and hugged it tight against her chest. Her stomach rumbled in complaint. *No food for you tonight, Monster.* The kids often joked about "the monster" that lived in their bellies – you had to keep feeding it to keep it happy. Her heart thumped against the pillow as the monster growled again.

Why didn't Jarón help me with coins for Opana? I probably didn't start trusting him soon enough. She began to think of all the things she could have done differently. *If only I'd trusted him sooner, he would've had more time to help me. If I hadn't stolen things that last day, I'd have left over coins. Jarón's making me pay now. Maybe he'll still keep Opana from kicking me out, though.*

She rolled over. *Jarón, if you're there, could you keep Opana from being mean to me tonight?*

She drifted into sleep where she dreamt she was still on Jarón's back, completely helpless, bouncing down the path in darkness.

Adan sat in his father's clearing, desperately hoping this would work. He had never summoned someone from the dead before by himself, though he'd seen his father do it tons of times. He set the incense burning and began to chant, calling his father's spirit. He drifted deep into the world of the spirits.

After a while, the smell of decaying flesh and rotten eggs filled the air and mixed strangely with the fragrant incense he had set. Suddenly his father's image materialized in front of him. He looked exactly as Adan remembered. It was all he could do to keep himself from getting up and trying to embrace the ethereal image. His father's eyes portrayed the same desire.

"Dad," Adan finally said.

"I know," Danjall answered back. "I am proud of you. You are doing well in keeping the power here in Sawtong. Your role here is crucial. I know of the threat in Jandro's daughter. Don't let her scare you."

Adan struggled to focus on his father's words. Overcome with grief and longing, he wanted to ask so many questions. *It'll be okay. He's proud of me.*

Danjall was continuing, "You must make a special sacrifice to Mahalan. It will give you and him the power to overcome Jandro, Yantir, Soliel and Ivah."

"A sacrifice? That's it?" Adan asked, relieved at the simplicity of it.

"There is a young girl."

Adan grimaced but his father continued, "A girl who was born for this very purpose, a girl who was born to be a sacrifice and bring power to our family. She escaped as an infant, but now that she is older and still pure, her death will grant you even more power."

Adan's gut tightened. He had never killed a young, innocent girl before. Yes, he had killed Felirnu, but Mahalan had used him for that. He had put spells and curses on deserving enemies of his own and others that had resulted in death, and he'd offered up other small helpless creatures, but a young girl, as a sacrifice? That was a new one. He wasn't sure he was ready for that.

"It's the only way!" Danjall reverberated in front of him. "It's the only way you'll keep the power in this town!"

The sound of his father's voice sent cold determination down his spine.

"Who is it?" Adan asked.

"Graisia."

The girl that laughed.... Adan's courage faltered. Then he remembered the dream he had about her. "She's the one I dreamt I was trying to kill before you died," Adan said quietly, looking at the ground.

"Yes... you see? You are meant to kill her to gain power. Mahalan knew you would need it soon.... She was born for this purpose."

Her laughter floated through his mind and mixed with the memory of his mother's and a fleeting thought of Ivah.

"It's the only way!" Mahalan's voice shouted in his head along with his father's.

Adan looked up at his father again.

"If you do not offer her as a sacrifice, all I have worked for... all that your fathers have worked for, will be lost! Do not let a moment of weakness or daydreams tear down all we have done! You are stronger than that, my son."

Adan could feel his determination to rule slowly winning over. His mind began focusing again on the goal.

"She lives in that small wooden space you tried to destroy the other night, next to the altar of Harapkan."

Now it made sense why he felt the way he did at her shack. He was *meant* to kill her. He was destined to, in order to gain the power he needed to rule.

"Now let me be in peace.... Do not summon me again."

Adan looked at his dad in dismay.

"You must learn to rule for yourself. You are the new Spirit Priest. If you are in grave danger, I will come to you." His father's image faded into the midnight air.

Graisia wakened to pitch black and the banging of Opana's metal bucket on her roof. A moment later Opana's scowling face appeared in her doorway.

"Found you, you little rat. Think you can get away with free rent, do you?" Opana grabbed Graisia by the hair and dragged her out. "I warned you!"

Graisia screamed and tried to pull Opana's hands out of her hair, but to no avail. Opana's hands were strong and clamped as hard as a rabid dog. She pulled Graisia to her feet then yanked her head back to look into her face.

"I knew you were here." Opana's spittle sprayed all over Graisia's face as she talked. "You know why? Every time I try to talk with Harapkan, when *you're* here, she says nothing! You're not only worthless, you've offended her! And you're bringing me bad luck. What have you done?" She glared at Graisia and gave her head another yank.

Looking into Opana's threatening face, Graisia was so afraid she couldn't have gotten anything out of her mouth even if she had an answer. She shook her head as much as Opana's grip would let her, trying to show she had no idea how she'd offended the goddess.

Adan wanted to ask his father so much more. What was his weakness? Who killed him? And how did he handle Mahalan living in him for so long? Adan cursed at the darkness, wishing it would bring his father back. *Don't summon me again?* Had his father really said that? He stared at where his father had been until Mahalan stirred him from his stupor.

"What are you waiting for? You must act quickly!" Mahalan's voice carried urgency.

Adan stood up and focused on his assignment. *Kill Graisia.* He didn't like it. It wouldn't be quite as clean and easy as Felirnu... but he had to focus on what needed to be done. He strode toward his shack. If her death was to bring the needed power, he would have to sacrifice her with the proper ceremony, not just kill her with a simple spell, focusing *lakás* on her or by smashing her little space to smithereens. *But... if that's all it takes to be able to fight Jandro, Yantir, Soliel and Ivah, I guess that's not too bad.*

He knew no one would stop him walking through town dragging Graisia after him, even if she was screaming her head off. They wouldn't dare. When he reached his shack he angled to the right and, quickening his pace, headed off toward Harapkan's altar. Even as he went, he knew that by killing Graisia, he would be putting a final stake through any other option that was even presented to him. Not just by strengthening his bond with Mahalan through such a sacrifice, but also by nailing shut his heart to any hope Ivah or his mother might be trying to offer him.

"And to think I took you in because you had the gift," Opana spat in disgust, not entirely missing Graisia's face. "You're not going to take advantage of me anymore! I've had patience with you long enough!" Opana took the bucket in her other hand and hit Graisia hard across the head with it, knocking her to the ground. Graisia reeled in shock even as a stabbing pain shot through her knee. She had landed on a piece of broken glass.

This wasn't how it was supposed to work out. Jarón was supposed to help her....

"Lazy trash girl!" Opana proceeded to kick and hit Graisia anywhere she could land a blow. Graisia tried to guard herself, but she never knew where Opana would strike next. Her head pounded and her body throbbed all over.

"I don't want to *ever* see your face again! Or I'll drown your worthless head in this bucket, and no one will even miss you!" Opana paused for a moment, breathless and red with fury. "Go join the dogs where you belong, piece of trash!"

Graisia limped and stumbled painfully as fast as she could down the path, wiping her blood-soaked hair out of her eyes and trying to see through the tears. She paid no attention to where she was going; she just knew she had to get away; far, far away.

20

Adan found Opana ranting and raving inside her shack, throwing her weight around and striking out at anything and anyone in her way. He gave her no more than a glance and then made his way around the shack to find Graisia. To his surprise, he didn't feel the same anger and electric sensations as he did before. A young girl peeked around the corner at him. She gasped in terror and darted out of site into Opana's shack. Adan followed.

Opana was like a ferocious lion interrupted from feeding on her prey. The little girl tried to hide behind her imposing form. When the big woman realized it was Adan, she toned her expression to one of mild surprise. He'd never had any direct dealings with her before. There'd never been any reason for it.

"What can I do for you?" Opana asked relatively calmly, though still breathing heavily.

"I'm looking for a young girl. You have any others older than her?" asked Adan, motioning to the one hiding behind her.

"One way older and the rest are boys." Her eyes

narrowed. "Actually... I just got rid of one, though. You looking for Graisia?"

Adan raised his eyebrows, and Opana continued, "She was making a fool of me, so I kicked the rat out just before you got here. She went off that way." Opana pointed down the path. "If she did something to wrong you, I wouldn't be surprised, and I'd say good riddance! She's a worthless piece of trash."

The corner of Adan's mouth turned up in a smile. Without saying a word, he spun around and took off in the direction Opana had pointed.

After looking for almost an hour, with no sign of Graisia, he was about to give up and head home when he finally glimpsed a girl darting in and out of the shadows up ahead. She seemed to be injured or carrying something heavy.

He had just about reached her when she stepped into a pool of moonlight. It wasn't Graisia at all, but a young lady carrying a child. Disappointed, he watched her hurry into a shack a few doors down.

That's when he realized whose shack the lady might have just disappeared into. Soliel was supposed to live somewhere nearby here, and rumors were spreading that Soliel had started healing people with Ivah's power. Using healing to rally a following irked Adan. It was like she was luring *his* people away with candy.

With Graisia momentarily forgotten, he crept closer to Soliel's shack so he could hear what they were saying inside.

"Please, can you help my son? He's sick again.

He's had this fever for days, and he's hallucinating now, he's all I have left!"

Adan felt sick listening to her whimper.

"Give him to me," Soliel replied gently. "You must believe, Yesenia, in the power of good and of love. Anything is possible."

Yesenia? Wasn't that Felirnu's wife? That must be Vic she's got in there, the one Soliel asked us to curse for her father! She's such a scammer! There was silence for a few moments. Adan could imagine Soliel putting her hands on the young boy's head, channeling power into the boy to drive out the sickness. After a few moments he heard Soliel speak again, "Teach him to seek love with his life, to live sacrificially. Teach him to work for unity."

"I will, I will. Praise be to Ivah," Yesenia replied gratefully. "Thank you so much. How can I repay you? I... I have no money."

"You have paid enough at the hands of my family. Give. If there is some service you can do for someone else, do that. If you live sacrificially and give, you will better your life and the lives of others, and the cycle will continue."

Adan couldn't believe what he was hearing. *A bunch of soft, do-good, crazy advice! Soliel's a fool to trick people into thinking that's how power works. She can't take the town's allegiance with that!* Or maybe she could.

He ran his fingers through his hair. *If that boy recovers, it'll be trouble for me.* Adan was the one who had cursed Vic. If Soliel could undue his curses.... He *had* to keep the boy from recovering.

He wasn't ready to face Soliel yet directly. His father had made that clear. He needed the power from Graisia's death, and then he needed to find Ivah's weakness. *But until then, I can still control the people in his town.* He felt Mahalan's pleasure with his idea.

Yesenia backed out of Soliel's house, carrying her now-sleeping son. Adan followed, keeping his distance until they were a ways away from Soliel's shack. Then he came up and grabbed her shoulder, stopping her instantly. Yesenia looked up. Her brown eyes went wide in alarm.

He smiled at the panic in her face. There was something so satisfying about making people squirm. He enjoyed it just as much as his father had. He knew it guaranteed him future power. The young boy stirred in his mother's arms. She wrapped her arms around the boy tighter – as if it would help to shield him.

"So, you think Soliel and Ivah deserve your allegiance more than me or Mahalan? You think they're more powerful?"

The woman trembled. Sweat beaded on her face and she shook her head slightly.

"Your family will continue to be an example to anyone else who thinks they can find more power with someone other than me or Mahalan." Adan looked down at her son. He could feel Mahalan's power ready to be released. Mahalan gave him instructions, as well. *"Curse her womb, too. Let her have no more children after this."*

Adan reached out and flattened his hand

against the boy's chest. The boy's breathing instantly became labored and raspy. Yesenia tried to pull back, blood draining from her face, but Adan still had his hold on her shoulder. The boy's breathing sounded like more of a gurgle. Then he stopped breathing altogether. Yesenia let out a sob and crumpled to the ground holding her lifeless son.

Still gripping Yesenia's shoulder, he spoke a curse that insured the boy would never be replaced.

"Now you can tell your friends how powerful Soliel is to protect you," Adan sneered. Satisfied he had done what was needed, he turned and headed home. He'd have to find that blasted Graisia another way.

Graisia dodged a group of drunken men and kept hobbling as fast as she could – up alleyways, through shadows – stumbling over the uneven ground. She moved as fast as her aching legs would carry her until her side hurt so much she was forced to stop. She slid down onto the ground next to a shack and slumped wearily against the wall. She didn't care if the owner would be mad. She had no idea where she was, or if she was even in Sawtong anymore.

Her arms longed to hug her cloud or lean against Jarón's back, but she'd left her pillow at Opana's... she'd never get to see Jarón again. *If only I'd trusted Jarón earlier, or hadn't stolen at all. I'm getting what I deserve. I even mess up the goddess of fate with my mistakes!* She pulled her knees up close to her. Her entire body screamed in pain at the simple movement. *Opana is right, no one would care if I died.* Ignoring the blood smeared on her injured knee, she rested her throbbing head on her bruised arms and the knee that wasn't cut. It didn't take long before she was drifting off into the welcome escape of sleep.

Graisia awoke in the forest, sitting at the edge of the path, practically in the thorns. Although she was wearing her beautiful, velvety, petal dress that sparkled with gold, her knee was bleeding, and the thorns nearby had blood on them. Tears streamed down her face. More intense than the pain in her knee was the heaviness of confusion that weighed in her heart. She thought she'd done what was right, what Jarón wanted, but this whole mess seemed to be her fault.

She pressed her hand on her knee, trying to stop the bleeding and the pain. Strangely, even through her tears, she could see the drab forest more clearly than the last time she was here. The golden path was visible under the splay of her dress, and... *Jarón's feet!*

She looked up to see him kneel down. He tenderly placed a hand on her shoulder and her worries lightened just at the sight of his smile and the sense of his touch. Her knee did not stop aching though.

"The pain is real, isn't it?" he asked. "You were unjustly hurt. It's not a pain you deserved, Graisia."

"But I trusted you!" Graisia blurted out. "And look what's happened!"

"Yes, but did you trust me to use whatever happened for good? I didn't promise there wouldn't be pain." He covered her fingers with his strong warm hand. "I didn't want her to hurt you, but will you let me use it for good?"

Graisia blinked at him through her tears, wondering how pain could ever be used for good.

At her silence, Jarón continued, "Lots of people choose to live in the thorns, and in their pain they use the thorns against others." He brushed a strand of her matted hair away from her eyes. "They don't know any other way." His penetrating gaze melted more of her worries and fear. "Could you forgive Opana for hurting you, and let me take care of the consequences?"

Graisia scrutinized his face. Could he be serious? Forgive Opana who had treated her cruelly from the day she moved in? Opana, who had beaten her and hardly gave her enough to eat? The vines along Graisia's side pricked and poked at her leg and hip.

Jarón glanced down at the blood-smeared thorns beside Graisia, stained by the drops escaping under her hand. When he turned back to look into her eyes, they reflected her pain. He felt it too. He carefully lifted her hand away from the wound, exposing it to the stinging air. "Don't try to cover up the pain. You need to let some of the blood out so it can cleanse itself."

It hurt even more now without her hand putting pressure on it. Graisia watched as her falling tears mixed with her blood and dripped together onto the thorns.

Graisia didn't think it was possible for Jarón to see deeper into her heart, but he did, enough to leave her speechless. He had shown her so much love – even when she'd stolen from her friends – so much that he let these merciless vines kill him.

"Graisia, if you respond to Opana in my love, the pain will be turned around for good. If you respond in anger and hatred, the thorns will grow even more." His warm voice surrounded her with comfort even as his eyes spoke of limitless love beyond comprehension. She knew without words that he would always be there for her.

"Yes!" The word spilled from her lips before she could stop it. She could forgive Opana. Jarón could and would take care of everything.

That's when she realized something was happening to the thorns coated in her blood. They were melting and turning golden like the rest of the path! Her blood and tears were actually widening the path. She looked up at Jarón. "I didn't know *my* blood could do that too."

"Neither did Opana." His smile widened. Then he softly placed his hand over the gash on her knee. Immediately the liquid warmth of Uri's light flooded over it. Streams of light gleamed through Jarón's fingers. When he lifted his hand, she had a golden scar where the wound had once been.

A rooster crowed from a distant cage in someone's window. With her eyes still closed, Graisia could still feel the warmth of Uri's light on her knee.

She tried to soak up the lingering feeling of Jarón's presence before opening her eyes.

Finally, she raised her head and looked around. The early morning sun had turned the ever-present smog to a dirty shade of pink and the shacks were taking on the same hazy glow. A few people were beginning to stir in nearby shacks. A bleary-eyed man shuffled by, probably heading off to work somewhere, even as another stumbled home. It took her a moment to remember why she didn't recognize her surroundings.

She sighed as it all came back to her. She was about to hang her head down on her knees again when she noticed that the faintly warm gash on her knee was not the gold of her dream, but a bumpy scab. She let her head rest on her good knee. At least she'd made it through the night. *What's Jarón going to do now? He said to trust him to use everything for good....*

Graisia felt a tap on her shoulder. Expecting that she was going to be shooed away by the shack's owner, she was surprised to feel refreshed from the touch. When she looked up, she found herself staring at a girl of about her own age, who also wore a too-small dress and had hair just a little darker than Graisia's. The girl smiled and laughed, beckoning Graisia to come, as if she wanted Graisia to play with her. *What does she want with me?* Graisia looked around. There was no one else the girl could be motioning to except her. When Graisia looked back, the girl waved again for her to follow, then ran away.

Graisia's curiosity got the better of her. Even though she was still incredibly sore and achy, and probably quite a mess to look at, she stood up and hobbled after the girl as best she could. It was hard to catch up, though. The girl always seemed to stay about five shacks ahead. Graisia followed her down little alleyways, across ditches and under laundry lines. Every now and then, the girl would look back and make sure Graisia was still following. They rounded a bend in the path, and just as Graisia was about to catch up, the girl disappeared between two shacks.

Determined not to lose her, she mustered a burst of energy and followed. When she came out of the shadows, she found herself in a small clearing, right in front of another little shack, and with no other outlet. *It's a dead end!* She stood turning in circles, trying to figure out where the girl had disappeared to. Maybe she had gone inside.

The only person around was an old man sitting on the crude front porch hunched over and busily working on something. The porch, a platform made of scrap wood, with a little metal roof, barely sheltered the old man from the now risen sun.

He lifted his head. Graisia shuddered. *Did he use that girl to trick me into coming back here?* It was the crazy, old witch-man, Salim.

21

Salim seemed to be emerging from his own distant world as he looked up and focused on her. His thick white hair had a trace of stubborn black that must have been striking when he was younger. He could have been taller once too, and maybe even strong, but now, he was simply withered and tired. He was so stooped over he seemed to be hiding behind the old tennis shoe he was repairing, even as he sat perched precariously on a little stool that was missing one leg. A twig stuck out from his mouth at an odd angle and bobbed up and down as he gnawed on it.

In an instant, she took all of this in. Her next thought was to turn and run before he could capture her and lock her away, like she'd heard he would do. But there was something about his presence that actually made her feel safe. And he didn't seem like he even wanted to talk with her, let alone jump up and grab her. *Maybe it's his magic.... Maybe he's using it to make me not be afraid.* But she *did* feel oddly safe. The fear she usually felt from even just thinking about him and his wife had melted as she looked at him.

"What are you looking for?" Salim finally asked after clearing his throat.

"Um... did you... did you see the girl that came back here?" She was still trying to catch her breath.

Salim remained on his little stool, chewing slowly. It seemed like her words were taking a few moments to sink in. Although he had some light in his eyes, deep creases folded across his brow and marked his temples with strong crow's feet as if he'd suffered through many monsoons. "Just saw you," he finally answered and then turned back to the tennis shoe.

He obviously wasn't interested in capturing her. *He could just be trying to make me feel safe though first,* she told herself again. Maybe he wanted to lure her into their shack.

Against her better judgment she found herself speaking again. "No, there was this girl, I don't know who she was, but she kept wanting me to follow her. She ran back here, I'm sure of it. She doesn't live here?" She paused and added, "She kinda looked like me."

The man looked up again with his eyebrows raised, peering at her as if trying to get a feel of what kind of person she was. She turned her eyes toward the ground.

"You say she looked like you?" he asked. "And you don't know her?"

"Yes," Graisia affirmed hesitantly. Should she run now, while she still had the chance? *Maybe he's got a whole cage of kids behind his shack where he keeps them for his magic, like Opana said.*

Salim stared at the shoe on his lap. "Hmmm..." He tilted his stool back and leaned even more unsteadily against a flimsy wall, still chewing his twig. "You didn't tell me she'd be so little," he muttered. "I don't know how she can..." Then he looked at Graisia again, but he seemed to be talking to someone else. "Oh, alright," he mumbled, agreeing with whoever it was he was talking to. This man really was crazy.

Salim looked Graisia in the eye. "I can tell you who that little girl was. She's one of your *aysh*." He turned his attention back to the shoe and pulled back the loose rubber sole.

"My what?" Graisia asked. He really was talking crazy now. She'd heard people talk about *aysh* before, but no one she'd known had ever claimed to have one for themselves. Opana had mentioned them now and again. She said they were messengers of Harapkan, worker spirits, or something like that.

He slapped a blob of glue on the loose sole. "Your *aysh* – a spirit being who follows you around. There are good and bad ones. The good ones watch out for you and every once in a while, they take on human form – if they have to do something special." Looking up, he added, "Sometimes they look kind of like the person they help. That way, they don't scare you so much." He turned back to his shoe again, clothes-pinning the sole in place.

The whole explanation seemed a bit absurd... and it *was* coming from Salim. *But then where did the girl go if he's lying?* she wondered. "So... why would this... *aysh*... bring me back here?" According to Opana, she had offended Harapkan. "Why would Harapkan send me *here*?" Maybe this was Opana's way of getting revenge.

"Harapkan?" The old man looked at her from the corner of his eye while still adjusting the clothespins.

Graisia looked down again.

"Not all *aysh* are from Harapkan," he said. "But why here? Well... you need a new place to live, don't you? And we could use an extra hand. Besides, now we have a place that needs filling, too. Problems solved."

Graisia stared at him her mouth agape. *How did he know?*

Salim continued, "We got a little space up on the roof we just closed in for you. I thought it would be a bit too small, but now that I see you, I didn't need to worry." He smiled slightly as he set the shoe down to dry.

Live with them! The thought would have terrified her yesterday, but now, looking at Salim, it just sounded bizarre. He talked about weird things, and he knew things she hadn't told him.

He put his hands on his knees. "Seems like you could use some washing up, too. You've got some nasty bruises."

Graisia self-consciously reached her hand up to touch her head, wincing at the pain as she did so. Her hair felt like a matted mess too. She'd almost forgotten about all her aches and injuries. "How'd you know I needed a place to sleep?" she stammered.

He started pulling himself up, muttering again about how he couldn't imagine she could be so important, since she was so small. Then louder he answered Graisia, "Uri told me this morning. Said someone important was coming today and needed a place to live."

"Uri? You know Uri!?" Relief flooded through her, and suddenly it all made sense. She took a few steps closer to Salim. "Is that why they call you crazy?" Maybe... maybe everything would work out okay.

He raised his eyebrows. "Yes, I know Uri." He sighed deeply. "And I guess you could say that's *one* reason they call me crazy." The creases on his face deepened and he seemed to withdraw into his own thoughts for a moment. Then quietly he told her, "But you'll have to decide for yourself if I'm crazy or not." He turned towards the door. "Com' on, I'll show you your new home." He called toward the back of the shack, "Estar! Our new boarder is here! She's a mite one!"

Graisia hadn't said she was staying, but she couldn't think of any reason to object now, so she followed Salim in. This turn of events bewildered and amazed her. It seemed so odd, but a smile still crept onto her face. Who would have guessed she'd be moving in with the crazy, old witch-couple? *Lio maybe,* she thought ironically.

She stepped into the dusty one-roomed-shack. It had only the sunlight from two windows and another door for light, a simple room made out of scrap wood and metal. The floor sagged in the middle – but it wasn't dirt! She saw a roughly made ladder off to one side, and assumed it went up to the loft where she'd be sleeping. A pile of repaired shoes took up one whole corner. Old fruit crates nailed to the opposite wall held some food, old dishes and a pot. A well used sleeping mat was rolled up neatly against the wall underneath the crates, and another fruit crate lay nearby on the floor, turned upside down, with a book lying on top of it.

As soon as Graisia saw the book, she walked straight toward it. "This looks like the one I saw with Uri! Where'd you get it?" She gently rubbed her hand over the cover. It was beautiful, even if it was old, well-used and worn. No lights came out of it though, but the writing on the front was still in gold.

While Salim was taking down a piece of bread and an overripe banana from one of the crates on the wall, Graisia opened the book and looked for her name. There were only a bunch of markings she didn't understand.

Disappointed, she closed the book and turned to Salim. He didn't offer an answer, but held out the fruit and bread to her. She took them and began to eat ravenously. She'd forgotten how long it was since she'd fed the monster. Swallowing her second bite of bread, she remembered what people said about how food from the witch-couple could make you go insane. She paused for a moment and looked at the bread and banana. They looked normal, and Salim followed Uri... and she was starving. She took another huge bite of the bread.

Salim smiled somewhat sadly at her then turned and headed out the back door. A moment later, he came in again following Estar, a slow-moving woman in a faded dress. She had clothespins pinned down the right side of her dress, ready to use whenever she might need them. Since Graisia had always been afraid of her, she'd never taken the chance to actually look at her. Estar's eyes seemed tired, but her sun-weathered skin was lit by a gentle smile that revealed a number of missing teeth. The old woman brushed some wisps of gray hair away from her face as she looked at Graisia. The rest of her hair was held back with a few randomly placed clothespins.

As soon as she saw Graisia up close, her smile turned to a frown. "My goodness, you're a mess! Come here, lovey, we should get you cleaned a bit."

Graisia moved toward her and Estar took a rag, wet it with water from a bucket and then attempted to wash Graisia's face and head while Graisia attempted to cram the last bit of bread in her mouth.

Estar turned to her husband and commented, "She *is* a mite one. You sure she's the one Uri was talking about?"

"Yup, positive. Uri hasn't spoken to me that clear for a long time... and an *aysh* brought her. Besides, look at the bright light coming from her." Salim waved a hand at Graisia.

"What light?" Graisia asked with her mouth full of mushy banana.

"I don't see it, lovey, if it means anything to you." Estar kept cleaning. "But Salim here, he's been known to see things... in times past anyway." Estar glanced at Salim from the corner of her eye as she kept washing.

Graisia looked to Salim for an explanation, but it was Estar who explained further.

"We all give off various kinds of light – colored, white, darker or gray – even if we don't see it." She paused. "Do you see any light or colors coming from Salim?"

"No," Graisia answered. *Both of them might just be crazy, after all.* She winced as Estar attempted to clean the blood from her hair. She must have a ton of goose-egg bruises on her scalp.

Estar looked at her more intently and said, "If you could *imagine* light or colors coming from him, what would it look like?"

Graisia looked at Salim, wondering if Estar was serious. Estar wiped some dirt from around her right eye.

Graisia decided to give it a try. She'd experienced so many new things lately, why not this? She scrunched her face and thought. "Okay, if he had a color coming from him, I think it would maybe be kind of a blue, like the sky, but a dark blue, like just at the end of a big storm."

Salim raised his eyebrows. "You've got quite an eagle eye." Then he furrowed his brow in thought, and Graisia could have sworn some of the clouds from the storm crossed over his eyes momentarily. He turned away.

Estar looked at Salim for a moment then turned back to Graisia.

"What's your name, lovey?" Estar dipped her rag in the bucket and set to cleaning Graisia's knee.

"Graisia."

The lady turned to her husband. "Did you hear that, love? Her name is Graisia."

"Mm hmm." Salim mumbled something else unintelligible and went out the back door.

Turning back to Graisia, Estar said, "I guess you know who we are, at least our names anyway." She sighed and looked off in the distance, then smiled again. "I'm glad Uri's brought you. It will be nice to have some new company. We don't get many visitors. We spend most our time fixing old shoes, and then we resell them. We could use your help. I'm getting too old to be washing them all. Uri obviously brought you here for some other reason too, but until we find out more about that, you can at least help me with the washing."

Graisia nodded, delighted. *No more trash!* She was feeling more comfortable with Estar by the minute. She couldn't imagine how or why anyone would have started such horrible rumors about this couple. *I wonder what they did... and why Salim seems so sad.*

Estar continued, "So what's your story? How'd you come to be needing a place to live?"

Graisia looked up, a bit startled. She wasn't sure she wanted to answer. She chewed a moment on her lower lip thinking how she should reply.

Estar noticed her hesitancy. "No doubt you've got your tale. You can tell us when you're ready, love."

Relieved, Graisia relaxed again.

Estar motioned for Graisia to sit on the floor and then quietly went to work attempting to comb Graisia's tangled hair. It was a painful process. Graisia couldn't remember the last time a comb touched her hair. But she also couldn't remember ever being treated with such gentleness. Estar used some of the clothespins from her dress as temporary barrettes while working through the knots. Graisia almost didn't mind the pain. She felt like she was a princess on her bed in one of her dreams, and she didn't want to wake up from this dream.

When Estar had cleaned Graisia to her satisfaction Salim rejoined them on the floor. He had another shoe to work on and was still chewing on his twig. He placed a cup of water in front of Graisia. "So what brought you to needing a new home?"

She drank the whole cup empty before answering. She was afraid to tell them everything. Maybe they'd kick her out if they knew all she'd done – stealing from her friends, making the goddess of fate angry – and then there was Jarón. She'd left the pillow behind. She'd never see him again. She hung her head as she thought about all of these things.

"Do you have any parents or family?" Estar encouraged gently.

Graisia shook her head, looking at the floor. She could at least start with that. "Opana found me when I was small, along the road. She said I had the gift, I think she meant for collecting garbage, so she took me in. She made me work at the dump." Graisia turned her head and looked off into one corner. "She kicked me out last night, because..." She stopped.

"Because...?" Estar leaned in. "It's okay, lovey, were not going to kick you out. Uri sent you here, and we're going to trust that Uri knows best."

That gave Graisia the courage she needed.

"Because I didn't pay her enough money, because I had to pay back my friends I stole from, and she said I had offended Harapkan," it all came out in a rush. "I didn't mean to.... I was trying to do what Jarón told me to do." She pulled her hands to cover her face as tears slipped down her cheeks.

"Don't worry." Estar squeezed her shoulder gently. "Especially about that goddess, she's a good one to offend."

"Mmm..." Salim agreed. "You do have the gift."

"What gift?" Graisia burst out through her tears.

"I don't know all what your gifts are, but one of them is seeing. You've obviously got eagle eyes," Salim responded.

"What do you mean, seeing?" Graisia wiped her face gingerly with her hands, avoiding the bruises. "Everyone can see."

Estar shook her head. "You can see more than others see, lovey. Beyond the ordinary into the world of spirits, like Salim does."

Graisia wrinkled her forehead in thought. She wasn't sure she wanted to see spirits, from what she knew of them.

"It's why you have lots of dreams, too," Salim commented. "You're seeing beyond the ordinary in those dreams, into a fuller picture of what's really going on."

How did he know about her dreams? She was about to ask when he turned to his wife and asked, "Have you ever seen someone so young with so much light and such strong gifts? She can't be more than 12!" He shook his head. "Haven't seen the gift so strong in someone since..." He stopped himself, and his voice faded. He stood up and busied himself momentarily with moving some dishes around. After clearing his throat, he spoke up again. "I'm surprised Opana didn't mention the light coming from you, too. I'm sure she saw it. Had to. That's what was bothering Harapkan, I'm sure."

"I thought you said everyone had light." Graisia said turning to Estar.

"True, everyone gives off light, but there's a brighter light placed deep within a person when they've truly met the king," Estar replied, tilting her head a little. "You know, his light is the brightest and purest, and it's in you now. That can upset other beings, and people."

"The king?" Graisia asked surprised and confused. She'd never met any king.

"Jarón," Estar stated matter-of-factly.

Graisia was shocked. "I didn't know he was a king. He didn't tell me that." But she definitely remembered the light coming from Jarón into her – Uri's incredible light!

"He's not just *a* king, he's the *High* King, lovey, with many kings and queens under him."

"But I left my cloud pillow at Opana's! How am I going to see him again?" Then she remembered, "Wait, how did I see Jarón last night without the pillow?"

"Pillow? What do you need a pillow for?" Estar interjected. "And how in Sawtong, did you get one in the first place?"

"Don't you need a pillow to be with Uri or see

Jarón in your dreams?" Graisia asked.

"Where did you get such an absurd idea?" Estar chided.

Salim shook his head as if everything was easily clear to him. "What does a pillow mean to you, Graisia?"

"It's what queens and princesses use. And it's really soft to sleep on. You sleep with it." Graisia couldn't see why that was important.

"There you have it," Salim said as he lowered himself onto the floor and leaned back against the wall. His twig bobbed up and down sticking out between his lips. He reached over to inspect his work on another shoe.

"Have what?" Graisia was finding it easier to see why people called him crazy.

He took the twig out from between his teeth momentarily. "That's why Uri must've used a pillow to take you to the Realm. To show you you're royalty, that you can rest in Uri and rule with Jarón. You don't *need* the pillow. Uri was just using it to teach you something."

Graisia looked at him skeptically. "It isn't magic? And what's the Realm?"

"No, it's not magic." Salim took a deep breath and looked up thoughtfully. "The Realm... the Realm is where everything can be as Uri meant it to be. It's a kind of place – where Jarón rules and where we can rule with him for all of eternity. It can be everywhere, but isn't yet. It's a place where you can enter timelessness, eternity; the real depths of love... and live out of that in unity with Jarón. It's seeing and experiencing the most powerful of what really is. We can be in it, it can be in us, and we can spread it to others. Your life really seems to begin when you enter the Realm.... It's where you are truly *being* who you were meant to be...." Salim's voice trailed off and he suddenly seemed somewhat distant, like he was wondering if he even really believed what he had just said.

Graisia tingled all over though. Jarón had said they had lots to "be."

Salim took a resolved yet shaky breath. "It is a realm above all other realms, and the only realm that will last forever."

Whether he truly believed it or not, Graisia felt Salim was right. It seemed like something Jarón would tell her, even if she didn't understand it all. She was too worn out to figure it all out now though, and suddenly became very aware of the aches in her body. She closed her eyes to rest her brain and try to relieve some of the tension in her head.

Estar must have noticed. "We should let her rest, Salim. She's been through a lot, and here we are, trying to explain all of existence and eternity to her."

She gently nudged Graisia and ushered her up the ladder. The new little space did appear to be made just for her. It was a bit longer than she was tall, with worn wood boards for walls and a scrap of metal for a roof, just high enough that she could sit up. There was a real reed sleeping mat, not cardboard, covering her floor. At one end was a small window-type opening with a board next to it that could be used to cover the hole when it rained.

Graisia gratefully stretched out on the mat, feeling unusually safe and content. She only wished she still had her cloud pillow for her head.

She heard Salim head out the front door down below, probably to work on a shoe. He called back, "You left the clothespins in her hair, Estar."

"What clothespins?" Estar's voice came from just under Graisia. "I got all my clothespins right here."

Graisia smiled at Estar's absentmindedness and pulled the clothespins out of her hair to make sleeping more comfortable. *These people are strange, but I don't think they're crazy, at least not in a bad way. I think they'll be alright to live with. Definitely better than Opana. They are so different than Opana. Jarón's right, he can use anything for good if I trust him. Thanks, Jarón.*

She drifted off into the most peaceful sleep she'd had in a long time.

Graisia awoke into Uri's room of light that she loved so much; all the weariness of the last few days forgotten. Excited to see what new things she would discover, she parted the shimmering curtains and was greeted by the warm breath of light she had come to long for. She sat for a moment on the edge of the bed, eyes closed, bathing in its radiance.

Gradually she became aware of a soft whisper traveling through the room. Opening her eyes, she saw no one. The whisper, unintelligible, came again like a gentle wind blowing from one end of the room to the other, swirling playfully in its dance. Glancing off a wall behind her, it came back in a whoosh, traveled through the curtains on the opposite side of the bed, and blew right toward the back of her head. It swirled around her body like a rainbow ribbon of air, and suddenly, as clear as a fresh, mountain stream, the whisper became intelligible. It sounded like the crystal singing part of Uri's voice, "I am the Spirit of Jarón and Uri, come to live and stay with you, to make my home in you. Will you take me?"

"Yes!" Graisia enthused. Who would want to resist anything from Jarón and Uri? And to live with her forever? "Yes!" she said again, bouncing lightly on the bed in her excitement.

The ribbony breeze lighted on the top of her head then breezed down into her mind, sailed gently down through her neck and heart, coming to rest in her belly. It hadn't settled for more than a moment when it bubbled up again like fizzing soda, and she quickly became a gurgling, bubbling fountain of laughter.

Days passed, and no sign of Graisia. Adan was getting desperate. The pressure was mounting from all directions. Despite his efforts to scare people by killing Yesenia's son, Soliel's following actually seemed to be growing. He wouldn't admit it, but it seemed killing the boy had actually made people like her more. Efrin had informed him that Jandro was finalizing plans with his loyal *basyo* (who were also growing in number), and planning to challenge him at the next ring gathering in three days. And then there was Yantir, who could strike at any time. Things were not looking good. He *had* to find Graisia.

From his various sources, he learned that Graisia had no real family – that would make life easier for him – and he already knew that she worked at the dump with Kaly and the rest of her *bandhu*. However, he also discovered Graisia hadn't been seen with them for several days. No one knew where she was. He figured since she had been pretty tight with at least one member of her *bandhu*, she would probably try to return to them as soon as possible, if she were still in the neighborhood. He purposefully didn't interrogate or threaten her *bandhu* in case they might somehow warn her. He *wanted* her to return to them.

With no other leads, he could only keep his eyes on the dump. He hated spending his days loitering around mountains of garbage watching Kaly and the rest of her *bandhu*. The whole scene disgusted him: people, mostly kids, sifting through the refuse of the rest of the world. It was the pit of humanity where people scavenged alongside the animals. He preferred to focus on controlling the people who lived around it, never admitting he was just one rung up on the food chain from these dump diggers.

But he had to find Graisia. His whole future depended on the power to be gained through that girl's death.

Graisia woke up to the playful chirping of the tiny cinnamon-colored sparrow that liked to perch outside her rooftop window. Life with Salim and Estar had fallen into a simple routine, and every morning, without fail, her dusty, feathered friend greeted her with the sun. Graisia enjoyed watching it fluff its feathers and sing in the early light. Sometimes other sparrows would come too, especially when she put out a few crumbs for them, but this one seemed to have chosen her roof as its favorite place.

Graisia rolled over on her back, and just as the sparrow basked in the morning sun, she tried to soak in the light and love that surrounded and welled up within her every time she focused on Jarón or Uri. It was a wonderful feeling, and magnificently addicting. She could spend all morning laying in it.

Life was now uncomplicated and pleasant. She couldn't believe the difference. In the mornings, the three of them ate a small meal together of rice or flat bread and some kind of mushy bruised fruit. Then she'd help Estar wash and scrub old shoes until they looked as new as possible. After that, the shoes were hung to dry with the ever-present clothespins. She had discovered clothespins were really quite useful for lots of things and had taken to wearing them down her dress too. In the afternoons, when the sun was the hottest, Estar would lie down inside while Graisia sat with Salim on the front porch. She pestered him with questions and listened to him read or tell stories. Sometimes though, he wouldn't talk much and seemed lost in his own melancholy world.

After a couple hours of rest it would be back to work for all of them until they had their second meal in the evening. They didn't have enough food for three meals, and it was cooler to cook in the evening. Graisia liked living with Salim and Estar; they were amazingly kind and generous. She wanted to pinch herself with the clothespins sometimes, to make sure she really was still awake. But when she remembered that Estar and Salim had both met Jarón and Uri, it made sense that they were kinder and more generous than Opana.

They hadn't explained to her how they met them, but Graisia gathered they had known them for a very long time. Salim once mentioned an old man named Nandan, who had taught him much of what he knew. Then there was the book they had in the shack with lots of stories about Uri and Jarón – that was the book Salim read out loud from sometimes.

So far, her favorite story from the book was about a man who gave messages to people from Uri. He stood up to an evil king and queen and showed them Uri was more powerful than their gods. Uri saved the man's life many times. One time he had to get somewhere really quickly to deliver a message. Uri helped him run so incredibly quick, he ran faster than a horse and its chariot! She wondered if she could be a messenger for Uri, and if Uri would ever do things like that for her.

Graisia turned over and looked out the window at the sparrow, wanting to enjoy its company for a few moments more. As she watched, a crow swooped down, scaring the tiny bird.

Graisia let out a cry.

The sparrow darted under a piece of overlapping metal. The crow circled, landing on the roof. It hopped over to the little bird cawing angrily. The little sparrow backed into the eaves even further where the crow was too big to reach. Finally the frustrated crow took flight with a jaded screech that sent chills down Graisia's spine. It circled a few times and then flew off.

Graisia knew exactly what it meant. Adan was still after her, but at least for now, she was safe. She had hoped she could forget about him, living here, but apparently not.

She called out softly to her sparrow friend, "It's okay, little bird, you're safe now." She hoped it was true. She hoped Uri would watch out for her too.

The sparrow tentatively made its way out from under the eaves, tilting its head this way and that to make sure the crow really was gone.

When Graisia came down for breakfast, Salim stood next to two full bags of repaired shoes.

"Later this morning, you can help me take these to the man who sells them for us," he said, "and then we'll get some more shoes to work on from Pouyan."

A thrill went through her. "You mean Pouyan at the dump?"

Salim nodded.

She'd wondered how her *bandhu* friends were, and whether they missed her. Mitina had probably been worried sick. But to Kaly, she'd probably just become the latest topic of gossip. Usually, Estar and Salim kept Graisia so busy that by the end of the day, they were all too tired to go anywhere. If Salim took her to the dump, she'd learn the way and be able to go on her own at other times too. "Do you think I could see my friends while we're at Pouyan's?" she asked cautiously.

"I suppose so." Salim shrugged. "No reason why not."

Graisia beamed. "I can't wait!" Breakfast couldn't be eaten fast enough.

When they finally set out around mid morning, Graisia knew she had an enormously silly grin on her face, but she didn't try to wipe it off. She even attempted to add a little skip to her step, despite the heavy bag of shoes slung over her shoulder.

Adan stood near Pouyan's shack watching the scavengers with disgust. He glared at people now and then who dared to show they noticed him. He could tell some were whispering nervously about him out of his earshot. *Let them wonder.* Eventually he got tired of standing in the sun with sweat dripping down his back. Pouyan would have to share.

He made his way into Pouyan's shack, and once inside, maneuvered around various piles of odd and reusable materials. It didn't smell any better inside, but at least he was out of the sun.

Pouyan raised his eyebrows and looked as if he was about to protest to Adan's presence, but then thought better of it and shut his mouth. Adan made himself comfortable near the back of the shack on a big bundle of clothing. He had a good view of Kaly and her friends through Pouyan's window. It was still early in the day and not many were bringing finds over yet, so Pouyan kept himself busy sorting and ignored Adan.

"Pouyan!" an old man yelled through the window. "I need to get some more shoes. You got any?" It looked like Salim. Adan ignored him, keeping his gaze settled on Kaly and the others.

"Just for you, old man. Come around to the door." Pouyan yanked at a sack buried amongst the piles.

A girl's voice piped up from somewhere outside

the window, "Salim, can I go see my friends?"

A wave of hatred and anger washed over Adan at the sound of her voice. It could only mean one thing. He sat up straight. His mouth went dry and his heart pounded. *She's been hiding with crazy old Salim?*

Salim looked off to his right, presumably to where Graisia stood. "Sure, Graisia. Don't take too long, though. We've got to get back."

Graisia darted off towards her friends, totally unaware she was being watched.

Salim came around to Pouyan's door and let himself in. In the lightless shack, Salim probably couldn't see him sitting in the back. As he entered, Adan felt the same electrical current rolling off of Salim that he'd felt at Graisia's place. Adan's mind spun with hatred as he sought Mahalan's counsel and tried to contain his fury. *How should I get Graisia?*

Like a spider, Mahalan's instructions crept through his mind, *"Follow them home. Take her tonight. The less people who know how she disappears, the less trouble you will have later."*

Adan nodded absently, continuing to gaze at Salim and trying to keep from unleashing his emotions at that moment. He would get her and secure his rule, tonight.

"Graisia!" Mitina dropped her bag and ran, throwing herself into her friend's arms. She practically knocked Graisia off her feet.

Graisia laughed, equally as happy.

"*Kosa,* where have you been?" Mitina asked. "We've been so afraid for you! Did Opana really chase you out? Kaly thought you were dead, but I knew you couldn't be." Mitina took in a breath and looked up at Graisia with eyes bright and alive.

Graisia let out a sigh of relief. It was so good to see Mitina again. The others in the *bandhu* made their way toward them, Kaly last of all. Lio had picked up Mitina's sack and was dragging it behind him.

"So, oh disturber of fate, where have you been hiding?" Kaly asked somewhat sarcastically when she finally reached where they were standing. "Opana's been telling everyone what bad luck you are."

Graisia couldn't decide if Kaly's smile was one of amusement or mocking. "Um... well, it's a long story."

"You're healthy at least," Kaly stated. Was Kaly actually relieved? Was she forgiven? "Who's been feeding you?" Kaly asked.

Tayzor looked Graisia up and down as well. She had been eating more than she used to, and it showed.

"I... I've been living with..." Did she really want to tell them? What would they think of her when they found out? Lio could really play it up if he wanted to. She looked down at the trash beneath her feet. A scruffy doll with a missing head looked like it was reaching out to her with its pudgy pale arms. "Umm... I've been with Salim and Estar." She raised her head to see their reaction.

The look of shock on all of their faces was just as she expected.

"They haven't killed you?" "They let you come out?" "Did you eat their food?" "Did you escape?" "What happened?" The questions came all at once. She even thought she caught a glimpse of awe on Lio's face.

When they gave her room to talk again she continued, "They're actually very kind. They're not really crazy – a little weird maybe, but not crazy. And their food's alright – it doesn't make you go insane. They just worship Uri. I think that's why people think they're crazy. They fix and sell old shoes, and I help them now."

They stared at her as if she had told them she had spent the week walking on the moon.

"I wanted to come back and see you guys, but I didn't know how to get here, and we've been really busy!" She pointed toward Pouyan's shack. "Salim's over talking with Pouyan right now, getting more shoes."

"Where Adan is?" Mitina asked, eyes wide.

"Adan? I didn't see him." Graisia's chest tightened. She thought of the crow from this morning.

"Yeah, he went in there a few minutes ago." Kaly glanced over her shoulder in the direction of the shack. "He's been hanging out here a lot the last few days. No one knows why. But he hasn't hurt anyone." Kaly shrugged causing her too big t-shirt to slip off one of her bony shoulders. She yanked it up again.

"He hasn't hurt anyone here," Lio said looking sidelong at Kaly and then turned to Graisia. "But did you hear what he did the other night – the night you disappeared?"

Graisia shook her head.

Lio continued, "He killed Vic. His mom took him to Soliel to heal him. Adan was furious, and killed him right after Soliel made him better."

"Why would someone go to Soliel?" Graisia asked, confused.

"*Lakás!* You don't know anything anymore, do you?" Mitina exclaimed.

Looking exasperated, Kaly took over the explanation. "Soliel went and made an alliance with Ivah. Now she supposedly has power to heal and help people." She wrinkled her nose indicating how foolish she thought this was. "Adan's not happy about it. He's probably afraid she's going to take over the town."

Graisia glanced back at Pouyan's shack concerned for Salim. Salim stood just inside the doorway, filling their bags with old shoes. "I don't think Adan would want to hurt Salim. He's not trying to take over Sawtong or anything." She turned back to the others, trying to believe her own argument.

"Soliel just says she wants to do good," Kaly warned, "and it sure isn't keeping her out of trouble. You better be careful going after some other spirit god, whoever this Uri is. I'm sure Salim isn't called crazy for nothing."

Despite a growing fear, Graisia also felt a little happier. Kaly actually seemed concerned about her.

As if Kaly realized her feelings had shown, she hardened her face again. "But it's up to you if you want to get into more trouble. At least we got our money out of you before you skipped on us."

Graisia swallowed. Maybe she wasn't totally forgiven. In the distance, she saw Salim waving at her. "Oh, I gotta go! Salim's done...." She looked at all of them. "You could come visit me sometime."

"Yeah, right." Kaly's voice dripped with sarcasm.

Graisia quickly gave them directions anyway, hugged Mitina one last time, and then ran back toward Salim.

As she left, Graisia heard Kaly muttering something about how there must be a story about Salim and Estar's past. Graisia had no doubt Kaly would ask her gossiping Aunt Lindi for another history lesson tonight.

While waiting for Graisia to make her way back to him, Salim bent down to make sure the sacks of shoes were tightly closed, and then stepped further into the shack to pay Pouyan. It was at that moment he noticed someone shifting in the back. The face was unmistakable. Salim blanched and stiffened at the sight of Adan's dark chiseled features. He had felt uneasy when he arrived. Now he knew why. Anguish and shame coursed through Salim's heart before he could stop their rush. His hands were clammy and trembling when he placed the money in Pouyan's hands.

"Thanks," Salim barely muttered then turned quickly to go outside. Graisia stood next to the shoe bags, looking concerned.

"Everything okay, Salim?" she asked.

"Fine, fine," Salim muttered – too rapidly, he knew. He motioned for Graisia to take one of the sacks. He picked up the other and grabbed her hand. They walked briskly along the ring road to the smaller path leading off into their part of the town maze. He was glad she didn't ask any more questions.

He looked sidelong at her and noticed she was biting her lip. She seemed so fragile and vulnerable. *Why did you give me her to protect, Uri? Why must I always be reminded of my failures?*

23

 After dropping off the new stock of shoes and sorting them out, Salim and Graisia took some buckets down to fill them at the nearest water pump. When they returned home and rounded the last bend before their alley, water sloshed out of Graisia's bucket onto her feet making her flip flops muddy and slippery. She walked a bit more carefully so she didn't slip.

Salim turned into their alley and came to a complete stop. Graisia was pleased she was able to pull up short behind him without spilling.

Salim stared at the ground. She peered around his arm to see what he was looking at so intently, and then stumbled backwards causing the water to slosh on her feet again. She hoped desperately she hadn't seen what her eyes told her she saw. *No! Please, not that.* But when she looked again, sure enough, that's what it was. Someone had drawn the *dusanays* symbol in the dirt path leading to their shack. Only one person would have drawn that – the Spirit Priest. And when he did that in front of someone's house, it meant only one thing. He had placed a curse on the people or a person in that home. It was a sign of death.

Salim wiped it out with his foot, whispering something under his breath. Graisia thought wiping away the symbol and muttering wasn't going to do anything. "What are we gonna do?" Her voice had risen in near panic.

Salim didn't answer. He headed back toward their shack carrying his water pails. After dropping them off on the porch, he went in the front door and headed straight out the back. Graisia started to follow, but Estar stopped her, looking concerned.

"What was it?" she asked.

"*Dusanays* in the dirt," Graisia stated.

Estar put her hand on Graisia's shoulder. "Let him go, love. He needs to be alone for a while."

Dinner time came and went. The air was full of shadows more than light, and still, Salim could not bring himself to move. The metal of his neighbor's shack radiated lingering heat from the day against his back, but gave little solace. He felt more alone than ever, like a tree lost in the throes of yet another monsoon.

It barely registered that Estar came out the door and was heading toward him. She eased herself down at his side with difficulty, and once situated, placed her hand on his knee.

Why is she so good to me? He wondered for the

millionth time. Salim's throat felt strained by insurmountable pain and weariness. "I've tried and I've tried, Estar, but I can't bring myself to talk to Uri about Adan. I can't ask for Uri's help."

Estar spoke slowly in her weariness. "You can't go on forever holding the past over your head, Salim. The past is the past and what has been done has been done." She patted his knee gently.

But it affected our entire future, Salim wanted to argue.

Estar looked toward the doorway of their shack and added, "But that doesn't mean you have to stop fighting for the future."

Estar's words, though gentle, felt like a slap across the face. Had he really given up on the future? Of course he had. For over twenty years, he'd had no reason to try and make anything more of his life other than keep Estar and himself alive. Alive for what, he didn't know.

He knew Estar was trying to look him in the eye, but he continued looking at the doorway. It hurt too much to look into her eyes and see his disappointment reflected back.

She spoke quietly. "Maybe Graisia coming here is Uri's way of showing us we're being given grace for a new future."

A new future.... He let out a deep sigh and looked down at his hands, callused and wrinkled with age. They mocked any thought of hope and a future.

Estar said nothing more. She patted his knee one last time and then struggled to stand, leaning heavily on his shoulder to do so.

Salim watched her trudge inside, even as her words settled deeper into his heart – like water blanketing a seed and making its way down into ground that had not been tilled for many years, ground that was desperately hungry for water and for life. *Maybe Graisia is a sign. Maybe... maybe you are giving us a second chance, Uri.* A single tear slipped down his face and a determination began to rise up in his heart. He wasn't going to let another life be stolen from him, his own or anyone else's in his house.

Now he was ready to fight. He closed his eyes, slipping deeper into the Realm, ready for battle in the forest alongside Jarón.

Ever since Adan ran into Salim and Graisia earlier that day, Mahalan's wrath had flared and subsided like a rumbling volcano ready to blow. Adan wasn't sure he could handle it much longer, even though Mahalan's anger was becoming more and more his own. He was determined to get Graisia tonight, not just because his life and authority depended on it, but to satisfy his own growing hatred and rage.

Darkness settled in with clouds blocking the moonlight. Adan was glad for the additional cover. He wanted as few witnesses as possible of him taking Graisia away, not that anyone would stop him. But he didn't need extra trouble right now. The crazy old couple would be pushovers; he saw how terrified

Salim had been of him earlier. *It will be easy*, he kept telling himself. He had already taken what he would need for the sacrifice down to his father's clearing by the river – his clearing now – he had to remember that.

He wondered if Salim or Graisia had seen the *dusanays* symbol he left. If they had, he laughed inwardly, they were probably petrified. He retraced his steps back toward their alley. Mahalan and the other spirits living in him increased in agitation and excitement. He rounded the last corner.

As Salim and Estar's flimsy shack came into view, he stopped abruptly. In front of him was something he had never seen before, or for that matter, felt. The whole ramshackle building seemed to be engulfed in a sphere of fire. In front of him – almost as tall as the shack itself – were two flaming, fireball spirit creatures with fiery wings, *aysh* like he'd never seen. They had human looking faces with streaming white hair that flowed like pale flames. The air reverberated with every beat of their wings of fire. Between them, Adan could have sworn he saw the crazy old man holding a sword, and it too was blazing.

But what he saw wasn't nearly as hideous as what he felt. The fire that wasn't consuming the shack, seemed to be penetrating through his skin. Mahalan and the other spirits shrieked inside him from sheer torture. Adan yelled out, feeling the same excruciating pain and staggered backward out of the alley, gasping.

Graisia was startled awake by a blood curdling yell from somewhere outside the shack. She had fallen asleep sitting with Estar's arm wrapped around her. Estar's hold tightened and Graisia stared at the front door, trembling. Then she heard someone running down the alley and off into the distance. She let out her breath slowly, wondering where Salim was and if there was still anyone else out there.

"*Lakás!* What was that?" Adan kept asking over and over. It was beyond any display of power his father had ever shown, beyond what Mahalan could even seem to handle.... *Who* is *that man! And how did he do that?* Of course he knew it was Salim... but that gave absolutely no explanation of what he had just seen.

Adan lay back in a heap on the floor of his shack, exhausted and struggling not to feel humiliated. How could he get his hands on power like that? "The girl must be the key," he muttered to himself.

"*Yes, the girl is the answer,*" Mahalan whispered as the familiar spine-tingling needles prickled up and down Adan's back.

"But how? She's still alive," Adan wondered.

"*She has power from the spirits, and he is feeding off it. When you sacrifice her, your power will reach a level far beyond either of theirs.*"

Adan rolled over and grabbed a nearby jug of water. He couldn't understand how Graisia could have so much power to feed off of, but he wasn't going to argue. His throat felt scorched from the fire. A long drink brought no relief. He lay back again on the floor.

He had to have that power, no matter what.

Graisia jumped when Salim entered through the back door. He looked drained. His shoulders were stooped and the shadows under his eyes were darker, but there was a peace about him she hadn't noticed before. He walked to the front door and looked out. Satisfied with what he saw, he sat down heavily on the floor, leaned his head against the wall and closed his eyes.

After a few moments of silence, Graisia finally blurted out, "What happened?"

"He's gone for now. But I don't think we've seen the last of him." Salim could only be referring to Adan. "The boy couldn't handle Uri's power. I don't expect he's seen anything like it,"

"What did he see?" Graisia replied.

"Something you'll see if you need to, Graisia." Salim stretched his long legs out in front of him. They reached almost to the middle of the shack.

Graisia wondered what could have been so terrible that it scared Adan away. Before she could come up with what it might have been though, she noticed an unearthly coolness filling the shack. It was an eerie feeling, under her skin, like she used to feel sometimes when Opana summoned Harapkan. The sensation grew until it felt like a cyclone of ice trying to take her breath away – yet there was no breeze and the air remained humid and still. She kept her eyes on Salim, hoping he knew what was going on and what to do.

He scanned the room intently as if looking for something. "He's come back... just his spirit though this time."

Graisia's entire body went stiff with fear as she grasped Estar's hands hard. How many ways could Adan come back?

Salim struggled to his feet. Just above the ground, Adan's spirit hovered in the middle of the room – his face tormented with rage.

An image of Adan's father, wearing the same spirit-induced anger, flared in Salim's mind like a hot coal sprayed with gasoline. Salim stammered, trying to form words that would stop Adan from harming them, but the image of Adan's father was so real... so painful; his thoughts turned to ashes.

In the old man's hesitation, Adan summoned the spirits inside of him and swept his hand in a forward command. *Throw!* A crate burst off the wall. Its dishes crashed to the ground as it flew toward Salim and glanced off his arm. Adan grabbed a pot and sailed it at Salim's head, but the old man ducked at the last second.

Salim staggered slightly and straightened his back. The icy cold of the room was creeping into his soul. How could he carry through with this? *What am I doing? I lost to his father. How can I ward off Adan? I'm an old man. I'm weaker. I'm a failure.*

Lies of the past flapped around him like crows returning to nest. He dodged a knife that whizzed by his ear.

Graisia sat on the floor, cowering next to Estar. Out of nowhere, she felt an invisible hand grab her leg and pull her toward the front door. Screaming, she tried to hang on to Estar's hands, but even together, they were no match for the unseen force pulling at Graisia. Her hands slipped loose. Frantically she grabbed for Estar's leg, but that too was torn from her grasp. She saw Salim, stammering and trying to avoid flying objects, unable to help.

Trying to take hold of the doorframe as she was dragged through it, Graisia finally cried out, "Jarón! Help!"

A voice from somewhere deep inside jolted Salim out of his stupor. *"You did not lose to his father. You chose not to fight, and he chose not to follow you."* A tantalizing feeling of peace lingered on the echo of the words.

Salim leaned against the wall, short-winded, watching Graisia being dragged away. He could believe this voice and choose to fight, or he could succumb to failure once again.

He would choose the voice this time.

Instantly peace flooded through his bones, forcing out the icy air he had allowed in.

He pushed himself off the wall and focused his stare on Adan's eerie, half-visible presence, now on the front porch. With a steady sure voice, he commanded, "By the council of Jarón, the High King, and his Realm, let her go!"

Adan recoiled as streaks of light came streaming toward him from Salim's mouth then jolted through his body. He stumbled backward cursing and letting go of Graisia as he fell.

He glared at Salim as Graisia scrambled back inside. He would come back to her in a moment, she couldn't get far. But this man needed to be dealt with once and for all.

He focused on Mahalan and on summoning the spirits for another onslaught. *No one is stopping me from getting her this time.*

24

Graisia only knew that whatever grabbed her leg had abruptly let her go. Back in Estar's arms, she peered out the front window – and suddenly began seeing and hearing in a whole new way.

Adan's spirit hovered in the air just outside the door. She screamed at the sight of his hideously contorted face, distorted by the beastly spirits that swarmed around him like a hurricane gathering strength. Strong and foreign guttural words spewed from his twisted mouth. They made her insides shake and filled her ears with a raspy, staticky noise that even covering her ears didn't help. She watched as his face and body disappeared behind the glimmering image of the creepy man she'd met in the forest. In the midst of all the confusion, she realized that creepy man must be Mahalan.

She wanted to bury her face in Estar's shoulder, but as she glanced at Salim, her attention was arrested. Salim gleamed with vivid blue light and was surrounded with various sizes of glittering orbs floating like bubbles that sparked and sizzled with flashes of bright white light... and was that a golden crown on his head? This sight of Salim was as splendorous to look at as Adan was dreadful.

She noticed Estar was glowing too! Soft and yellow. It looked like there was a faint golden crown on Estar's head as well, but she couldn't be sure. Graisia blinked and looked down at herself, seeing her own light for the first time. It was a deep purplish shade that reminded her of the colors of her dress in the forest.

"By the council of Jarón, the High King, and his realm!" Salim shouted. Graisia looked up to see him pointing at the figure that now looked more like Mahalan than Adan. Salim's voice resonated with authority, "Leave and do not come back! We are servants of Uri, and you may not harm us!"

Brilliant rays shot out of Salim's mouth and burst from the orbs at the same time, spraying like arrows into Mahalan, Adan, and the storm of spirit beasts surrounding them. The intruders flew backward together, screeching into the midnight air.

Salim stepped back into the shack and pointed at the walls, sweeping his arm in a circular movement. "By the authority of Jarón, I declare a ring of Uri's fire around our home, going out two meters in all directions. Nothing wicked can enter in." He dropped his hand, leaned against the wall and took in a slow shaky breath, suddenly looking very frail and weary again.

For a moment, the shack walls seemed fainter and Graisia could see through them. Sure enough, there was a curtain of fire surrounding the entire shack, even above and beneath.

Trembling from the emotion of all she had witnessed, she leaned back into Estar's arms. Her added vision faded and everything looked normal again. She let the peace and warmth from the fire-shield, that she knew was now there, soak into her heart. As she did, the fullness of what just happened hit her. In awe, she stared at Salim, the only man she'd ever heard of showing more power than Adan and Mahalan put together. "Why don't *you* rule Sawtong?" she blurted out.

Salim gasped and took a moment to recover from the shock of her question. "It's not that... easy...." He turned away from her.

Estar stood up slowly and gathered up a broken dish, giving a sidelong glance at Salim that Graisia didn't understand.

Salim bent down to pick up a shattered crate, his hands shaking. "In this dimension, or world, we can only rule where we have authority, where people honor Uri, and over nature." He paused and took the broken crate outside. When he returned, he added, "If people don't want to be under Uri's rule, we can't force them. Some have tried, of course, but it doesn't work. That's not Uri's way." He turned away from her to gather up objects strewn all over the floor.

"But you told Adan what to do!" She leaned forward, excited. "Didn't you just force him to leave?"

He looked over his shoulder at her. "I didn't force him to serve Uri. He was in our place and attacking us. So Uri's power could overrule his power." He turned away again. "Uri's power and love sometimes works differently though too.... Sometimes Uri's way of love, and ruling, is through suffering. He works in many ways – but always in love."

Graisia thought of Jarón letting the thorns get him and how he used Opana's cruelty to bring her here. "But –" She still couldn't let it go. "Couldn't Uri make it so Adan wouldn't bother anyone anymore?" That would be perfect. "If Uri loves us, why couldn't everyone be protected from Adan?"

Salim sighed. "Uri's way *is* love. Love gives choices. It doesn't force its rule. We have to choose to rule with Jarón and be ruled by him. As people, anyone can rule, either with Jarón or without him. But where Uri's rule is honored or requested, when we rule with and under Jarón, when the Realm is looked for and sought, then Uri can protect."

"I don't get it," Graisia stated simply.

Salim took a deep breath and let it out slowly. "Uri created people to rule the world, Graisia, to be in charge of all Uri placed in it. Uri also gave us all the choice, to rule with Jarón or without. But it's a choice. Uri won't force us to choose Jarón as our High King. And we can't force people in Sawtong to choose Uri's ways either."

"But... it doesn't seem like love when Adan can still..." Her words trailed off.

Salim rubbed his hands over his eyes, looking wearier than ever. Leaning against the wall again, he gazed down the alley way through the open door.

"The people in Sawtong have given Adan power because of fear," he said. "If they were to all choose Uri's way of love, Adan wouldn't have any power at all." He looked down at his hands and spoke softer, almost as if he had a hard time believing what he was saying. "Love is the opposite of fear, and infinitely stronger. Love is the only way that works. It's how we're designed to live." He stopped and abruptly busied himself with unrolling the sleeping mat.

He didn't seem to want to talk about it anymore, but Graisia wasn't quite ready to give up. She had just seen the person she feared the *most* beaten in a battle. "But then, shouldn't we be telling everyone about Uri's Realm, and love, and shouldn't we be trying to convince them that Jarón has a better way? Can't we convince them?" Graisia's mind raced. *Maybe this is what Uri meant about defeating Mahalan! Maybe I'll get to help convince the town! How can Salim be so uncaring about this?*

Salim looked up. Was that pain, hope, or a wound that flashed deep in his eyes? He seemed rocked to the core, like she'd touched something long buried. Then it was totally replaced with a blank, unreadable stare. He shook his head. "We tried..." he whispered.

And that was all he would say. By the look on his face, Graisia knew he wasn't going to answer any more tonight. He finished rolling out the mat, and Estar took the clothespins out of her hair.

Graisia reluctantly headed toward her loft.

"Sleep well, lovey," Estar called softly as Graisia climbed the ladder.

Sleep was the farthest thing from her mind. Shouldn't they be trying to tell other people about Uri's way, if ruling with and under Jarón really was so much better and so much more powerful – and the way they were designed to live? Graisia couldn't help wondering if this was what she was meant to do with her life. Somebody needed to do it.

Adan's spirit slammed back into his body, still stinging from the needles of light that had shot through him. He rubbed his hand across his chest, wishing it would help. *What is going on?* Mahalan, who he thought was the most powerful being there was, couldn't stand up to the crazy, old witch-man? That went against everything he knew. The old man had mentioned two names, Uri and the High King Jarón. Just thinking about those names made him dizzy.

Mahalan raged inside him, *"They are the enemy!"* Adan covered his ears instinctively. Adan felt like he was going to be sick. He opened the door and leaned out to throw up. All he had just experienced – was it possible? What if Mahalan wasn't strong enough to stand against Yantir and the rest of his enemies?

He tried to keep a coherent line of thought. *Who are those Uri and Jarón spirits?* He leaned back into his shack and closed the door. *Didn't Dad once say they were imaginary beings made up by weak and deluded people? Or – was it that Jarón was Mahalan's weaker brother?* He couldn't remember. Another wave of nausea swept over him. For some reason, his father hadn't seen them as a threat. *My father must have sacrificed someone like Graisia to get his power. I've got to get a hold of that girl!* Just two more days until the next ring gathering, where Jandro would challenge him face to face.

Two days.

25

The next day, Graisia woke up still wondering what had happened to make Salim so sad and quiet. Why wasn't he as excited about the idea of telling everyone in Sawtong about Uri and Jarón as she was? Why wasn't he thrilled that he'd defeated Adan and Mahalan last night? *There's someone more powerful than Mahalan! We could change the town! Everyone should want to know this!*

Graisia scrambled down the ladder, hoping Salim would be in a more talkative mood this morning.

He wasn't.

She found him so unusually quiet and withdrawn he didn't even acknowledge her.

She sighed. As much as she wanted to ask, she kept quiet through breakfast. *Something really bad must have happened when they tried to tell people in Sawtong,* she finally decided.

Later, as Estar took the empty dishes away, Graisia spoke up, "Salim, isn't there *something* we can do to tell people?"

Salim's head shot up and his eyes opened wide.

He looked like a rat caught eating in a rice sack.

Before he could answer, Estar interrupted. "Lovey, there's something I want to teach you today."

Graisia watched Salim take the opportunity to escape her question and head out the front door.

Estar laid down the dishes and went over to the big book that sat on the overturned crate. She opened the book and turned to a page somewhere near the middle. "There are lots of ways Uri can talk to us, like the dreams you have, or things you might see that not everyone sees... but all of it, if it doesn't match this Sacred Book of Truth... then you know it can't be from Uri."

"Really?" Graisia's interest was piqued.

"Yes, and if you want to be able to read the book for yourself, I need to teach you how to read."

Graisia looked through the window at Salim, already busy with a shoe. She wasn't going to get anything else out of him for now so she might as well learn to read. She also remembered what Uri had said about the book. She gave a small smile of agreement to Estar.

They spent the rest of the morning scratching with sticks in the dust as Estar taught her the alphabet. Shoes could wait.

At their midday break, Graisia was exhausted from study and the late night before so she decided to take a nap with Estar. She drifted into dreams almost the moment her eyes shut.

She stood on a golden path near the edge of the forest. Not far from where the trees stopped in front of her, she could see the bright expanse of a brilliant empty sky. Behind her everything was dim, but in front of her, all was glowing faintly.

She walked forward closer to the edge of the trees. From somewhere just out of sight, she heard what sounded like two men wrestling – grunting, shuffling, and whacking noises. She reached the end of the forest and was surprised to find the rim of a cliff that looked deep into a chasm.

To her right, the cliff jutted out and showed that the forest actually grew on top of an amazingly beautiful rock. It was like a solid rainbow, with flecks of gold reflecting light from across the chasm. The vivid splash of color was a harsh contrast to the cheerless forest above it clothed in vines of relentless death.

She looked down into the chasm. It wasn't as frightening as she expected. Though there was a steep vertical drop, the bottom was hidden in clouds and steam rising from within them. Across the wide chasm was another cliff shrouded in stunning swirls of light and color, too bright for her to see the details, but beautiful enough to be breathtaking. She wondered if that was Uri's place.

The sound of the men wrestling drew her attention away to her left, where the cliff edge continued on as far as she could see. The men's voices were clearer now.

"I will *not* kill my son! Never!"

The other growled back, "You are weak... useless to me! You will pay!"

A man burst out at the edge of the forest,

staggering and seeming to fight with some unseen force – it was Danjall, Adan's father! Graisia normally would have been terrified, but she felt somehow safe and invisible. But then things started getting confusing. She saw who Danjall was wrestling with. Just as she'd seen Adan's spirit overlaid with Mahalan, now she saw Mahalan in a hideous rage *inside* Danjall. Mahalan didn't look completely human. His hands had turned to claws, and his teeth to fangs. Raging like an animal, he clawed and ripped at Danjall's insides.

Graisia could barely watch. Through squinted eyes and between fingers laced over her face, she saw Danjall struggle to take a breath through lungs that were being torn apart. Danjall turned his face toward the chasm, and his eyes suddenly widened – as if for the first time, seeing the glorious lights and colors on the other side. His final cry of agony suggested pain as well as desperate regret over the beauty he could never reach – and then he stumbled toward the rim and threw himself over the cliff. His cry echoed in Graisia's ears as he disappeared into the clouds below.

She closed her eyes in sorrow. Even though she had lived her entire life in fear of Danjall, it hurt to watch another person endure such a painful end, especially with such beauty so close.

Gradually, she became aware that someone was holding her hand. She opened her eyes and looked up to find Jarón, eyes full of pain beyond depth of knowing, looking into hers. Graisia knew instantly that Jarón had taken her into the past. Here was the truth of how Danjall had died. Adan had not been the one to kill Danjall.

When Graisia woke in the afternoon, she found her cheeks wet with tears. She lay quietly, letting the reality of the dream settle over her and some of Jarón's feelings become her own. When she finally sat up, she wondered why Uri would show her, of all people, about Danjall's death.

Estar stood nearby, looking concerned. She handed Graisia a small bowl of watery rice soup left over from the morning. "What's the matter, love?"

Graisia took the bowl and began slowly slurping it up, forgetting to touch her fingers to her lips and then heart before eating, as Estar and Salim were in the practice of doing. Estar had said they did it out of gratefulness to Uri for having something to eat and to honor those who labored over it.

Salim walked in and set down a finished pair of shoes.

"I had a sad dream," Graisia said with her mouth full, "and I don't know why."

Salim was about to head back out front when Graisia continued.

"It was about Danjall."

Estar almost dropped the dish in her hand. She set it down slowly and Salim turned around looking at Graisia intensely. Startled by their response, Graisia went quiet and swallowed. She looked back and forth from Estar to Salim.

Salim cleared his throat. "And...?"

Graisia told the dream. When she got to the part

about Danjall falling off the cliff, Estar let out a quiet sob. Graisia quickly told about Jarón appearing, but Estar only raised her hands to her face to cover a rush of tears. She fled out the back door where Graisia could still hear her sobbing.

Graisia looked back at Salim, who seemed pale and pained as well.

"Why is she so sad?" Graisia asked softly. Why did this couple have such an incredible love for the worst people? Somehow, their pain reminded her of the look in Jarón's eyes. Yes, it was sad to see someone die in pain, but the kind of love that would make Jarón and Estar, and even Salim, so heartbroken over Danjall, was beyond the depth that Graisia knew.

In a daze, Salim slowly walked toward the back door, muttering something about, "At least it wasn't Adan's doing...." He stood at the door, looking out at Estar, as if he was unsure if he wanted to go to her. He hung his head, turned around and went out the front door to busy himself with his work again.

Graisia felt like she'd ruined the afternoon for everyone. *Why would Uri give me a dream that would do that? Maybe I shouldn't have told them. But how was I supposed to know?* She went around and around in her thoughts as she set her bowl down on the floor. She didn't feel like finishing it now. She couldn't help Estar, and Salim clearly didn't want to talk to her, so she got up, took her writing stick and went into the alley way that led to the main path. In the little bit of shade she could find, she squatted on the path and half heartedly practiced her letters in the dirt.

She was so lost in thought that she didn't notice footsteps coming up behind her until someone bopped her on the head playfully. "What the heck are you doing?" That tone of voice could be none other than Kaly's.

Graisia swung around with a smile on her face, glad to hear a familiar voice that wasn't sad. She brightened even more when she saw that Kaly wasn't scowling at her, and that Mitina was there too, beaming next to Kaly.

"Teeny! Kaly!" Graisia stood up. Maybe Kaly had forgiven her now.

"Came to visit the deserter. The mouse here wouldn't let me come without her. So, what's all your scratching?" Kaly asked again.

"Oh... Estar's teaching me to read, I'm practicing letters," Graisia responded, glancing back at her work on the ground.

"Read! What are you planning to be? Some rich, city lady – better than us? It's that queen thing again, isn't it?" Kaly's lips curled in a sneer in the only way she knew how to be friendly.

"No. I just wanna be able to read a certain book...." Graisia trailed off, looking at Mitina. Mitina's smile widened, and Graisia smiled in response to their shared secret.

"Whatever." Kaly suddenly remembered why she had come. "Hey, have I got something to tell you!" Then her voice got quiet as she looked behind Graisia to make sure Salim and Estar wouldn't be able to hear. "I asked my aunt about Salim and

Estar, I *knew* there had to be some juicy story behind them...."

As Kaly talked, Mitina's eyes narrowed with concern.

"I found out why they hide so much and keep to themselves.... I'm surprised they didn't leave Sawtong... or aren't dead by now." Kaly glanced around again, then leaned over and whispered in Graisia's ear so not even Mitina would hear, "Danjall was Salim and Estar's son. He hated his parents so much he promised to kill anyone who mentioned they were related. Adan doesn't even know – it was so long ago."

Graisia felt the blood drain from her face. Her jaw dropped. She quickly covered her mouth with her hand. She wanted to say something but couldn't. *Oh... lakás! w*as all she could think to herself. Suddenly all the pieces of the puzzle fit together. She steadied herself against the shack nearby.

"Are you *sure*?" Graisia finally asked, knowing deep down it had to be true.

"I swear it, *kosa*, on our *bandhu*. Aunt Lindi knows everything about everyone in this town, and she made me swear I wouldn't go telling everyone. But I figured it wouldn't hurt to tell you. Danjall's dead, and you *need* to know." Though more than likely, Kaly was telling Graisia for her own motives. She loved knowing more than others – and showing that she did.

"What? Tell me! What is it?" Mitina pleaded, still frowning. She tugged impatiently on Kaly's shirt.

Kaly didn't even look at Mitina when she

answered her, "Don't worry about it mouse, it's over your head."

Graisia just stood there, wondering what she should do now. *No wonder Salim was so upset and didn't want to talk about things. Poor Estar.*

Kaly interrupted her thoughts. "We gotta go, but I'll see you around."

"Yeah..." Graisia replied in a daze.

"Don't do anything stupid!" Kaly said, meaning goodbye. She took off running toward the dump. Mitina trailed, glancing back over her shoulder every few steps. Graisia knew Mitina wanted to stay, but she had to keep up with her protection.

Practicing letters was completely forgotten. She spent the rest of the afternoon just sitting in the shade, absently drawing things in the dirt with her fingers as she turned this new information around and around in her mind, wondering what in the world she was supposed to do with it.

When evening came and the three of them were eating together, it was very quiet. And after their meager dinner and cleaning up, they all went to bed without much more than a word.

"You go." Mahalan's voice interrupted Adan's thoughts.

"What?" Adan asked aloud.

"Go and meet Yantir. It will serve our purposes."

Before he could ask Mahalan how he was to do this, someone knocked on his door. Adan yanked it opened impatiently. Candle light from inside his shack barely illumined the face of Yantir's messenger. He asked if Adan would meet Yantir under the bridge at midnight, alone.

Adan frowned. He didn't like the "alone" bit of that request.

While he paused, the messenger explained, "He has an offer to make, but he wants to do it in person."

Adan tried not to show his surprise. That wasn't exactly what he expected when Mahalan gave the instructions.

"Yeah, tell him I'll be there – and that I was expecting the meeting." He shut the door and took a deep breath. It couldn't hurt to appear knowledgeable to one's enemies. He wondered if Yantir really did have an offer, or if Yantir just wanted to get him alone so he'd be easier to kill.

Either way, Mahalan apparently had a plan.

Adan sat on the floor and leaned against the plank wall. It was still warm from soaking all day in the sun. *Mahalan! Why won't you tell me who killed my dad?!* It would make life a whole lot easier if he knew. Every time he asked he got only silence in reply. This time, however, Mahalan gave an answer.

"Some difficulties make you stronger," Mahalan's voice wafted through his head like rancid smoke. *"There are certain things you must trust me with. If you trust me, I will make you as strong and powerful as possible."*

"At least it's an answer," Adan muttered.

He turned his mind back to Yantir. *Did he kill*

Dad? It seemed possible. *But then why didn't he try to take over the town right away? Why is he waiting?* Something didn't seem right. He wished he had killed Graisia already. Then, no matter what Yantir might throw at him, he'd be able to fight him. But she hadn't been away from home all day, and he already found out he couldn't get her at her home. She wasn't likely to be leaving at this time of night, either. He'd have to wait until tomorrow.

He had to catch her somehow, away from Salim. It was all so absurd. If crazy old Salim had power enough to keep him away from her, then why didn't Salim try to take over the town?

Adan leaned forward and massaged his temples, trying to soothe the tension that never seemed to go away. A thought occurred to him, and he sent a spirit to summon Efrin and Hydal, another loyal *basyo*.

He would go to meet Yantir, but not alone.

26

Just after midnight, Adan arrived at the river's edge in view of the bridge. He'd hidden Efrin and Hydal nearby, out of sight and hearing range for the coming conversation. He could call on them, though, if he needed their assistance. As he approached the underbelly of the yawning structure, his heartbeat accelerated with each step.

He spotted Yantir standing confidently, like a sentinel in the shadows beside the riverbank. Adan had never really seen him up close. He guessed Yantir was in his mid-forties. He had dark, bushy hair and a few days' growth of beard stubble. As Adan walked forward, flashbacks of the night he found his father assaulted him. He looked out to the river. The end of life as he'd known it lay tied to a rock in its depths.

Adan looked around him casually, trying not to appear worried, yet wondering if Yantir also had men hiding nearby and was planning the same fate for him. Did Yantir know he had used the river for his dad's grave? Maybe he had even watched Adan discover his dad. He trembled at the thought but continued walking forward. He set his face as firmly as he could, reminding himself that Mahalan had told him to come. He hoped Mahalan knew what he was doing. There'd been no further instructions.

As Adan arrived under the bridge Yantir smiled warmly in welcome. "Thank you for coming. Your trust in my request speaks of a deep heart." Adan wished Yantir would skip the empty flattery.

Yantir placed what seemed like an attempt at a fatherly hand on Adan's shoulder, but Adan looked down at it and scowled. Yantir removed his hand without altering his smile. "I know you have many problems that have arisen in your town," Yantir continued, "and even though you now are the rightful heir to the priesthood, it may be more of a burden than you imagined."

Adan stood stoically, not willing to give any indication of how true this was. "What is your offer?" Adan asked.

"You *are* wise, though." Yantir turned slightly and looked at the river. "So I think you will see the value of my offer." He turned back to Adan. "I will not live forever. You know I'm an old man for these parts, and my son has chosen to live in the city." Yantir glanced at Sawtong over Adan's shoulder. "He wants no part of my ways and will not carry on the worship of Verhor when I am gone."

Now Yantir gazed directly into Adan's eyes. Being confronted with the power of Verhor living in Yantir, Adan felt like he and Yantir were two north-pole ends of magnets resisting each other, even as they had pushed themselves into such close proximity. Instability hung in the charged air between them. Something fatal could happen if they weren't careful.

Yantir spoke again, "You could be like a son to

me, Adan. If you are willing to come under my authority and change your allegiance to Verhor, we could both double our territory. I would help you perfect your training. When I die, you will have both Sawtong and Trakston to rule." Yantir smiled again. "You see, the deal works well for both of us."

For the briefest of moments, Adan allowed himself to think about how nice it would be to easily gain power over an additional town, and even more, have a father and mentor again. The desires rose up so quickly they startled him, but just as speedily, they wilted in the reality of unanswered questions. *Did he kill my father just so he could join our towns? Would he kill me after I gave him authority over Sawtong? Mahalan would not have brought me here to switch allegiance. But will Yantir kill me if I turn down the offer?* One thing he knew for certain, Mahalan would never let him change allegiance.

Mahalan's voice rasped in his head, *"He could help you get Graisia. And then you won't need him."*

Adan suddenly saw the immense wisdom of Mahalan's command to come tonight. *Yes,* Adan agreed, *he wants to use me, but we can use him.*

"Your offer has some worth," Adan started hesitantly. "Together we could easily defeat Jandro and Soliel." He looked Yantir straight in the eye with growing calm and assurance, despite the uncomfortable force still present between them. "However, if you want me to join you, I have one request."

Yantir tilted his head with a curious smile. "Let us do business, *kaibigan.*"

The next evening, when Graisia came in for dinner, Estar announced she and Salim would not be eating.

"Why?" Graisia asked, spotting a cockroach that needed squishing.

"We're doing it for Adan. If we don't eat, Uri gives more power to the good *aysh* around Adan."

"He's got *aysh* from Uri?" The cockroach suddenly lost her interest.

"He does now, at least. We're asking Uri to do all that's possible to try and help Adan to see that Uri's way is better." Estar flicked the cockroach out the door.

"Oh." He was a lost cause as far as Graisia was concerned. They should focus on helping other people learn about Uri, not Adan. He had so much hatred and pure evil in him that she couldn't imagine wanting to try and help him. Why didn't they just tell everyone else about Uri, so he wouldn't have power anymore?

Only when she thought of Adan as their grandson, did their desires make a bit more sense.

Estar motioned to a bowl of rice on the crate. "You can choose to eat or not. It's up to you."

Graisia went over and picked up the bowl. She wasn't going to do something sacrificial for Adan, not when he was trying to kill her. She took her rice out front where she could sit and enjoy the slightly cooler dusk that was enveloping the town.

She was just scraping the last bit of rice into her

mouth when she thought she spotted Lio half way down the alleyway. With the bowl close to her face, she strained to see if her eyes were playing tricks on her in the darkness. No, he really was there, and he was beckoning to her anxiously.

He must be too afraid of Salim and Estar to come back here. She put her empty bowl down on the stoop and ran over to him, wondering what would bring him to see her at this hour.

"It's Mitina," Lio explained, his face strained with worry. "She's sick and keeps calling for you. Her mom sent me to get you. I... I don't know if she's going to make it, Graisia. She's really bad."

No! Not Teeny! Most kids she'd known who got really sick never recovered. "Where is she?"

"She's at home. Com' on, I'll take you there. I know a short cut," Lio said urgently.

Graisia turned back to go and tell Estar or Salim, but Lio grabbed her hand. "There's no time, com' on! I'll come back and tell them later where you are."

"Alright." She glanced back at the softly lit shack and then turned to Lio. "Let's go." They took off running as fast as they could through the web of shadows darkening by the minute.

27

Evening was settling in with the heaviness of a thick soggy blanket. At least that's the way it felt to Adan. The ring gathering, where Jandro was supposedly going to confront him, was at midnight. Everything had to work like a precision machine, or... Adan didn't want to think of the alternative. He made his way down along the river heading toward his father's clearing. He wasn't supposed to meet Yantir under the bridge for another hour, but he wanted to be away from the townspeople.

He tried not to think of what he had to do tonight. He tried not to think of what could go wrong if Yantir didn't show up. But he wasn't having much luck. If Yantir didn't come through with his end of the deal, Adan wasn't sure what he'd do. He didn't have a backup plan. *If it doesn't work, maybe somehow I could work with Yantir and follow Verhor anyway.* Adan didn't see any other option. Salim's power was too strong for him to get to Graisia, and Jandro and Soliel were amassing followers. Everything was unraveling precariously far.

He wondered briefly if he should look into the god Salim mentioned. *What was his name? Jarón?* A wave of nausea swept over him at the thought. *No, Salim just has power because of Graisia. She's destined as a sacrifice. I* have *to get her. And if I don't...* He thought again of Verhor, and then what Mahalan might do to him if he tried to change allegiance and shuddered.

When he got to his father's clearing, Mahalan was crouched down in front of a fire, poking at it with a stick that dripped blood from its tip. Adan froze on the path and stared. Mahalan seemed as real as his heart pounding in his ears.

"There's no decision to make, Adan." Mahalan's voice was firm like a father speaking to a foolish child. "Even if you wanted to follow another god and change alliances, you cannot. You have given yourself to me with your blood." He turned to look at Adan with glowing red eyes that bored into his soul. "You can *never* get out of your contract with me.... Never." He stood up, pointed the stick at Adan and walked toward him. "If you even try to leave, I will kill you... like I killed your father."

A burst of pain shot down through Adan's chest and his lungs went tight. His mind reeled. *Could it be possible?* He barely had time for the thought before the agony became unbearable. Claws scraped down the inside of his lungs, poised to rip him open at the slightest provocation. Adan let out a cry of astonishment, both from the pain and from Mahalan's confession. The image of his father torn apart, seemingly from the inside out, had been burned into his memory. Through pain-filled eyes, Adan could only watch Mahalan mock him and laugh in wicked enjoyment.

"Stop!" Adan cried out in rasps of desperation, "Please, stop!" He could barely breathe. He clutched at his chest and buckled to his knees. "I'll do whatever you say...." His voice trailed off weakly.

Mahalan's laughter halted abruptly. "Then kill Graisia."

The razor claws inside him vanished, though a raw throbbing remained. Adan fought for breath, blinking away the stars at the fringes of his sight.

Mahalan threw his stick toward the fire, and a tongue of flame licked the air, consuming it. The vision disappeared and all that was left was a barely noticeable pool of dried blood in the center of the clearing.

Adan collapsed, sobbing. It all made too much sense; the scratch marks on his father's body, the fact that no one else knew how he had died, the silence of the other spirits, who had been too afraid of Mahalan to tell... and Mahalan's silence. Adan felt betrayed; betrayed by his father who would leave him to this heartless god, and betrayed by his god who killed the only person that cared for him. Adan felt like he was free-falling in an abyss that had no end. Maybe he should just kill himself. Everything would be over then.

How could I have been so stupid? Adan berated himself.

Mahalan answered inside his head in sickening consolation, *"Don't blame yourself. Your father had a weakness that you do not have. He was punished justly for his disobedience. You, however, still have the opportunity to redeem yourself and your family."*

Adan wasn't sure he wanted to. "What did my father not do?" he sobbed. "Why did you kill him?"

"Get up," Mahalan commanded.

Adan tried once more, "What was his weakness?"

Mahalan ignored his plea. *"Prepare yourself for the sacrifice."*

Adan didn't feel like doing anything. But Mahalan's force inside him compelled him to stand and walk toward the bridge. As Adan staggered in a daze, Mahalan continued to build strength within him like billowing thunderclouds, whispering words of promise, and dulling the very pain he'd created only moments ago. The ache in Adan's chest went numb and a new sense of deadness to everything around him filled its place.

Then, suddenly, something clicked. In an instant, Adan was resolved. He realized he had nothing left to lose, and still everything to gain. An indomitable determination set in. If Mahalan could use him, he could use Mahalan. If there was no way of backing out of being Spirit Priest, then he'd soak Mahalan for all the power he could get.

Graisia tried hard to keep up with Lio. He was smaller, but definitely faster. Graisia wasn't totally familiar with this area of town yet either. They rounded a corner and then dodged a young couple to race around another. *I hope we get to Mitina in*

time....

Lio let go of her hand so he could run faster. She called out to him as he darted into a narrow path, but he ignored her and kept running. She pictured her beloved little friend suffering, and it made her run harder. She followed Lio into the narrow path that quickly led to another broader one. When she reached the broader one, she looked right and left to see where he had gone, but he had disappeared into the shadows.

Before she could decide which way to go, she felt a yank on the back of her dress strong enough to lift her off her feet.

Adan paced under the bridge, waiting for Yantir. *What is keeping him? He must –*

His thoughts were cut short by the sound of footsteps in the mud. He looked up and saw Yantir striding toward him, alone.

Adan's anger began to boil, but instantly turned to panic. He had to have Graisia, now!

Graisia tried to scream, but a hand clamped hard over her mouth. Horrified, she watched people walking or standing nearby look the other way, pretending not to see her. She tried to squirm free, but the man's monster-like arms held her tight. Another man appeared and gruffly forced something powdery into her mouth. Then he tied a gag over her mouth so she couldn't spit out the awful substance.

It tasted bitter and icy as it burned and spread over her tongue and throat.

Graisia panicked. *What are they going to do to me?* Stories of torment she'd heard from Kaly flashed in her mind. Then everything started getting hazy. A monster-arm threw her over a shoulder. They tied her feet and wrists tightly together. She tried to twist again against the chords and scream through the gag, but she was losing consciousness.

"You're a feisty one." The man laughed a deep throaty laugh. "And cheap too."

Graisia heard the second man chuckling through her fog. "Yeah, a few *donyas* to her friend, we wait, and she comes to us... that wasn't hard."

What? Lio...? She tried to grasp at the thought, but her world went completely black.

Adan struggled not to show his rising dread. "Where's your end of the deal?" he asked Yantir.

"Patience, son. I will not disappoint you." Yantir was as calm as a cat licking its paws after eating a large rat.

With timing that couldn't have been planned better, rustling came from the reeds behind Yantir, accompanied by men's voices. Two men tramped up, one carrying Graisia slumped unconscious over his shoulder.

Adan let out his breath in relief. He even felt the tug of a smile pull at his lips. Then he steeled himself for what must happen next.

"She was sitting out there just a minute ago. Salim, I don't like this." Estar puttered around the shack, nervously putting Graisia's dirty dish in the wash pail. It clanged loudly.

Just moments before, Estar had walked outside to get Graisia's bowl from her but found Graisia gone. Together, Salim and Estar had called up and down the path for her but received no answer.

"Salim, do you think Adan got her somehow?" Estar wrung her hands apprehensively.

Salim's empty stomach growled. "How could he? We would have heard – or at least sensed him." He sat down on the rough floor and pulled his knees up against his chest so he could cross his arms and rest his forehead on top of them. "Maybe she went off with one of her friends. Maybe she got tired of us." Salim felt in his spirit that wasn't true though. "I don't know, Estar. I don't know."

"What'll we do? We can't just do nothing. Something must've happened to the little love." Estar absently opened and closed a clothespin on the edge of her dress.

"You're right." Salim pushed against the floor and struggled to his feet. "I'll go look for her."

"I'd go too," Estar offered, "but as weak as I am from not eating, I think I'd do more good sitting here with Uri."

Salim gave a small smile of agreement and slipped out the door. They would each do their part.

The man carrying Graisia dropped her in front of Yantir like a sack of rice. Her eyes were closed. Adan looked closely to make sure she was still breathing. It wouldn't do to sacrifice someone who was already dead. *They must have drugged her.* Satisfied and relieved, he looked back at Yantir. Adan could hardly believe it. Everything *was* going to work out.

"Thank you," Yantir said to the men who brought her. He motioned for them to leave and then turned his attention back to Adan. "I've done my end of the deal. I'll expect yours tonight at the gathering." Yantir paused. "May I ask what you want with this girl? Why her?"

Adan's voice was steady, "Sacrifice."

Yantir raised his eyebrows.

"She was destined for it," Adan continued.

"Ahh... I see." Yantir looked Adan in the eye. "Then you won't mind offering her to Verhor tonight as your proof of loyalty, will you? Your *basyo* must be shown you are serious."

Adan swallowed, wishing he hadn't been so foolish as to reveal her significance. This was not part of the plan. He meant to sacrifice her *before* the gathering, so he could have power to stand up against Yantir and Jandro *during* the gathering.

Yantir must have noticed his hesitancy. He turned to pick up Graisia's limp body. "I will guard her for you and have her brought to you when it's time."

Adan cursed in his mind. How would he get out of this one? What choice did he have? Maybe he could sacrifice to Mahalan while appearing to offer her to Verhor.

Yantir slung her easily over his shoulder. "I will see you at midnight."

"Yes." Adan cleared his throat. "Midnight."

Maybe it didn't matter who he sacrificed her to. If he simply sacrificed her, he could gain the power. *I hope that's the way it works....*

28

When Graisia woke up, she felt hazy, groggy, and very constricted.

Then she remembered being grabbed. Adrenaline shot through her like a bullet. She opened her eyes and tried to focus on her surroundings. It was dark, and everything was blurry. Blinking and straining to see up through a thick patch of weeds, she heard people talking – a lot of them, and not far off.

She heard the river, gently swooshing nearby. Pebbles, sticks and trash poked uncomfortably into her shoulder, arm and her leg that was angled awkwardly beneath her. She was tied and gagged, and her right arm had fallen asleep. She tried to wiggle it awake, but the ropes were too tight.

She could sense unseen beings swirling around her, pressing into her brain, trying to seep in with their oppressive heaviness and make her go crazy. Her panic was easily turning to terror.

Where are you Jarón? You said you'd be with me all the time. With her inner eyes, the eyes of her imagination, she tried to focus on Jarón. As she did, she felt the fiery beings around her fly away about half an arm's length. She felt like she was in the middle of a ring of fire. Not a pleasant fire though, but a fire that wanted to burn her up. She took the eyes of her imagination off of Jarón and was immediately engulfed again by the fearful insanity trying to pry her mind apart. She quickly focused on Jarón again, and the fire once more became a ring set out at a distance.

Okay, Jarón. I just need to stay focused on you. Only you.... Help me!

Adan stood half-way between the *basyo,* who were gathering under the bridge, and the limp pile that was Graisia lying on the ground. One of Yantir's men had deposited her there only moments ago. He was tempted to take her and run to his father's clearing and sacrifice her before anyone could stop him. He had his knife. It was in its sheath, attached to his belt. But Yantir had said he would reveal himself when Adan made the announcement, and that meant Yantir was already somewhere nearby, watching.

He could just kill her where she lay, but it wasn't a sacred or dedicated place and that wouldn't be following protocol. Who knew if the sacrifice would be honored if not in a sacred place? He didn't want to find out the hard way. Adan let out a deep breath. *It better go right, or...* Again, he didn't finish the thought.

In the distance, the *basyo* were casually, yet

distinctly, spreading into two groups, those loyal to Adan and those who had apparently formed alliances with Jandro. Soliel of course was absent, and Efrin stood with neither group. Efrin was attempting to feed the bonfire Adan had started in the center of the circle. In front of where the fire was being built, Adan had constructed a waist-high altar out of broken cinderblocks. He'd spent the last hour dragging the blocks from where he had been planning to use them, at his father's clearing, to where they stood now.

The weeds rustled off to his right. Graisia was stirring. He watched her with a mixture of dread and anticipation. He had been hoping she wouldn't wake up but it looked like Yantir hadn't wasted any more drugs than he needed to. *I could use some of those myself.* He cursed himself for forgetting his supply of snake eye. Efrin could get him some. The bonfire now seen to, Efrin strode toward him. Someone stopped Efrin to ask him a question, so Adan turned his attention back to Graisia.

He pulled the knife out of its sheath and walked over to her.

Graisia looked up and saw Adan's head in and out of focus, swerving slightly above her. She pulled back instinctively and even more so as he lifted a menacing blade over her face and began to twist and turn it slowly. It was long enough to go straight through her, she was sure. His eyes gleamed unnaturally with the reflection of flames from a fire somewhere nearby. *Jarón!* she cried in her mind.

Adan stopped twisting the knife and looked into her eyes. "I'm going to kill you tonight, Graisia, one way or another. I won't let you get away this time."

Adrenaline squeezed her heart, and the unseen beings around her snarled in a frenzy of laughter. She shook her head and tried to plead with her eyes.

A man's head appeared above Adan's shoulder. "Everything's ready," the man said.

How could Jarón let Adan go through with this? *Jarón must not be real.... Jarón! Help!* Her mind was stuck in a frantic limbo.

Adan stood up and turned toward the gathering. "Carry her to the ring. Make sure no one tries to rescue her."

"Of course," the man replied. Once again, Graisia found herself thrown over someone's shoulder.

Salim was weak and exhausted. It was near midnight and he'd walked much of Sawtong calling Graisia's name. None of the neighbors claimed to have seen or heard anything about Graisia that evening. He'd gone by Adan's shack, and it had been empty. Even Kaly and Mitina knew nothing of where she might be.

Salim circled around to Adan's home again, somehow knowing Adan must be connected to her disappearance. It was still empty. None of his neighbors were any help either. As soon as he mentioned wanting information relating to Adan, their lips shut tight and their doors were not far behind. *Of course they won't talk,* Salim thought begrudgingly, *especially to me.* They knew better.

There was only one place left to look and he'd been trying to ignore the idea all evening. He hadn't let himself think it was possible. He wanted to check everywhere else first. But even as he headed toward the bridge that led into town, he knew he should have gone there first. He heard a buzz of activity coming from the direction of the bridge. Though the area was hidden from view, he knew what it was used for. Everyone did.

"Oh, please Uri, not..." Salim couldn't bring himself to say it. He paused on the path. Should he go? He was only one man, and they were the whole ring of *basyo.* It was practically suicide to show himself there. Even though the younger ones didn't know his story, the older ones would. Never mind it would be one of the largest gatherings of spiritual forces opposed to Uri in the area... and on their own territory. He thought of Estar backing him up within the Realm, sitting beside Jarón. He tried to sense Uri too. He wasn't totally alone. He could feel the connection, both with Estar and with Uri; both in the darkest depths of the forest and in the throne room of Jarón.

"Uri help me..." Salim whispered, "for Graisia's sake." Trembling, he set off again, making his way down to the riverbank.

Adan stood in front of the altar with the river to his back. The *basyo* stood in their two distinct clusters on the far side of the altar. Jandro stood prominently in front of his faction, with his arms crossed casually as if he were simply biding time. Efrin stood beside Adan, and Graisia lay on the ground nearby. Adan thought she looked pathetic, her face and clothes dirt-smeared and her hair plastered to her face. Her eyes looked wildly around the circle, probably hoping someone would come to her aid. He knew no one would.

Let her squirm, he thought. *She deserves it for all the trouble she's put me through.*

Adan lifted his eyes to look above the heads of those gathered where he knew Yantir would be hidden with his own *basyo,* waiting to join him when he made the announcement.

He looked back down at his *basyo.* They were *his.* And if he could help it, by the end of tonight they would still be his, and only his.

Churning inside him, Adan could sense Mahalan's growing excitement in the pending sacrifice.

It was time to begin.

He raised his hands toward the sky. *"Kaibigan."* He had only to say the word and all drew quiet. Without wavering, he began reciting the ceremonial invocation. "We are gathered to honor the sacred god of this land."

As one, the *basyo* intoned the appropriate

response. "We come to offer him gifts and ask his favor."

"We ask for protection from our enemies," Adan said.

"We dedicate our lives to his rule," their answer was louder.

"May it be so." Adan lowered his hands, infused with a fresh release of power already.

Confidently, he continued, "Many of you came with great expectations tonight." He allowed his gaze to linger on Jandro's side of the assembly. "I do not think you will be disappointed. Many of you have thought I am unfit to rule... too young, too inexperienced, not powerful enough. Don't play me as a fool. I've heard your secret conversations. I know your plans. And they won't work."

Jandro stared back calmly. Either he truly was not worried, or he was an incredibly good actor.

"Our generous neighbor, Yantir, has also been concerned for us. Perhaps some of you have seen him around." *Here it goes*, Adan thought, *this better work.*

He turned to Efrin and motioned for him to hoist Graisia onto the makeshift altar. Efrin picked her up and set her roughly on the pile of tottering broken cinderblocks. Efrin quickly bound her to the blocks and un-gagged her mouth before stepping back.

Adan wished an uncovered mouth was not part of the traditional ritual. At least she seemed to be in so much shock that she wasn't talking or screaming hysterically. He didn't want to be reminded of her voice, the one he would silence forever. He stuffed memories away and turned to the matter at hand.

"Yantir and I have come to an agreement that is beneficial for both of us." The *basyo* looked around uneasily. They weren't expecting anything to do with Yantir tonight. "We both are not satisfied with ruling only one town, and he has offered a solution. He has offered to rule both our towns through Verhor, in return for calling me his eldest son and leaving both towns to me when he is gone." Gasps and whispers rippled through the crowd. "He is here, at this moment," Adan spoke louder to be heard over the din, "to hear my acceptance. You are all here as witnesses."

Heads turned toward the slopes. Yantir and about thirty of his *basyo* stepped out of the shadows. They strode forward and surrounded the assembled crowd.

Jandro narrowed his eyes.

Mahalan, if you don't get me out of this one, we'll both be in trouble. Adan couldn't help but wonder if Graisia's life would truly give him enough power to stand against Yantir *and* Jandro's groups – 45 or so people who would soon turn against him.

"*Kaibigan,*" Adan called for their attention again. It took longer this time, but everyone eventually quieted down. "Yantir, you have made a generous offer. Your god, Verhor is powerful...." Adan pulled his knife out of its sheath and, as was customary before slitting the neck of a human sacrifice, he raised it high above her head, blade down, for all to see.

He ignored the desperation on Graisia's face,

though it sought to tear through his own heart. He focused instead on the knife. Just before drawing it downward, he yelled, "But this is for Mahalan!"

"Stop! By the power of Jarón! Stop!"

Adan's grip froze in midair, grasped by a burning set of floating hands that appeared out of nowhere. He let out a yell in frustration. His arms wouldn't move. The knife hung a full foot above Graisia's neck. He looked wildly around for the voice.

"Salim!" Graisia shrieked.

Adan turned his head enough to see the crazy, old witch-man beyond Efrin and near the water's edge. He looked haggard and frail, but Adan could sense, and see, power coming from him. Salim glowed bright blue like the light surrounding the core of a lit match.

No one made a sound.

Salim continued to approach slowly. "Adan, I know you did not kill your father."

How could he know? Adan was stunned. "What?" was all he could think of to say.

Voices around him murmured in astonishment at this bold declaration.

"Graisia has seen it in a dream." Salim waved a shaky hand toward Graisia. "She knows. Mahalan is the one who killed your father."

Adan gasped. No one else besides him was to know this.

"Is this true?" Yantir pushed his way forward toward the center of the circle, closer to the fire.

Before he could figure out how to answer, Salim spoke again, "And yet..."

Efrin maneuvered to block Salim from coming any closer.

"And yet you would give Mahalan the life of someone else? You would continue to serve a god who killed your father... and drove away your mother?"

Adan could feel his resolve quaking and close to crumbling. The old man was getting too close to a raw nerve.

"Choose whom you will serve, Adan," Yantir challenged from across the fire. "Don't listen to this crazy man. If you don't go with Verhor tonight, your life will be over."

Adan knew he couldn't go with Verhor, Mahalan would kill him. Yet now he couldn't move his arms to kill Graisia for Mahalan! This old man was ruining everything! If he didn't kill Graisia, he would be killed by Yantir, Jandro or Mahalan before morning!

"Don't sacrifice her to Mahalan, Adan." Salim's voice had turned quieter, almost fatherly.

Adan spoke to Salim almost in agony, "I have to, or I won't have the power to survive."

"Her death and Mahalan cannot give you the power you're looking for," Salim said. "She doesn't have power, it comes from Uri. Only Uri's power can satisfy. Uri's power is love and is beyond all other powers. You've seen it, Adan. You can serve Uri too."

Jandro barged over to Salim and pushed the old man back toward the water, reciting incantations and curses over him.

"If I don't kill her," Adan said just loudly enough for Salim and those around him to hear, "Mahalan will kill me. I have contracted my life to him, I have no choice." The burning grip on his hands started to loose its hold.

Before he was pushed into the river, Salim shouted out one last time to Adan, "Jarón can break the contract for you. He's more powerful!" There was a splash as Salim fell back into the river and started to float down stream.

"Enough of your crazy talk, old man!" Jandro spat on the ground.

 If Graisia didn't speak up now, she knew she might never again. "He's not crazy! Don't you know who he is?"

"Don't listen to her, Adan." The man who had put her on the altar stepped closer.

The slight glow of flames she had seen around Adan's hands was fading fast. She didn't have much time. Graisia looked from Adan's quivering hands to his unsettled face.

"He's your grandfather!" she blurted. "Your dad chose not to follow his ways. He married the Spirit Priest's daughter. Your dad hated Salim and told everyone never to speak of him again, or he would kill them." Her words tumbled out like water from a spilled bucket. "Your dad started rumors about them, said they were crazy. But he loves you, Adan. Salim and Estar love you, and the power they have in Uri is stronger than yours."

Adan's mouth dropped open and he looked

around the gathering, asking with his eyes if what she said was true.

Jandro stepped up next to the man who'd tied her to the blocks. "It's true, Adan," Jandro spoke evenly. "Salim is your grandfather. You come from a long line of failures. Give up now and we'll let you leave Sawtong alive."

When Adan didn't move, Graisia closed her eyes. *Jarón!* She had to focus on him. She thought of Estar and Salim not eating for Adan's sake. Now, would be a good time for Uri's *aysh* to help. She opened her eyes in time to see Adan's knife coming down toward her neck. *Uri!*

Jandro grabbed the knife out of Adan's hands and backed away. "You aren't going to sacrifice here tonight, boy!"

Chaos erupted. Knives and sticks appeared and curses came from every direction. The man who tied her to the altar grabbed Adan and wrestled him to the ground.

Frantically, she squirmed and wriggled her arms and legs. But she couldn't move without the cords cutting into her. Desperately, she looked around for someone who might help her... but all the *basyo* were fighting one another. Then, off to the left of the fire, Graisia spotted the same young girl who had led her to Salim and Estar's home! She was walking straight toward Graisia in the midst of all the chaos. Either from the mayhem, or perhaps because the girl was invisible to everybody else, no one seemed to notice her, but still, she held a finger to her lips indicating Graisia shouldn't say anything.

When the girl reached Graisia's side, she stood on her tiptoes, reached out to touch the cords binding Graisia's wrists and ankles... and then vanished. The ropes slipped easily onto the cinderblocks. Graisia's right arm tingled painfully now that it was able to wake up.

Cautiously, she turned her head toward where she'd last seen Adan. In all the madness, she couldn't tell who was who. But for the moment, no one seemed to be paying her any attention.

Thank you, Jarón! She rolled off the cinderblocks into the weeds and darted between two clusters of fighting men.

Efrin had knocked Adan pretty far from the altar, but using Mahalan's strength, Adan easily tossed Efrin to the side. As far as Adan was concerned, he still only had one choice, and it was to kill Graisia. He fought his way back to the altar.

When he reached the empty cinderblocks, it took only a second to glimpse Graisia disappearing into the fray. He headed after her, knocking everyone in his path out of the way. Mahalan hurricaned insanely inside him. Adan grabbed someone's knife out of their hand and jammed it into his sheath as he ran.

Graisia could hardly see the uneven path, and her legs wobbled unsteadily. Weeds whacked at her legs. She stumbled and caught herself. Footsteps pounded behind her. She turned to see who it was.

Adan!

She spun around and tried to run harder, but the footsteps were gaining on her. Her foot slipped on the muddy path. Before she could catch herself, she went sprawling into the mud.

Adan barely stopped himself from falling on top of her. As she wrestled to her feet, he grabbed her arms and sent her sprawling again, relief coursing through his body like a drug. Mahalan laughed inside him with delight and Adan let the laughter spill out of his own mouth.

Darkness pressed in on Graisia's mind. She kicked and squirmed, spitting mud out of her mouth.

"Let me go!" she squealed. She tried to grasp for Jarón in her mind.

"Yeah, right, and you're the queen of Sawtong," Adan retorted.

Adan laughed again. Then all of a sudden, he felt someone grab the yoke of his shirt and yank him up off the ground. His breath caught in his throat, and he watched in astonishment as Graisia scrambled back to her feet and took off running again. Adan spun around to see who had yanked him up.

There was no one there. Confused, but not

deterred, he ran after her again.

She hadn't gotten far and he was gaining easily. He was close enough to grab her. He reached out.

His hand was closing around her arm when – somehow she seemed to shift into fast-forward – and zoom away like a speeding vapor. She was gone!

Graisia felt as if a huge hand had gripped her waist and yanked her forward so fast she could barely breathe. Everything around her whooshed past in a blur.

The next thing she knew, she was falling onto her hands and knees in the alleyway leading to Salim and Estar's place. Inside, she could see Estar's silhouette in the welcoming light.

She jumped up and ran toward the shack. "Estar!"

Reeling, Adan looked in all directions for the blasted girl then let out a string of curses. It felt like Mahalan was about to explode inside him.

Turning to the wide expanse of sky, he yelled with all the fury and frustration he felt, "Uri!!" It was sinking in – the power behind Graisia would never let him get to her.

There was no hope. He was finished. "Uri..." he called out again, this time in almost a desperate plea. He fell to his knees. He had no one else to turn to.

The name had barely left his lips when

something like warm honey began to seep into the gaping cracks of his soul. *Could there really be hope?*

He heard squashy footsteps behind him. He twisted his torso to see who it was. Salim, dripping wet, swayed to a stop at his side. *The witch-man – my grandfather?* Salim reached out a hand and laid it on his shoulder. It seemed to burn his skin, but the heat quickly changed to the same unspeakably radiant, honey-like warmth attempting to penetrate his soul.

"Only through experiencing love can you experience true power," Salim whispered.

The thought terrified him. This incredible feeling – so breathtaking – could it really be from one greater than all the other gods – greater than Mahalan?

"It is weakness!" Mahalan screamed inside his head, but with no claws extended. *"You can never trust love. It will always let you down. Your father, mother, Soliel – and remember, you easily overruled her work on the boy."*

Adan stared into Salim's eyes, startled to see how much the old man really did resemble his father. He was ashamed he had never noticed it before. But there was more, something different that was genuine and deep in Salim's eyes – peace.

Mahalan pressed in on Adan's lungs, forcing him to gasp for breath. *"I will kill you,"* Mahalan threatened.

"Stop," Salim said firmly.

The pressure on his lungs lightened instantly.

"Do you want it?" Salim asked softly.

Adan continued staring into his eyes, unsure of

what to say.

"Do you want Jarón's way out?" Salim repeated.

Adan nodded his head slowly.

Like a molten waterfall of gold, a new voice reverberated in Adan's head, *"Find your home in my love."* At the word *"love,"* it felt like electrified arrows shot through his heart, shattering his last defenses, and he yelled out in exhilarating pain.

Inside him, Mahalan and myriads of other spirits screamed and cursed at Adan. Mahalan's command came through clearly, *"Get up! Run!"*

But Adan had no desire to do any such thing. His legs felt like they'd turned to liquid. The warm honey-gold flowed through his limbs and he crumpled forward into the wet earth. He writhed and yelled. This liquid love scalded his insides, uncovering more and more darkness in him. It was overwhelming, yet he didn't want it to stop. He wanted more of the light, but it burned. He felt like he was being kissed all over – but with a hot iron that seared the very essence of who he was. He didn't want to keep facing this darkness inside him, but he would give anything for it to continue.

Mahalan and the other spirits were still screaming, but their cries were getting fainter. The last thing Adan heard was a hideously desperate shout from Mahalan, *"I am not finished with you! You are still mine!"* But Adan was hardly aware of it.

He wept at the deepness of this love. He was already slouched on the ground, but he curled into a ball sobbing in agony, forehead in the mud. His hands were so limp he couldn't even hold them to his face.

After a time, he felt Salim's arms wrap around his shoulders. The warmth that had flowed from Salim's hand, now poured through Salim's arms, filling Adan's body with cleansing comfort. Salim held him until his weeping finally came to a stop and Adan could barely lift his head – all his muscles felt like jelly. Salim helped him sit up and let him lean against his chest.

Even as he could hear the battle for power raging in the distance, a quiet peace settled over Adan. He felt like a child again in his father's arms.

"Come home with me, Adan," Salim said as a gentle command.

Home? Adan allowed himself to be lifted onto his feet. Salim swung Adan's arm over his shoulder, and they headed up the path away from the river.

As they staggered together, Adan saw Mahalan out of the corner of his eye, following at a distance. Strangely, he had no fear. Rather, he was stunned that Mahalan was no longer in him. He'd survived Mahalan leaving!

Mahalan watched for a moment, then condensed and darkened into a solid shadowy mass before flying straight up and speeding off toward the other end of town.

The battle was bloody, and lives were being lost on all sides. Jandro managed to escape in the middle of the tumult and make his way home. He could feel it in his soul – there was a position open, and he wanted it.

He sat in the roofless room behind his shack with the partial moon casting silvery rays on his sacrifice. Spicy incense helped to calm his frazzled nerves and heighten his senses as he plunged deeper into the world of the spirits.

It wasn't long before an icy chill crept up his back, spreading over his shoulders and into his skull. *"Your sacrifice pleases me, Jandro."*

Jandro smiled at the low, wicked voice of his chosen master.

"The position you have wanted is yours for the taking."

Jandro's smile widened and a thrill of pleasure washed over him. The stirring of Mahalan's power swirled in his head and mind so strongly he could taste it. The power was his!

Whispers and shrieks churned the air.

He laughed with abandon. *And they thought they feared Danjall!*

TO BE CONTINUED…

GLOSSARY AND MEMORY JOGGER

Adan (AY-dun): 15-year-old son of Danjall. As son of the Spirit Priest of Sawtong, he is feared by most, and sought out for assistance in placing spells, curses and getting revenge.

aysh **(AYSH):** A type of spirit being that is either good or bad.

bandhu **(BAN-du):** A group of friends, somewhat like a gang, that looks out for one another and works together. Some have more tendencies toward violence and drugs.

basyo **(BAW-see-o):** A spiritualist, one who seeks to control *lakás* through actions such as chants, spells, incantations, and sacrifices. There are many *basyo* in Sawtong as well as in other towns and in the city. They are all subordinate to the local Spirit Priest in their town or region.

Cuni (KU-nee): Opana's youngest son.

Danjall (dan-JAWL): Adan's father and Spirit Priest.

donya **(DON-yuh):** A unit of money, a coin, equal to about half the amount of what the people living in the dump town could make each day.

dusanays **(doo-SAN-ays)** The symbol of the Spirit Priest who serves Mahalan. The symbol consists of two overlaid, broken triangles. The Spirit Priest of Mahalan often leaves the symbol where he has made a curse.

Efrin (EF-rin): A *basyo* particularly close and loyal to Danjall. He acts as a messenger, spy, and assistant.

Estar (ES-tar): Wife of Salim. She and her husband wash and repair old shoes so they can be resold.

Felirnu (fel-EER-new): A *basyo* who owed money to Jandro and would not pay.

Graisia (GRAY-see-uh): An orphan that Opana found along the side of the road as a toddler. Graisia is allowed to stay with her if she gives Opana the money she makes working at the dump. Graisia is about 12 years old, but no one knows for sure.

Harapkan (har-awp-KAWN): The goddess of fate. Opana is the keeper of a shrine to her in Sawtong.

Hydal (HY-dawl): A *basyo* loyal to Danjall and a friend of Efrin.

Isela (ee-SEL-uh): Opana's oldest daughter.

Ivah (AI-vah): A goddess known for her generous rule through the Spirit Priest's family generations ago, until their allegiance changed to Mahalan.

Jandro (HAHN-dro): A well respected *basyo* in Sawtong. He would do anything to become Spirit Priest himself. He has raised his daughter, Soliel, to be a *basyo* as well.

Jarón (Jah-RON): The High King

Kahitsa'an (Kah-HEET-suh-AHN): The island nation where this story takes place.

kaibigan (Kai-BEE-gahn): A term for a family friend – singular or plural.

Kaly (KAY-lee): A fellow member of the *bandhu* that Graisia is a part of. Kaly is 14 years old and lives with her mother's sister, Lindi.

kosa (KO-sah): A term meaning friend, companion or fellow gang member. Used amongst children in the same *bandhu* when referring to one another.

Kutah (KU-tah): The capital city of Kahitsa'an.

lakás (la-KAHS): The power offered by many of the spirit beings to be used for controlling, helping or hurting people.

Lindi (LIN-dee): Kaly's mother's sister. Kaly chose to live with her, rather than her mother and her mother's boyfriend in the city. Lindi has also taken in many kids from relatives' families where the parents have died of "slim." Lindi is also known as the "town gossip."

Lio (LEE-o): A nine-year-old boy who becomes a member of Graisia's *bandhu*. He lives with his mother. Lio takes care of his mother more than she takes care of him.

Mahalan (mah-hah-LAHN): The spirit being that the ruling Spirit Priest's family in Sawtong has given their allegiance to. He rules Sawtong through the Spirit Priest.

Mitina (mee-TEE-nuh): The youngest member of the *bandhu* Graisia is in. She is about seven years old. She moved with her parents and younger brother closer to the city from the countryside when they lost their farm. Her nickname is Teeny.

Nala (NAH-lah): Soliel's *aysh* name.

Nandan (NAHN-dahn): An old man who once taught Salim much about the Realm.

Opana (o-PAWN-uh): A washer lady who found Graisia as a toddler and allows her to stay in part of her shack. She forces Graisia to work at the dump and hand over all the money she makes.

Pouyan (POO-yawn): The man who gives money to the kids who work at the dump in exchange for useful trash they collect that can be recycled.

Ramél (ra-MEL): Adan's Grandfather and the first

Spirit Priest among Adan's ancestors to serve Mahalan. He dedicated his family to serve Mahalan.

Rawiya (rah-WEE-yuh): A "crazy" lady who supposedly communicates with ghosts and spirits. She is the keeper of many of the local legends. Most people think she is a bit insane. Children like to listen to the stories she tells.

The Realm: The Realm is where everything can be as Uri meant it to be. It's a kind of place, where Jarón rules and where someone can rule with him for all of eternity. It can be everywhere, but isn't yet. It's a place where a person can enter timelessness, eternity; the real depths of love... and live out of that, in unity with Jarón. It's seeing and experiencing the most powerful of what really is. People can be in it, it can be in them, and they can spread it to others. A person's life really seems to begin when they enter the Realm. It's where a person is truly *being* who they were meant to be. It is a realm greater than all other realms, and the only realm that will last forever.

Salim (SAY-lim): Husband of Estar. Along with his wife, he repairs old shoes so they can be resold.

Sawtong (saw-TONG): The unofficial name of the dump town where Graisia and Adan reside. The meaning of the name is "so what."

"Slim:" A disease officially known as AIDS. It's called "slim" in Kahitsa'an because the people who contract the disease often get incredibly thin before they die.

Soliel (so-LEE-uhl): Teenage daughter of Jandro whom he has raised as a *basyo*.

Spirit Priest: An unofficial town leader who rules an area with the power of their spirit god and through fear or threat.

takra **sticks (TAWK-ruh):** A set of sticks held in the hand and released onto a flat surface. Omens are read from the patterns made by the fallen sticks.

Tayzor (TAY-zor): The 15-year-old leader of the *bandhu* Graisia is in. He is particularly weak and sickly, the youngest son of five. He lives with his mother and two of his brothers.

Trakston (TRAKS-tuhn): A slum town bordering Sawtong, separated only by train tracks. Train tracks also run through much of Trakston.

Uri (YUR-ee): The great dreamer who sang all of existence into being.

Verhor (ver-HOR): Yantir's spirit god. Verhor is worshiped and served in Trakston.

Vic (VIK): Son of Felirnu and Yesenia.

Vivi Sel Luan (VI-vee SEL luu-AHN): Prime Minister of Kahitsa'an.

Yantir (yan-TEER): The Spirit Priest of Trakston who worships Verhor.

Yesenia (ye-SEN-ee-uh): Wife of Felirnu and mother of Vic.

Inspiration

    K.L. Glanville has traveled to countries where people are as poor as those you have read about in this book. She has also heard lots of stories from people around the world who have lived and worked in areas much like the one described in this book. Not every child has the luxury of living in a wealthy city or neighborhood, or is even able to go to school. Many children live in poverty that can hardly be imagined. Inspired by what she has heard and experienced, K.L. Glanville created the imaginary country of Kahitsa'an you have just read about.

    As for the reality of the supernatural elements in this story... that is for you to discover on your own journey.

www.KLGLANVILLE.com

Acknowledgements

Armloads of thanks to all who have read various drafts along the way and given feedback that has helped to shape the book into what it has become today:

- ❖ FTS writing group that helped me take some of the first steps of trepidation

- ❖ Inklings West, especially Bob, Elaina, Dori and Gary, encouragers all!

- ❖ Kathy Tyers for her incredible editing job that (hopefully) took my writing up a notch

- ❖ Mom, Dad, Becky, Lou, Kathy, Gramma, Suzanne, Kristiana, Kathleen, Danielle, Kristi, Rick, Jeff and all the other friends and family who took first peeks and gave their helpful input

- ❖ Kevin Miller for his beneficial advice

Special thanks to:

- ❖ Dad, for being my formative writing instructor and believing I could do anything, and Mom, for giving me things to write about and showing me no dream is out of reach

- ❖ Jenny and Nels for taking my imagination soaring to places I never would have gone on my own

- ❖ Cora Alley, for her entertaining advice on creative writing and for being a great encouragement

- ❖ Beth Nixon, for her excellent legal and business expertise

- ❖ Vanessa Lindstrom for assistance on "corrupting" the seal on the cover

- ❖ Jeff Milam for his tireless efforts on the cover

- ❖ And all the P.I.'s, for being awesome advocates in higher places

INFORMATION ON ORDERING MORE COPIES
CAN BE OBTAINED FROM

LUMINATIONS
MEDIA GROUP INC.
Monterey Park, California

WWW.LUMINATIONSMEDIAGROUP.COM

Don't Miss Out!

Sign up to find out more about The Realm.

Be among the **first to be notified** of the sequels.

Sign Up At:

www.EnterTheRealm.com